Peter Lovesey began his writing career with *Wobble to Death* in 1970, introducing Sergeant Cribb, the Victorian detective who went on to feature in seven more books and two TV series. Of his fifteen mysteries, three suspense novels, and two short story collections, *Waxwork* won the Crime Writers' Association Silver Dagger, *The False Inspector Dew* the Gold Dagger, *The Secret Lover* the Veuve Clicquot Prize for best short story, *Swing, Swing Together* the French Grand Prix de Littérature Policière, *A Case of Spirits* the Prix du Roman d'Aventures and *The Last Detective* the prestigious Anthony Award, a prize rarely given to a British author.

Peter Lovesey was Chairman of the Crime Writers' Association in 1991/92.

'One of the very best of the current generation of crime writers, and he controls his plot like clockwork – everything timed to perfection'
Evening Standard

'Too few writers seem capable of delivering a crime novel that is not only entertaining but also delicate and witty. An exception is Peter Lovesey'
Sunday Express

PETER LOVESEY

The Crime of
Miss Oyster Brown
and Other Stories

WARNER FUTURA

An *Warner Futura* Book

First published in Great Britain in 1994
by Little, Brown and Company
This edition published by Warner Futura in 1995

A CIP catalogue record for this book
is available from the British Library.

ISBN 0 7515 1571 X

Printed in England by Clays Ltd, St Ives plc

Warner Futura
A Division of
Little, Brown and Company (UK)
Brettenham House
Lancaster Place
London WC2E 7EN

Acknowledgements

Curl Up and Dye was first published in Ellery Queen's Mystery Magazine, 1986; *The Curious Computer* in *New Adventures of Sherlock Holmes* (Carroll & Graf), 1987; *Friendly Yachtsman, 39* in Woman's Own, 1988; *The Pomeranian Poisoning* in *Winter's Crimes, 19* (Macmillan), 1987; *Where is Thy Sting?* in *Winter's Crimes, 20* (Macmillan), 1988; *A Case of Butterflies* in *Winter's Crimes, 21* (Macmillan), 1989; *Youdunnit* in New Crimes (Robinson), 1989; *The Haunted Crescent* in *Mistletoe Mysteries* (Mysterious Press), 1989; *Shock Visit* in *Winter's Crimes, 22* (Macmillan), 1990; *The Lady in the Trunk* in *A Classic English Crime* (Pavilion), 1990; *Ginger's Waterloo* in *Cat Crimes* (Donald L. Fine), 1991; *Being of Sound Mind* in *Winter's Crimes, 23* (Macmillan), 1991; *The Crime of Miss Oyster Brown* in *Midwinter Mysteries, 1* (Scribners), 1991; *Supper with Miss Shivers* in Woman's Own, 1991, as *The Christmas Present; The Man Who Ate People* in *The Man Who . . .* (Macmillan), 1992; *You May See a Strangler* in *Midwinter Mysteries, 2* (Little, Brown), 1992; *Pass the Parcel* in *Midwinter Mysteries, 3* (Little, Brown), 1993; *The Model Con* in *Woman's Realm Summer Special*, 1994.

Contents

The Crime of Miss Oyster Brown and Other Stories

The Crime of Miss Oyster Brown

MISS OYSTER BROWN, A DEVOUT member of the Church of England, joined passionately each Sunday in every prayer of the Morning Service – except for the general Confession, when, in all honesty, she found it difficult to class herself as a lost sheep. She was willing to believe that everyone else in church had erred and strayed. In certain cases she knew exactly how, and with whom, and she would say a prayer for them. On her own account, however, she could seldom think of anything to confess. She tried strenuously, more strenuously – dare I say it? – than you or me to lead an untainted life. She managed conspicuously well. Very occasionally, as the rest of the congregation joined in the Confession, she would own up to some trifling sin.

You may imagine what a fall from grace it was when this virtuous woman committed not merely a sin, but a crime. She lived more than half her life before it happened.

She resided in a Berkshire town with her twin sister Pearl, who was a mere three minutes her senior. Oyster and Pearl – a flamboyance in forenames that owed something to the fact that their parents had been plain John and Mary Brown. Up to the moment of birth the Browns had been led to expect one child who, if female, was to be named Pearl. In the turmoil created by a second, unscheduled, daughter, John Brown jokingly suggested naming her Oyster. Mary, bosky from morphine, seized

1

on the name as an inspiration, a delight to the ear when said in front of dreary old Brown. Of course the charm was never so apparent to the twins, who got to dread being introduced to people. Even in infancy they were aware that their parents' friends found the names amusing. At school they were taunted as much by the teachers as the children. The names never ceased to amuse. Fifty years on, things were still said just out of earshot and laced with pretended sympathy. 'Here come Pearl and Oyster, poor old ducks. Fancy being stuck with names like that.'

No wonder they faced the world defiantly. In middle age they were a formidable duo, stalwarts of the choir, the Bible-reading Circle, the Townswomen's Guild and the Magistrates' Bench. Neither sister had married. They lived together in Lime Tree Avenue, in the mock-Tudor house where they were born. They were not short of money.

There are certain things people always want to know about twins, the more so in mystery stories. I can reassure the wary reader that Oyster and Pearl were not identical; Oyster was an inch taller, more sturdy in build than her sister and slower of speech. They dressed individually, Oyster as a rule in tweed skirts and check blouses that she made herself, always from the same Butterick pattern, Pearl in a variety of mail-order suits in pastel blues and greens. No one confused them. As for that other question so often asked about twins, neither sister could be characterized as 'dominant'. Each possessed a forceful personality by any standard. To avoid disputes they had established a household routine, a division of the duties, that worked pretty harmoniously, all things considered. Oyster did most of the cooking and the gardening, for example, and Pearl attended to the housework and paid the bills when they became due. They both enjoyed shopping, so they shared it. They did the church flowers together when their turn came, and they always ran the bottle stall at the church fête. Five vicars had held the

2

living at St Saviour's in the twins' time as worshippers there. Each new incumbent was advised by his predecessor that Pearl and Oyster were the mainstays of the parish. Better to fall foul of the diocesan bishop himself than the Brown twins.

All of this was observed from a distance, for no one, not even a vicar making his social rounds, was allowed inside the house in Lime Tree Avenue. The twins didn't entertain, and that was final. They were polite to their neighbours without once inviting them in. When one twin was ill, the other would transport her to the surgery in a state of high fever rather than call the doctor on a visit.

It followed that people's knowledge of Pearl and Oyster was limited. No one could doubt that they lived an orderly existence; there were no complaints about undue noise, or unwashed windows or neglected paintwork. The hedge was trimmed and the garden mown. But what really bubbled and boiled behind the regularly washed net curtains – the secret passion that was to have such a dire result – was unsuspected until Oyster committed her crime.

She acted out of desperation. On the last Saturday in July, 1991, her well-ordered life suffered a seismic shock. She was parted from her twin sister. The parting was sudden, traumatic and had to be shrouded in secrecy. The prospect of anyone finding out what had occurred was unthinkable.

So for the first time in her life Oyster had no Pearl to change the light bulbs, pay the bills and check that all the doors were locked. Oyster – let it be understood – was not incapable or dim-witted. Bereft as she was, she managed tolerably well until the Friday afternoon, when she had a letter to post, a letter of surpassing importance, capable – God willing – of easing her desolation. She had agonized over it for hours. Now it was crucial that the letter caught the last post of the day. Saturday would be too late. She

3

went to the drawer where Pearl always kept the postage stamps and – calamity – not one was left.

Stamps had always been Pearl's responsibility. To be fair, the error was Oyster's; she had written more letters than usual and gone through the supply. She should have called at the Post Office when she was doing the shopping.

It was too late. There wasn't time to get there before the last post at five-fifteen. She tried to remain calm and consider her options. It was out of the question to ask a neighbour for a stamp; she and Pearl had made it a point of honour never to be beholden to anyone else. Neither could she countenance the disgrace of despatching the letter without a stamp in the hope that it would get by, or the recipient would pay the amount due.

This left one remedy, and it was criminal.

Behind one of the Staffordshire dogs on the mantelpiece was a bank statement. She had put it there for the time being because she had been too busy to check where Pearl normally stored such things. The significant point for Oyster at this minute was not the statement, but the envelope containing it. More precisely, the top right-hand corner of the envelope, because the first class stamp had somehow escaped being cancelled.

Temptation stirred and uncoiled itself.

Oyster had never in her life steamed an unfranked stamp from an envelope and used it again. Nor, to her knowledge, had Pearl. Stamp collectors sometimes removed used specimens for their collections, but what Oyster was contemplating could in no way be confused with philately. It was against the law. Defrauding the Post Office. A crime.

There was under twenty minutes before the last collection.

I couldn't, she told herself. *I'm on the Parochial Church Council. I'm on the Bench.*

Temptation reminded her that she was due for a cup of

4

tea in any case. She filled the kettle and pressed the switch. While waiting, watching the first wisp of steam rise from the spout, she weighed the necessity of posting the letter against the wickedness of re-using a stamp. It was not the most heinous of crimes, Temptation whispered. And once Oyster began to think about the chances of getting away with it, she was lost. The kettle sang, the steam gushed and she snatched up the envelope and jammed it against the spout. Merely, Temptation reassured her, to satisfy her curiosity as to whether stamps could be separated from envelopes by this method.

Those who believe in retribution will not be in the least surprised that the steam was deflected by the surface of the envelope and scalded three of Oyster's fingers quite severely. She cried out in pain and dropped the envelope. She ran the cold tap and plunged her hand under it. Then she wrapped the sore fingers in a piece of kitchen towel.

Her first action after that was to turn off the kettle. Her second was to pick up the envelope and test the corner of the stamp with the tip of her fingernail. It still adhered to some extent, but with extreme care she was able to ease it free, consoled that her discomfort had not been entirely without result. The minor accident failed to deter her from the crime. On the contrary, it acted like a prod from Old Nick.

There was a bottle of gum in the writing desk and she applied some to the back of the stamp, taking care not to use too much, which might have oozed out at the edges and discoloured the envelope. When she had positioned the stamp neatly on her letter, it would have passed the most rigorous inspection. She felt a wicked frisson of satisfaction at having committed an undetectable crime. Just in time, she remembered the post and had to hurry to catch it.

There we leave Miss Oyster Brown to come to terms with her conscience for a couple of days.

*

We meet her again on the Monday morning in the local chemist's shop. The owner and pharmacist was John Trigger, whom the Brown twins had known for getting on for thirty years, a decent, obliging man with a huge moustache who took a personal interest in his customers. In the face of strong competition from a national chain of pharmacists, John Trigger had persevered with his old-fashioned service from behind a counter, believing that some customers still preferred it to filling a wire basket themselves. But to stay in business he had been forced to diversify by offering some electrical goods.

When Oyster Brown came in and showed him three badly scalded fingers out in blisters, Trigger was sympathetic as well as willing to suggest a remedy. Understandably he enquired how Oyster had come by such a painful injury. She was expecting the question and had her answer ready, adhering to the truth as closely as a God-fearing woman should.

'An accident with the kettle.'

Trigger looked genuinely alarmed. 'An electric kettle? Not the one you bought here last year?'

'I didn't,' said Oyster at once.

'Must have been your sister. A Steamquick. Is that what you've got?'

'Er, yes.'

'If there's a fault. . .'

'I'm not here to complain, Mr Trigger. So you think this ointment will do the trick?'

'I'm sure of it. Apply it evenly, and don't attempt to pierce the blisters, will you?' John Trigger's conscience was troubling him. 'This is quite a nasty scalding, Miss Brown. Where exactly did the steam come from?'

'The kettle.'

'I know that. I mean was it the spout?'

6

'It really doesn't matter,' said Oyster sharply. 'It's done.'

'The lid, then? Sometimes if you're holding the handle you get a rush of steam from that little slot in the lid. I expect it was that.'

'I couldn't say,' Oyster fudged, in the hope that it would satisfy Mr Trigger.

It did not. 'The reason I asked is that there may be a design fault.'

'The fault was mine, I'm quite sure.'

'Perhaps I ought to mention it to the manufacturers.'

'Absolutely not,' Oyster said in alarm. 'I was careless, that's all. And now, if you'll excuse me . . .' She started backing away and then Mr Trigger ambushed her with another question.

'What does your sister say about it?'

'My sister?' From the way she spoke, she might never have had one.

'Miss Pearl.'

'Oh, nothing. We haven't discussed it,' Oyster truthfully stated.

'But she must have noticed your fingers.'

'Er, no. How much is the ointment?'

Trigger told her and she dropped the money on the counter and almost rushed from the shop. He stared after her, bewildered.

The next time Oyster Brown was passing, Trigger took the trouble to go to the door of his shop and enquire whether the hand was any better. Clearly she wasn't overjoyed to see him. She assured him without much gratitude that the ointment was working. 'It was nothing. It's going to clear up in a couple of days.'

'May I see?'

She held out her hand.

Trigger agreed that it was definitely on the mend. 'Keep it dry, if you possibly can. Who does the washing up?'

'What do you mean?'

'You, or your sister? It's well known that you divide the chores between you. If it's your job, I'm sure Miss Pearl won't mind taking over for a few days. If I see her, I'll suggest it myself.'

Oyster reddened and said nothing.

'I was going to remark that I haven't seen her for a week or so,' Trigger went on. 'She isn't unwell, I hope?'

'No,' said Oyster. 'Not unwell.'

Sensing correctly that this was not an avenue of conversation to venture along at this time, he said instead, 'The Steamquick rep was in yesterday afternoon, so I mentioned what happened with your kettle.'

She was outraged. 'You had no business.'

'Pardon me, Miss Brown, but it *is* my business. You were badly scalded. I can't have my customers being injured by the products I sell. The rep was very concerned, as I am. He asked if you would be so good as to bring the kettle in next time you come, so that he can check if there's a fault.'

'Absolutely not,' said Oyster. 'I told you I haven't the slightest intention of complaining.'

Trigger tried to be reasonable. 'It isn't just your kettle. I've sold the same model to other customers.'

'Then they'll complain if they get hurt.'

'What if their children get hurt?'

She had no answer.

'If it's inconvenient to bring it in, perhaps I could call at your house.'

'No,' she said at once.

'I can bring a replacement. In fact, Miss Brown, I'm more than a little concerned about this whole episode. I'd like you to have another kettle with my compliments. A different model. Frankly, the modern trend is for jug kettles that couldn't possibly scald you as yours did. If you'll kindly step into the shop, I'll give you one now to take home.'

The offer didn't appeal to Oyster Brown in the least.

8

'For the last time, Mr Trigger,' she said in a tight, clipped voice, 'I don't require another kettle.' With that, she walked away up the high street.

Trigger, from the motives he had mentioned, was not content to leave the matter there. He wasn't a churchgoer, but he believed in conducting his life on humanitarian principles. On this issue, he was resolved to be just as stubborn as she. He went back into the shop and straight to the phone. While Oyster Brown was out of the house, he would speak to Pearl Brown, the sister, and see if he could get better co-operation from her.

Nobody answered the phone.

At lunchtime, he called in to see Ted Collins, who ran the garden shop next door, and asked if he had seen anything of Pearl Brown lately.

'I had Oyster in this morning,' Collins told him.

'But you haven't seen Pearl?'

'Not in my shop. Oyster does all the gardening, you know. They divide the work.'

'I know.'

'I can't think what came over her today. Do you know what she bought? Six bottles of Rapidrot.'

'What's that?'

'It's a new product. An activator for composting. You dilute it and water your compost heap and it speeds up the process. They're doing a special promotion to launch it. Six bottles are far too much, and I tried to tell her, but she wouldn't be told.'

'Those two often buy in bulk,' said Trigger. 'I've sold Pearl a dozen tubes of toothpaste at a go, and they must be awash with Dettol.'

'They won't use six bottles of Rapidrot in twenty years,' Collins pointed out. 'It's concentrated stuff, and it won't keep all that well. It's sure to solidify after a time. I told her one's plenty to be going on with. She's wasted her money, obstinate old bird. I don't know what Pearl would say. Is

9

she ill, do you think?'

'I've no idea,' said Trigger, although in reality an idea was beginning to form in his brain. A disturbing idea. 'Do they get on all right with each other? Daft question,' he said before Collins could answer it. 'They're twins. They've spent all their lives in each other's company.'

For the present he dismissed the thought and gave his attention to the matter of the electric kettle. He'd already withdrawn the Steamquick kettles from sale. He got on the phone to Steamquick and had an acrimonious conversation with some little Hitler from their public relations department who insisted that thousands of the kettles had been sold and the design was faultless.

'The lady's injury isn't imagined, I can tell you,' Trigger insisted.

'She must have been careless. Anyone can hurt themselves if they're not careful. People are far too ready to put the blame on the manufacturer.'

'People, as you put it, are your livelihood.'

There was a heavy sigh. 'Send us the offending kettle, and we'll test it.'

'That isn't so simple.'

'Have you offered to replace it?'

The man's whole tone was so condescending that Trigger had an impulse to frighten him rigid. 'She won't let the kettle out of her possession. I think she may be keeping it as evidence.'

'Evidence?' There was a pause while the implication dawned. 'Blimey.'

On his end of the phone, Trigger permitted himself to grin.

'You mean she might take us to court over this?'

'I didn't say that—'

'Ah.'

' . . . but she does know the law. She's a magistrate.'

An audible gasp followed, then: 'Listen, Mr, er—'

'Trigger.'

'Mr Trigger. I think we'd better send someone to meet this lady and deal with the matter personally. Yes, that's what we'll do.'

Trigger worked late that evening, stocktaking. He left the shop about ten-thirty. Out of curiosity he took a route home via Lime Tree Avenue and stopped the car opposite the Brown sisters' house and wound down the car window. There were lights upstairs and presently someone drew a curtain. It looked like Oyster Brown.

'Keeping an eye on your customers, Mr Trigger?' a voice close to him said.

He turned guiltily. A woman's face was six inches from his. He recognized one of his customers, Mrs Wingate. She said, 'She's done that every night this week.'

'Oh?'

'Something fishy's going on in there,' she said. 'I walk my little dog along the verge about this time every night. I live just opposite them, on this side, with the wrought-iron gates. That's Pearl's bedroom at the front. I haven't seen Pearl for a week, but every night her sister Oyster draws the curtains and leaves the light on for half an hour. What's going on, I'd like to know. If Pearl is ill, they ought to call a doctor. They won't, you know.'

'That's Pearl's bedroom, you say, with the light on?'

'Yes, I often see her looking out. Not lately.'

'And now Oyster switches on the light and draws the curtains?'

'And pulls them back at seven in the morning. I don't know what you think, Mr Trigger, but it looks to me as if she wants everyone to think Pearl's in there, when it's obvious she isn't.'

'Why is it obvious?'

'All the windows are closed. Pearl always opens the top window wide, winter and summer.'

'That is odd, now you mention it.'

11

'I'll tell you one thing,' said Mrs Wingate, regardless that she had told him several things already. 'Whatever game she's up to, we won't find out. Nobody ever sets foot inside that house except the twins themselves.'

At home and in bed that night, Trigger was troubled by a gruesome idea, one that he'd tried repeatedly to suppress. Suppose the worst had happened a week ago in the house in Lime Tree Avenue, his thinking ran. Suppose Pearl Brown had suffered a heart attack and died. After so many years of living in that house as if it were a fortress, was Oyster capable of dealing with the aftermath of death, calling in the doctor and the undertaker? In her shocked state, mightn't she decide that anything was preferable to having the house invaded, even if the alternative was disposing of the body herself?

How would a middle-aged woman dispose of a body? Oyster didn't drive a car. It wouldn't be easy to bury it in the garden, nor hygienic to keep it in a cupboard in the house. But if there was one thing every well-bred English lady knew about, it was gardening. Oyster was the gardener.

In time, everything rots in a compost heap. If you want to accelerate the process, you buy a preparation like Rapidrot.

Oyster Brown had purchased six bottles of the stuff. And every night she drew the curtains in her sister's bedroom to give the impression that she was there.

He shuddered.

In the fresh light of morning, John Trigger told himself that his morbid imaginings couldn't be true. They were the delusions of a tired brain. He decided to do nothing about them.

Just after eleven-thirty, a short, fat man in a dark suit arrived in the shop and announced himself as the Area Manager of Steamquick. His voice was suspiciously like the one that Trigger had found so irritating when he had phoned their head office. 'I'm here about this allegedly faulty kettle,' he announced.

'Miss Brown's?'

'I'm sure there's nothing wrong at all, but we're a responsible firm. We take every complaint seriously.'

'You want to see the kettle? You'll be lucky.'

The Steamquick man sounded smug. 'That's all right. I telephoned Miss Brown this morning and offered to go to the house. She wasn't at all keen on that idea, but I was very firm with the lady, and she compromised. We're meeting here at noon. She's agreed to bring the kettle for me to inspect. I don't know why you found her so intractable.'

'High noon, eh? Do you want to use my office?'

Trigger had come to a rapid decision. If Oyster was on her way to the shop, he was going out. He had two capable assistants.

This was a heaven-sent opportunity to lay his macabre theory to rest. While Oyster was away from the house in Lime Tree Avenue, he would drive there and let himself into the back garden. Mrs Wingate or any other curious neighbour watching from behind the lace curtains would have to assume he was trying to deliver something. He kept his white coat on, to reinforce the idea that he was on official business.

Quite probably, he told himself, the compost heap will turn out to be no bigger than a cowpat. The day was sunny and he felt positively cheerful as he turned up the Avenue. He checked his watch. Oyster would be making mincemeat of the Steamquick man about now. It would take her twenty minutes, at least, to walk back.

He stopped the car and got out. Nobody was about, but just in case he was being observed he walked boldly up the path to the front door and rang the bell. No one came.

Without appearing in the least furtive, he stepped around the side of the house. The back garden was in a

13

beautiful state. Wide, well-stocked and immaculately weeded borders enclosed a finely trimmed lawn, yellow roses on a trellis and a kitchen garden beyond. Trigger took it in admiringly, and then remembered why he was there. His throat went dry. At the far end, beyond the kitchen garden, slightly obscured by some runner beans on poles, was the compost heap – as long as a coffin and more than twice as high.

The flesh on his arms prickled.

The compost heap was covered with black plastic bin-liners weighted with stones. They lay across the top, but the sides were exposed. A layer of fresh green garden refuse, perhaps half a metre in depth, was on the top. The lower part graduated in colour from a dull yellow to earth-brown. Obvious care had been taken to conserve the shape, to keep the pressure even and assist the composting process.

Trigger wasn't much of a gardener. He didn't have the time for it. He did the minimum and got rid of his garden rubbish with bonfires. Compost heaps were outside his experience, except that as a scientist he understood the principle by which they generated heat in a confined space. Once, years ago, an uncle of his had demonstrated this by pushing a bamboo cane into his heap from the top. A wisp of steam had issued from the hole as he withdrew the cane. Recalling it now, Trigger felt a wave of nausea.

He hadn't the stomach for this.

He knew now that he wasn't going to be able to walk up the garden and probe the compost heap. Disgusted with himself for being so squeamish, he turned to leave, and happened to notice that the kitchen window was ajar, which was odd, considering that Oyster was not at home. Out of interest he tried the door handle. The door was unlocked.

He said, 'Anyone there?' and got no answer.

From the doorway he could see a number of unopened

14

letters on the kitchen table. After the humiliation of turning his back on the compost heap, this was like a challenge, a chance to regain some self-respect. This at least, he was capable of doing. He stepped inside and picked up the letters. There were five, all addressed to Miss P. Brown. The postmarks dated from the beginning of the previous week.

Quite clearly Pearl had not been around to open her letters.

Then his attention was taken by an extraordinary line-up along a shelf. He counted fifteen packets of cornflakes, all open, and recalled his conversation with Ted Collins about the sisters buying in bulk. If Collins had wanted convincing, there was ample evidence here: seven bottles of decaffeinated coffee, nine jars of the same brand of marmalade and a tall stack of boxes of paper tissues. Eccentric housekeeping, to say the least. Perhaps, he reflected, it meant that the buying of six bottles of Rapidrot had not, after all, been so sinister.

Now that he was in the house, he wasn't going to leave without seeking an answer to the main mystery, the disappearance of Pearl. His mouth was no longer dry and the gooseflesh had gone from his arms. He made up his mind to go upstairs and look into the front bedroom.

On the other side of the kitchen door more extravagance was revealed. The passage from the kitchen to the stairway was lined on either side with sets of goods that must have overflowed from the kitchen. Numerous tins of cocoa, packets of sugar, pots of jam, gravy powder and other grocery items were stored as if for a siege, stacked along the skirting boards in groups of at least half a dozen. Trigger began seriously to fear for the mental health of the twins. Nobody had suspected anything like this behind the closed doors. The stacks extended halfway upstairs.

As he stepped upwards, obliged to tread close to the

15

banisters, he was gripped by the sense of alienation that must have led to hoarding on such a scale. The staid faces that the sisters presented to the world gave no intimation of this strange compulsion. What was the mentality of people who behaved as weirdly as this?

An appalling possibility crept into Trigger's mind. Maybe the strain of so many years of appearing outwardly normal had finally caused Oyster to snap. What if the eccentricity so apparent all around him were not so harmless as it first appeared? No one could know what resentments, what jealousies lurked in this house, what mean-minded cruelties the sisters may have inflicted on each other. What if Oyster had fallen out with her sister and attacked her? She was a sturdy woman, physically capable of killing.

If she'd murdered Pearl, the compost-heap method of disposal would certainly commend itself.

Come now, he told himself. This is all speculation.

He reached the top stair and discovered that the stockpiling had extended to the landing. Toothpaste, talcum powder, shampoos and soap were stacked up in profusion. All the doors were closed. It wouldn't have surprised him if when he opened one he was knee-deep in toilet rolls.

First he had to orientate himself. He decided that the front bedroom was to his right. He opened it cautiously and stepped in.

What happened next was swift and devastating. John Trigger heard a piercing scream. He had a sense of movement to his left and a glimpse of a figure in white. Something crashed against his head with a mighty thump, causing him to pitch forward.

About four, when the Brown twins generally stopped for tea, Oyster filled the new kettle that the Steamquick Area Manager had exchanged for the other one. She plugged it in. It was the new-fangled jug type, and she wasn't really certain if she was going to like it, but she certainly needed the cup of tea.

'I know it was wrong,' she said, 'and I'm going to pray for forgiveness, but I didn't expect that steaming a stamp off a letter would lead to this. I suppose it's a judgement.'

'Whatever made you do such a wicked thing?' her sister Pearl asked, as she put out the cups and saucers.

'The letter had to catch the post. It was the last possible day for the Kellogg's Cornflakes competition, and I'd thought of such a wonderful slogan. The prize was a fortnight in Venice.'

Pearl clicked her tongue in disapproval. 'Just because I won the Birds Eye trip to the Bahamas, it didn't mean you were going to be lucky. We tried for twenty years and only ever won consolation prizes.'

'It isn't really gambling, is it?' said Oyster. 'It isn't like betting.'

'It's all right in the Lord's eyes,' Pearl told her. 'It's a harmless pastime. Unfortunately we both know that people in the church wouldn't take a charitable view. They wouldn't expect us to devote so much of our time and money to competitions. That's why we have to be careful. You didn't tell anyone I was away?'

'Of course not. Nobody knows. For all they know, you were ill, if anyone noticed at all. I drew the curtains in your bedroom every night to make it look as if you were here.'

'Thank you. You know I'd do the same for you.'

'I might win,' said Oyster. 'Someone always does. I put in fifteen entries altogether, and the last one was a late inspiration.'

'And as a result we have fifteen packets of cornflakes with the tops cut off,' said Pearl. 'They take up a lot of room.'

'So do your frozen peas. I had to throw two packets away to make some room in the freezer. Anyway, I felt entitled to try. It wasn't much fun being here alone, thinking of

17

you sunning yourself in the West Indies. To tell you the truth, I didn't really think you'd go and leave me here. It was a shock.' Oyster carefully poured some hot water into the teapot to warm it. 'If you want to know, I've also entered the Rapidrot Trip of a Lifetime competition. A week in San Francisco followed by a week in Sydney. I bought six bottles to have a fighting chance.'

'What's Rapidrot?'

'Something for the garden.' She spooned in some tea and poured on the hot water. 'You must be exhausted. Did you get any sleep on the plane?'

'Hardly any,' said Pearl. 'That's why I went straight to bed when I got in this morning.' She poured milk into the teacups. 'The next thing I knew was the doorbell going. I ignored it, naturally. It was one of the nastiest shocks I ever had hearing the footsteps coming up the stairs. I could tell it wasn't you. I'm just thankful that I had the candlestick to defend myself with.'

'Is there any sign of life yet?'

'Well, he's breathing, but he hasn't opened his eyes, if that's what you mean. Funny, I would never have thought Mr Trigger was dangerous to women.'

Oyster poured the tea. 'What are we going to do if he doesn't recover? We can't have people coming into the house.' Even as she was speaking, she put down the teapot and glanced out of the kitchen window towards the end of the garden. She had the answer herself.

The Model Con

'COME ON, VICKY – JUST FOR a laugh.'

Just for a laugh. Those four short words undermined Vicky Simpson. All her instincts were against posing and parading. But when her friend Ella, her huge brown eyes glittering with anticipation, made her wild suggestion, Vicky couldn't bring herself to say a flat no.

'I'm not sure.'

'Why not?' demanded Ella.

Vicky laughed and tugged a wayward strand of blonde hair in front of her face. 'Look at me. I'm not exactly Jerry Hall.'

'Well, you've got a better figure than mine, and I'm willing to give it a try.'

'At your age?'

Ella stiffened her back and pressed a hankie to the corner of her eye like an offended dowager in a Jane Austen novel. It was one of her party pieces.

'Speaking for myself –' Vicky began.

'At thirty-something, as we're being brutally frank today,' Ella put in.

'Precisely. Who'd want to take me on?'

'You've got the wrong idea, my petal,' said Ella. 'Girls our age – elegant and sophisticated – are all too rare. Kids in short leather skirts with eyes like Bambi and no figure at all are ten a penny.'

'I'm not sophisticated,' said Vicky trying to be serious.

19

'People class me as NB before I open my mouth.'

'NB – what's that?'

'No background. Basically, I lack confidence.'

'Don't give me that. You came through your divorce with all guns blazing. No one had better pick a fight with you when you're angry.'

Vicky shook her head. 'I mean it. I'd die of embarrassment.'

'Why?'

'People looking at me.'

'They look at you all the time. You go temping and they look at you.'

'Not in the same way, Ella.'

'We might get into films.'

'Don't be daft.'

'They all started as fashion models. Brigitte Bardot, Audrey Hepburn, Marilyn Monroe.'

'Not at some tinpot agency in Swindon.'

'Now we're getting to it. This place isn't grand enough for Vicky Simpson.'

'You know it isn't that.'

'The money's terrific, I hear. Far better than temping, and you don't have to type boring letters. All you do is wear gorgeous clothes and take up poses.'

'Only if anyone hires you,' Vicky pointed out.

'So what's new? It works the same at a secretarial agency. We've nothing to lose.' Ella's eyes shone. 'Shall we give it a whirl? Just for a laugh?'

Vicky heard herself saying, 'Just for a laugh, then.'

Mrs Greatbatch, the woman at the agency, held out no prospects. She was willing to add them to her file of models, but she would need some good photographs, in colour and at least eight by ten, not the sort of thing you got from a passport photo booth.

'Forget it, then,' said Vicky when they got outside.

20

'Unless you happen to know David Bailey.'

'I know David Humphreys,' said Ella. 'He's got a good camera. He's an estate agent.'

'This gets more and more bizarre,' said Vicky. 'What do we do – stand holding a board saying Immaculate Freehold Property For Sale?'

Equipped with some quite professional-looking photos they registered properly with Mrs Greatbatch at the weekend. She worked her way down a card listing the usual personal details, plus colouring, vital statistics and finally – the KO punch – modelling experience.

'Mainly in London for Miss Selfridge, Next and Richard Shops,' said Ella without hesitation.

Vicky gulped.

'Really?' said Mrs Greatbatch, clearly impressed. 'Does that go for both of you?'

'Absolutely,' Ella said before Vicky could answer. 'Sometimes we work together, sometimes solo. When was your Harrods session, Vicky? Was it January?'

The only time Vicky had been to Harrods this year was for the Winter Sale when she'd tried on a couple of skirts and ended up not buying either. If that amounted to a 'session', she could reel off a few more names of Knightsbridge stores, but she merely nodded.

'How could you?' she demanded of Ella when they got outside. 'She thought we actually modelled for all those shops.'

'And we did,' said Ella solemnly. 'We tried on their garments, didn't we?' Then she burst out laughing. 'This is the rag trade, ducky. You have to put on frills.'

For the next three weeks Vicky dreaded a phone call from Mrs Greatbatch. She had visions of being asked along to some high fashion modelling assignment and shown up as inept, a total fraud. If it happened to Ella, she would think it a great hoot, but Vicky wouldn't be able to laugh it off. Her private fantasies of stalking elegantly up and down the catwalk were only wishful thinking. The reality would be sheer panic.

After five months she had forgotten about the whole thing. Which was when the call came.

'Miss Vicky Simpson?'

'Yes?'

'Greatbatch Modelling Agency here. Priscilla Greatbatch speaking.'

Vicky's blood ran cold. 'Oh.'

'A client has requested you for a modelling assignment next week.'

'Requested *me*?'

'Yes. Would you like to say which day you are available? It's a photo session and they're prepared to be flexible.'

'I, em, I've got a job now. Secretarial.'

'Let's make it Saturday in that case.'

'I don't think I can manage Saturday.'

'Why not, my dear? This is just what you've been waiting for. I've gone to no end of trouble to secure this assignment.'

'Couldn't you send someone else?'

'Impossible. Miss Darwin-Smith insists on you. She went systematically through the files and you're the ideal choice apparently. She's extremely keen. She'll pay top rates and all expenses. And I got the impression that it could easily lead to other work.'

Vicky was wavering. It was flattering to have been picked out from all the models on file. And in truth there hadn't been much secretarial work lately. 'What exactly does she want me to do?'

'It's a perfectly simple photo session, my dear. Do you know Christchurch?'

'A church?'

'No, the town, your location. Pretty little spot on the coast near Bournemouth.'

'All that way?'

22

'Your fares are taken care of – or do you have a car?'

'Yes.' Vicky thought of a day on the coast with all expenses paid. She hadn't seen the sea for over a year. It didn't sound so daunting as she'd first imagined. 'What sort of clothes will I be modelling?'

'Don't you worry. That's up to the client. Yachting gear, I shouldn't wonder. There's a lot of sailing down that way. All you need take is your make-up and a comb.'

She thought of ringing Ella to let her know. On further reflection she decided to wait until after Saturday. She could well imagine Ella thinking it a great lark to drive to Christchurch and peek at the performance.

Nervously she stepped into the bar of the hotel where she was to meet the photographer. She wasn't used to walking into bars alone. Several pairs of male eyes took stock of her pale pink blazer and white pleated skirt. A voice at her back said, 'The page three girl, I presume.'

She swung around.

'Joke.' He had a sports bag suspended from his shoulder and a light meter dangling on his chest, a grinning, blond, curly-headed hulk about ten years younger than she, quite smartly dressed in a black polo shirt and white slacks. 'Paul Jago, your friendly neighbourhood flasher.'

She didn't like his line in repartee and let him know with a stare.

'You *are* my model, buttercup,' he said. 'You've got to be.'

Nervous as Vicky was, she refused to be patronised. He was just a lightweight. 'My name is Vicky, and I'm not *your* model or anybody else's. Presumably you're here to do a job and so am I. Shall we start by respecting each other?'

He offered her a drink but she told him she'd rather make a start. 'Is anyone else expected?'

Paul Jago shook his head. 'You'll have to put up with me.'

'But what am I wearing?'

'Hold on, love.' He rummaged in his bag, tugged out a

23

camera and a lens and asked her to hold them. She was horrified. If the clothes had been stuffed in there under his photographic equipment, they'd be in no state to wear. Finally he unearthed a bright red garment.

A swimsuit. The blood rushed to her cheeks. 'Nobody told me I was to pose in that.'

'What do you expect at the seaside – a twin-set and tweeds?'

'I didn't agree to this.'

She examined the costume. It was a one-piece cut higher on the hips than anything she'd have chosen for herself and the top had no lining. 'Anyway, I've nowhere to change.'

'Get with it, Vicky. Why do you think we met in this place? Connie booked a room. You'd better ask at the desk.'

'Who's Connie?'

'The client. Miss Darwin-Smith.'

The receptionist gave her a key and she went upstairs with the costume. In the quiet of the room she sat on the bed and considered ways of escape. This whole adventure was ludicrous. Women her age didn't model swimsuits. She could have strangled Ella! She looked at the label. At least the size was right.

The phone rang.

'How are you doing?' Paul Jago asked. 'The light isn't bad now. If we leave it much longer it'll get too strong and then we'll have to mark time for a couple of hours.'

'I'll be down shortly.'

She tried the wretched thing on, hoping it would sag somewhere, so that she could honestly call off the session. It couldn't have been a better fit. She turned in front of the mirror. She'd never have chosen anything cut so high, but actually she looked very good in it. Positively stunning. Well, maybe I can get away with this, she thought.

After putting her face and hair right she wrapped the

blazer over her shoulders, slipped her feet into her white espadrilles, put on sun-glasses, picked up her bag and went downstairs. Her photographer was waiting in the foyer.

'Would it be unprofessional to say you look terrific?' he asked.

'Thanks.'

'It's only a short walk. The old cliché shot sitting on the deck of a yacht with your legs dangling and the sea in the background, but that's what the client wants.'

'Only the one pose?'

'Yes, and it's got to be spot on.'

He pointed out the sailing boat, a slim racing craft moored close enough to the harbour wall for her to step aboard. 'I'll take a polaroid first,' he told her. 'Just to be certain I've got it right.'

He showed her where to sit. To her great relief no one seemed interested in one more photographer taking shots of one more girl in a swimsuit. He was very clear about what he wanted. 'Hands behind you, flat to the deck. No, I said flat to the deck. Lean back a little more and swing your left leg just a fraction higher and hold the pose.'

She noticed that when he peeled off the polaroid picture he compared it with another photo from his pocket. 'Not at all bad,' was the verdict. 'Now we need a slight smile. No, less of the Edward Heath. Just a sexy grin, right? Beautiful. Now hold it.'

He took about ten shots of the same pose and then said, 'That's it, then. Playtime now.'

Vicky said, 'Don't you want any more?'

He twisted his face into what was meant to pass for a suggestive look. 'Are we talking about photography?'

She looked away, wishing she hadn't fed him such an obvious remark.

On the short walk back to the hotel he brushed his free hand against her thigh several times and she realized that

25

if she wanted information this was the moment to ask for it. 'That picture you kept checking the pose against. Could I see it?'

'Vicky, I'll show you anything.' He took the photo from his pocket and handed it to her.

To say that she was mystified when she saw it is an understatement. 'Thanks.'

At the hotel he started to walk upstairs with her. She said, 'The action is over for the day, Mr Jago. Why don't you trot back to your dark-room and print the pictures?'

He sneered. 'I didn't fancy you anyway, you scrawny hag.'

Ella's amazement had to be savoured. 'You're a slyboots. Modelling swimsuits!'

'*A* swimsuit,' said Vicky. 'One swimsuit and only one pose.'

'Funny.'

'You mean funny peculiar? I agree. I was paid and I suppose I shouldn't complain, but. . .'

'But what?'

'I'm suspicious, Ella. I told you he took out a photo of someone else and compared the pose. After we'd finished I asked to see it. It was a shot of some woman sitting on a yacht that I'm certain was the same one. She was in a red swimsuit exactly like the one I had on.'

'And did she look like you?'

Vicky shivered. 'This is the point. When I saw this photo I had a horrible shock. She *did* look like me, very like me. Same colouring and blonde hair cut just like mine. Only there was a difference. She was about three sizes bigger than I am. An eighteen, at least. You know that secret nightmare that your weight will go out of control? Or those distorting mirrors at fairs? I was shocked because I could see myself, and yet it wasn't me.'

'Spooky. Why would anyone set up a picture like that?

Did you ask the photographer?'

'He wouldn't have told me if he knew. I think I know the answer, and it's dodgy, if not criminal.'

'Get away!' said Ella.

'No kidding. I think some large lady – or someone else – has set this up to make it look as if she's done a slimming course. You know those pictures they always show of "before" and "after" the diet, or whatever it is.'

Ella's eyes widened. 'You could be right.'

'If I am, and someone plans to rip off the public, I could be part of a fraud.'

'No one could blame you,' said Ella.

'How can I be sure? I can see myself ending up in court over this, Ella, and having to face some ugly questions. I can't pretend it hasn't happened. I'm going to call Mrs Greatbatch.'

'Has she sent your fee yet?'

'Oh, yes. Over a hundred including expenses, which makes me even more suspicious that someone expects to cash in.'

Ella smiled. 'And make a fat profit?'

Mrs Greatbatch laughed down the phone. 'My dear, what an imagination you have! Oh, I understand your doubts, and you were right to mention them, but having dealt with Connie Darwin-Smith I'm sure the explanation is quite innocent, or the Greatbatch Modelling Agency wouldn't have any truck with it, believe me. As a matter of fact, I was trying to reach you anyway because the client was so delighted with your work that she wants to meet you. There's a strong possibility of more work.'

Vicky put her hand to her throat. 'I don't know.'

Mrs Greatbatch sighed. 'We went through this before, my dear.'

'Yes, and I'm still uneasy about it.'

'She'll pay you at the same rate and take you to lunch.'

'Just to talk?'

'Yes. No commitment – unless you are completely reassured, as I'm sure you will be.'

The place named for lunch was Eastland Park at Blandford Forum. Vicky couldn't find it in the book of hotels and restaurants she had, so she assumed it was either newly opened or too exclusive to be listed. Deciding that Miss Darwin-Smith wouldn't choose anywhere cheap, she put on the one really good thing she owned, her navy and white Chanel suit. With a red silk chemise plus chunky gold jewellery she hoped she looked the part of the top fashion model.

When she turned off the road and started along the drive to Eastland Park, she thanked her stars that she'd taken care with her appearance. This was quite some park. There were deer grazing under the trees. Her main concern was where to emerge inconspicuously from her little old Triumph Herald, for the forecourt of this place was certain to be bristling with Rolls-Royces and BMWs.

It was vast, stone-built and castellated. Inside the entrance hall was a small fountain in a jade-coloured bowl with silver fittings. The high ceiling had ornamental plasterwork and there were tapestries on the walls.

'Eastland was built for the first Duke of Wellington, but he never occupied it,' explained an elegant woman one would hesitate to call a receptionist. 'I was about to ask how I could help you, but it's obvious. You must be her sister.'

The woman blushed deeply and apologized on learning that she was mistaken. Once the confusion was over, it emerged that Miss Darwin-Smith was waiting in the library across the hall. Vicky went in. By the fireplace was a sofa and a blonde head turned as she entered. 'Vicky, my dear, it's got to be you! Amazing!'

Connie Darwin-Smith got up and gave Vicky several shocks. First, in these gracious surroundings she was

28

wearing a bright yellow tracksuit and trainers. Second, she was the woman in the photograph. And finally, she must have put on another three stone in weight since the shot had been taken. Even so, the resemblance to Vicky was weird, so striking that the women spent a moment staring at each other. It is a strange experience, looking at one's other self, give or take several stones in weight.

Connie spoke for them both. 'I'm gob-smacked.'

'Even our hair's the same,' said Vicky.

Connie giggled. 'That's a trade secret. Actually, I had mine styled like yours after I saw your picture.' She took Vicky's arm. 'Let's head straight for the dining room, little sister. I'm slavering for food.'

Other women in tracksuits passed them in the corridor.

'I should have warned you. Sports gear is the norm here,' said Connie.

'Is there a fitness centre somewhere?' Vicky asked.

'My dear, the whole place is a fat farm. I'm practically in permanent residence, and you can see why.'

Alarm bells rang in Vicky's head. 'You're a slimmer?'

'Don't laugh, will you? I'm trying to be.'

Later, at the table, whilst Connie champed steadily through a salad without any dressing, and Vicky did her best to consume a mushroom omelette discreetly, an explanation emerged. 'You may not think so, looking at me now, but I'm a feeble character, or I'd have a figure like yours. I'm fourteen stone twelve and I ought to be less than nine according to the tables. What are you?'

'Eight and a half.'

'Billy – my boyfriend – wants me to get what he calls a figure. What I've got is not a figure in his opinion.' She rippled with laughter. 'He wants a figure eight and I'm a ruddy great zero. He thinks I've been slimming for the past eighteen months. I don't know how to tell him I was putting it on. Well, it's panic stations now.'

Uneasy as she felt, Vicky couldn't help warming to

29

Connie's exuberant personality. 'Hasn't he seen you lately?'

'No, dear, he's away. But it won't be long before he's out, and I'm frantic.'

'Out,' repeated Vicky without registering.

Connie chuckled again and dimples formed. Her laugh was very infectious. 'He's in the slammer. Five years for armed robbery, but he'll only have to serve three. He's very well behaved. What they call a model con. You'd like my Billy.'

Vicky was so stunned that all she could find to say was a faint, 'Really?'

'It's a crying shame,' Connie went on. 'Because of the weight I've put on, I've been ashamed to visit the poor lamb. You can only get away with so much. I did my best to hide the flab with loose-fitting coats and stuff, but he knew. He kept remarking on it. You see, he had a photo of me pinned to his cell wall. It was taken a couple of years ago, when I was not much over eleven stone.'

'Taken at Christchurch on a yacht?' said Vicky, in a flat, frightened voice.

Connie gave a nod and her chins shook. 'I was a big girl then, but I was passable. Well, he wasn't ashamed to have me as his pin-up. Lord help us if he saw me now – and Lord help him if his fellow cons saw me. He'd be a laughing-stock. He's quite dishy in his way. And he keeps pestering me for a visit. I get these letters. Now I don't want you to take this amiss, Vicky. I sent him your photo.'

Vicky drew in a frightened breath. She'd guessed this a moment before, but it was still a shock to have it confirmed. 'You shouldn't have.'

'I know. It was a liberty, my dear, and I'm a naughty girl. I just thought it would keep the lad happy while I make an effort to slim down. He can put it on the wall and show it to the other fellows and tell them how his girlfriend is getting in shape for his release. Will you forgive me?'

'It's too late to object, isn't it?'

Connie smiled sweetly. 'I went through any number of agencies to find someone looking like me. You've got to understand what it's like for them inside. The mob turn on you for the slightest excuse. They'd give Billy a terrible time if they found out his girl is as fat as I am.'

Politeness is deeply ingrained. Vicky found herself saying, 'You're not so big as all that.'

Connie rolled her eyes and grinned. 'He'd be appalled.'

'It's all in the eye of the beholder,' said Vicky. 'That photographer called me a scrawny hag.'

'Paul? Did he – the ratbag.'

'We didn't get on too well.'

'Vicky, I'm sorry. I had no idea.'

'It doesn't matter now. But do you honestly think Billy will believe the photo is of you?'

Connie clenched her fist and punched the air triumphantly. 'He does! I've already had a letter. He's completely taken in. Wasn't it a brilliant idea to have the picture taken on the same boat as before?'

'But what happens next? What if he asks for a visit?'

Connie opened her hands and sat back. 'Darling, how did you guess? He's more keen than ever to show me off to his fellow prisoners. What am I going to do? I'm slimming like crazy, but I can't work the miracle overnight.' The blue eyes widening above the peachy roundness of her cheeks made her look childlike. Vicky couldn't dislike her, even though she'd taken such a liberty.

'You must be terribly in love with Billy.'

'Poor poppin, yes – and he's not short of a few pennies.' She laughed wickedly. 'He owns a big house in Bournemouth and in case you're thinking it was ill-gotten gains, it was inherited. His dad was something big in the diplomatic service.'

'What drove him to crime?'

'A stolen Cortina.' She threw back her head at this joke. 'Some guys he'd met years back at university talked him

31

into robbing a building society just to prove they could get away with it. You guessed. Billy was the one who didn't. Never committed a crime in his life and the judge sent him down for all that time to teach him a lesson. Would you mind if I finished your French bread?'

'Should you?'

'No, but if I don't I'll be slipping down to the village shop for chocolate. I know it.' She reached for the bread. 'I'll have a swim later. Burn off the calories.'

'How did you meet Billy?'

'On the beach at Bournemouth. Listen, my love, this is a thumping great favour to ask, but would you do something else for me? Would you visit Billy?'

Vicky gripped the edge of the table. 'In prison?'

'It will do so much for his morale.'

'Absolutely not,' said Vicky. 'Are you actually asking me to impersonate you?'

Connie gave a wry smile. 'That would be difficult.'

'Well, then.'

'Billy won't be taken in – but the others will. His reputation will rocket.'

'He'd be furious.'

'No, it's all about self-esteem. He'll be enormously grateful.' Connie reached across the table and put her chunky hand over Vicky's. 'I'll double your modelling fee, and you'll have the satisfaction of knowing you're getting two people off the hook.'

Vicky hesitated, and that, really, was that.

Shepton Mallet prison had granite walls almost twenty feet high. She was tempted to turn the car and drive straight home. Then she thought of the young man inside expecting a visitor.

'Name, please.'

'Miss Darwin-Smith – to see Billy Davenport.'

Connie had insisted that she use the name to sign in.

The prison officers had to be convinced just as much as the inmates.

'Sign the book, miss. He's waited some time for this.'

Her heart pounding, she waited with the other visitors until it was time to go forward and sit behind one of the narrow tables. Fancy being talked into this! The prisoners were led in. They all seemed to be looking directly at her. She shivered.

The young man who stopped at the table frowned.

Vicky said, 'Please sit down, Billy.'

He settled in the chair, saying nothing.

She gave the speech she'd spent most of the journey rehearsing in the car, knowing that everything can be overheard. 'I know what you're thinking and there's no need to say it. It's no good talking about old times.'

He stared back and said, 'No good at all, obviously.'

'I expect you want to know why I came, but don't ask. Just accept that it's all for the best, would you?'

Billy gave a shrug. Even in his prison uniform his rugged looks gave him a powerful presence. She was reminded of Mickey Rourke.

She talked about the weather and the price of petrol and the programmes on television. Billy contributed very little, but he was entitled to be dumbstruck. Towards the end a two-minute warning was given.

'I'll pass on the news that you're looking well,' Vicky offered.

He nodded. 'I could be out soon.'

'That would be wonderful,' she said, trying to sound thrilled for him and thinking at the same time of the panic this would cause Connie, with six or seven stones to shed.

Finally, to her astonishment he said, 'Come again.'

She answered in some confusion, 'I can't promise. It's not so simple. It depends—'

He gave her a long look and said, 'Please.'

33

She told Ella about the prison visit. 'He was thrown at the start, naturally, but he didn't object when he knew he was stuck with me.'

'I'm not surprised.'

'Well, it must have been a letdown.'

'I wouldn't put money on it,' said Ella. 'And you say he wants another visit?'

'That's the part that worries me,' said Vicky. 'I don't want to fall out with Connie.'

'She sounds to me like a lady who knows exactly what she is doing,' said Ella. 'If he were *my* boyfriend, I wouldn't let you within a million miles of him.'

'Hey, what are you saying – that I'm not to be trusted?'

The phone rang.

It was Connie. 'Darling, I've been trying to reach you,' she said. 'I've had another letter. Billy wants a repeat as soon as possible. How about Wednesday afternoon?'

'The deal was only one visit,' said Vicky.

'I know, dear, but reading between the lines not everyone believed it was me. Some of the inmates don't think you'll go again. You can prove them wrong. I'll pay you, of course.'

'It isn't that, Connie. It's basically dishonest, impersonating you.'

'It's buying me time, dear. I've lost nearly a stone in the last week. I'm deeply grateful.'

'What if we were caught out?'

'How?'

'Well, let's say someone was able to prove that instead of visiting the prison you spent the afternoon at Eastland Park?'

'I didn't. I went out shopping. I'll go out again on Wednesday. Sweetheart, you will do this for me – and for Billy?'

Vicky sighed. 'All right.'

After she had put down the phone she turned to Ella and said, 'Caught again.'

'Get away,' said Ella. 'Admit it, you find him attractive.'

Billy was more talkative on the second visit. 'Great to see you again. I really appreciate this.'

Vicky said, 'I thought when your letter arrived, it was obvious I should come again.'

'You bet. The other lads wanted to see you too, and looking so good.'

'That's nice.'

'I have to guard your photo. The one you sent a couple of weeks ago. That was taken at Christchurch, wasn't it?'

She was getting in deep water now. 'Christchurch, yes.'

'The same boat, apparently.'

'I think so.'

'Be nice to go there again. That's one of the first places I want to go when I'm out. Tell me, Connie, do you happen to remember the name of a girl who went to Christchurch, very beautiful, not unlike yourself?'

She reddened and said, 'I wouldn't remember.'

'Too bad.' He sighed. 'You get curious, banged up in here.'

She changed the subject to tennis.

At Connie's insistence, she made one more visit to the prison. 'I'm two stone lighter than when you first came,' Connie informed her over the phone. 'I almost have a waist. Well, I'll have one in another week or so. Billy's letters are so much brighter now. He'd really appreciate another visit.'

When Vicky took her place in the visiting room she found Billy elated. 'Terrific news!' he said. 'I saw the parole board. I'm being released on Monday.'

'Monday?' Vicky tried not to look alarmed as she counted the days on her fingers under the table. There was no way Connie could get down to a respectable weight by Monday. 'That's sooner than you expected, isn't it?'

'Not a day too soon for me.'

'Congratulations, Billy.'

'Thanks, love.'

She groped for words. 'Everything may not be quite the same as you remember it on the outside.'

'I understand. I've changed, too.'

She stumbled to another question. 'Will they help you get a job?'

'I'll find work.'

'It's not so simple.'

'I'm pretty stubborn,' he said looking steadily at her. 'I don't give up. I suppose you haven't remembered the name of that girl at Christchurch?'

She shook her head. 'Is there anyone you'd like me to contact about your release?'

'You wouldn't even remember where she lives?'

'Billy, it's best to forget,' she murmured.

They talked on until the end of visiting time, Billy trying artfully to get her to give away details of her journey, but she was determined to keep her identity a mystery. Finally, as she was leaving, he said, 'I'm going to wait for her down at Christchurch, just on the off-chance.'

He hadn't once addressed her as Connie. She smiled and wished him luck. She didn't look back because a tear was rolling down her cheek.

As soon as she got home she tried ringing Connie to give her the news, but the receptionist at Eastland Park said Miss Darwin-Smith had gone out for the afternoon and wasn't back yet. Vicky remembered Connie's promise to go shopping.

'Would you care to leave a message?'

'Yes, please tell her that Billy is coming home on Monday.'

'Certainly. Who shall I say the message is from?'

'It's all right. She'll know.'

Her cheque arrived a week later from the Greatbatch Agency and she got on the phone to Mrs Greatbatch and said she wanted her name withdrawn from the files. She no longer wanted to model.

Voices on the phone are incapable of concealing much. Mrs Greatbatch was frigidly businesslike. 'Very well. It's your decision.'

'I'm not ungrateful,' Vicky said.

'But I can't remove all reference to you, if that is what you are asking. It wouldn't be legal.'

'I understand.'

'If we are asked by a competent authority, we are obliged to make certain records available. You may rest assured that we observe the Data Protection Law.'

The tone appeared excessively formal considering that Vicky had done everything she had been asked and earned good commission for the agency, but she thought no more about it until she was passing Ella's house next day.

'Have you seen this?' Ella was waving a newspaper. 'You'd better come in right away, love. You're going to need a stiff drink.'

Vicky gasped when the paper was put in front of her. On an inside page was a report headed HEALTH FARM BODY HUNT.

'Murder Squad detectives confirmed yesterday that items of clothing found beside the A350 road between Blandford Forum and Poole belonged to Connie Darwin-Smith, 32, who disappeared from the exclusive health farm Eastland Park over a week ago. Ms Darwin-Smith was last seen alive on Wednesday, June 12th, when she left to go shopping in Dorchester. The clothes, which included items of underwear, have been

37

confirmed by forensic tests as belonging to the missing woman. A partially buried tracksuit top was unearthed by a dog being exercised in this wooded area by its owner and other items were recovered later by police. Det. Insp. Jeremy Turridge said, "Further tests will be carried out, but we strongly suspect that this woman is dead. Anyone who saw anything suspicious along this stretch of road in the last seven days should contact us immediately at Dorchester Police Station." '

Vicky put down the paper and covered her eyes.

'Drink this,' Ella said, pouring brandy into a glass.

'It's a nightmare,' said Vicky. 'Dreadful. Who could have done such a thing?'

'It's obvious, isn't it?' said Ella. 'The boyfriend. You said he was being released.'

'Last Monday. Oh no, I can't believe Billy would hurt her.'

'You may not believe it, but the police will. He's an ex-con, Vicky. You store up a heap of anger in those places. They'll pick him up as soon as they know Connie was the girlfriend who didn't come visiting.'

'How would they know?'

'They've only got to check with the prison. They keep records of visitors, don't they?'

'Yes, but I signed in as Connie.'

Now Ella turned pale. 'You didn't tell me that. Sweetie, you could be in deep trouble. If they were to trace you, they could even suspect you of killing her.'

'Why?'

'You fancied Billy. You practically told me you did.'

'I'm not a murderer, Ella.'

Ella put a supportive hand on Vicky's shoulder. 'I know that, love. But you're in one hell of a spot.'

'I don't believe Billy killed her,' said Vicky. 'But if I talk to the police and tell them the truth about those visits, I'll land him in real trouble.'

There was an anguished moment of silence.

'You'd better cover your tracks then.'

'How?'

'Get your name off the agency's books for a start.'

Vicky sighed. 'She won't co-operate. I don't think she'll go to the police because it's bad publicity for Greatbatch Modelling. But she won't wipe me from the records either. If they go digging, they'll find my name in the file.'

'What about Eastland Hall? Did they have your name? They'll have told the police about your visit, for sure.'

'Oh, damn, yes.' Vicky paused, thinking hard. 'But I don't think they had my name.'

'Well, your biggest source of danger is that photographer. If he sees Connie's picture in the papers he could go to the police. He had your name, didn't he?'

She found an advert for Paul Jago Photography in the Yellow Pages. A studio in Christchurch. She decided it was safer to go in person than to phone. She went at once, driving fast, and thinking frantically what she could do to get his co-operation.

The studio was above a pet shop in the main street. Halfway up the stairs she met Paul Jago coming down. He was obviously in a hurry.

'You?' he said, putting his hand to his neck. 'What do you want?'

'It's about Connie,' said Vicky. 'Have you seen the papers?'

'You must be crazy coming here.'

'Whatever has happened to her, I'm innocent. But I need to talk to you.'

'Have the police been on to you?'

'Not yet.'

He scraped his hand distractedly through his blond hair. 'We can't talk here. There's a teashop at the top of the street called Carly's. I'll join you there in five minutes.'

She wasn't sure if she trusted him, but at least the teashop would be neutral ground, safer than his studio. From his furtive conduct, he might have murdered Connie himself.

She found the place and sat at a table well away from the only other people in there. She ordered a pot of tea for two. She was beginning to think she had been duped when Jago walked in and came to the table.

'What do you want from me?' he asked, looking about him to see who else was in the shop.

'I'm frightened.'

'*You're* frightened?'

'The police could easily get the wrong idea about me. I visited Connie at Eastland Park. I don't think they know my name and I don't want to be involved. Would you do me a favour?'

'Forget I ever met you?' said Jago.

'Yes, and destroy the negative of that photo and any record you have of my name and address.'

His eyes locked with hers and seemed almost to bore into her. 'I can wipe you from my memory, yes – if you do likewise. If the law catches up with you, you never heard of Paul Jago, right?'

'Right.'

'That's a promise?'

'A promise.'

Vicky couldn't fathom why she felt such an over-whelming sense of guilt coming from the young man. Without another word he got up and left the shop. She sipped the tea to control her shaking. She drank two cups.

At least she had achieved what she had come for.

Still in turmoil, she walked back to where she had left her car. People were strolling the sunny streets of Christchurch in their shorts and teeshirts oblivious of the grisly search being conducted only a few miles up the road. She couldn't imagine herself ever feeling relaxed

40

again. She would listen to every news bulletin on the car radio.

Just as she was inserting the key into the car door, a man's voice spoke her name. She turned.

Whoever he was, she didn't recognize him. He was holding something in his hand, showing it to her.

'My name is Turridge,' he said. 'Detective Inspector Turridge. And this is Sergeant Morley. We'd like to ask you some questions.'

She leaned against the car and wondered if she would stay upright.

Sergeant Morley, who was a woman, helped her to a car parked nearby. They explained that they would be taking her to Christchurch police station. 'You want to know how we found you?' said Turridge. 'Through your car, ma'am. When you visited Miss Darwin-Smith at Eastland Hall the Triumph Herald stood out like the proverbial sore thumb. A security guard took the number and we tracked you through the police computer.'

'What do you want from me?'

'A statement at this stage, ma'am.'

'I've done nothing criminal.'

'Let's hope not.'

'Has Connie been found?'

He said after a pause, as if deciding whether to release the information, 'Yes, ma'am.'

Vicky lowered her head.

In the interview room Turridge asked her to give an account of everything she could recall about her dealings with Connie.

Matters had progressed too far for evasion. She unburdened herself of the entire story. They prepared a statement and she signed it. They offered to drive her back to where her car was, but she said she'd rather walk. 'May I ask something?' she added.

'Depends what it is.'

41

'Have you charged anyone?'

'Yes, ma'am. We have a suspect in custody. To put you out of your suspense it's Miss Darwin-Smith.'

'Connie?' she piped in disbelief.

He nodded.

'She's still alive?'

Turridge grinned sheepishly. 'She's been in custody ever since the day of her disappearance, which explains a lot. She was caught shoplifting in Dorchester. Strictly in confidence your ex-friend Connie has a long record of shoplifting. The shrinks would call her a kleptomaniac. It seems that on the afternoons you visited the prison you innocently provided Connie with an alibi, until she was caught with the goods in her possession. She was remanded in custody and, of course, being smart, she gave a false name. Not yours, by the way.'

'Why give a false name?'

'It's her previous.'

'Her what?'

'Previous convictions. She was dead scared they would be read out in court and she'd get a long sentence. As a first offender, she'd probably walk out with a warning and a promise of treatment.'

'Did this have something to do with her clothes being found?'

'That was the boyfriend laying a false trail to suggest she had been murdered.'

'Billy?'

Turridge shook his head. 'No. Couldn't be him. Those clothes had been buried for a week. Billy was still banged up a week ago. He only got out on Monday. It was the latest boyfriend, Jago. The one you came to see this afternoon. We picked him up an hour ago, stupid idiot. He'll be charged with obstructing the police and wasting our time. What a wicked old world it is, ma'am.'

Not quite so wicked as Vicky had imagined. She walked

42

out of the police station. She must have spent the best part of two hours having that statement prepared. The low evening sun, comfortingly warm on her skin, was adding richness to the colours of the sails in the harbour. The sea lapped at the wall.

She saw him ahead as she walked on. He was standing close to the spot where she had come to be photographed. She had only ever seen him in regulation blue before this. He had a white shirt and claret slacks. A grey jacket was slung over one shoulder. He was smiling.

She continued to walk towards him.

Where is Thy Sting?

THE STORM HAD PASSED, LEAVING a keen wind that whipped foam off the waves. Heaps of gleaming seaweed were strewn about the beach. Shells, bits of driftwood and a few stranded jellyfish lay where the tide had deposited them. Paul Molloy, bucket in hand, was down there as he was every morning, alone and preoccupied.

His wife Gwynneth stood by the wooden steps that led off the beach through a garden of flowering trees to their property.

'Paul! Breakfast time.'

She had to shout it twice more before Paul's damaged brain registered anything. Then he turned and trudged awkwardly towards her.

The stroke last July, a few days before his sixty-first birthday, had turned him into a shambling parody of the fine man he had been. He was left with the physical co-ordination of a small child, except that he was slower. And dumb. The loss of speech was the hardest for Gwynneth to bear. She hated being cut off from his thoughts. He was unable even to write, or draw pictures.

She had to be content with scraps of communication. Each time he came up from the beach he handed her something he had found, a shell or a pebble. She received such gifts as graciously as she had once accepted roses.

They had said at the hospital that she ought to keep talking to him in an adult way, even if he didn't appear to understand. It was a mistake to give up. So she persevered, but inevitably it sounded as if she were addressing a child.

'Darling, what a beautiful shell! Is it for me? Oh, how sweet! I'll take it up to the house and put it on the shelf with all the other treasures you found for me – except that this one must stand in the centre.'

She leaned forward to kiss him and made no contact with his face. He had moved his head to look at a gull.

She helped him up the steps and they started the short, laborious trek to the house. They had bought the land, a few miles north of Bundaberg on the Queensland coast, ten years before Paul retired from his Brisbane-based insurance company. As chairman he could have carried on for years more, but he had always promised he would stop at sixty, before he got fat and feeble, as he used to say. They had built ·themselves this handsome retirement home and installed facilities they felt they would use: swimming pool, Jacuzzi, boat-house and tennis court. Only their guests used them now.

'Come on, love, step out quick,' she urged Paul. 'There's beautiful bacon waiting for you.' And tirelessly trying for a spark of interest she added, 'Cousin Haydn's still asleep by the look of it. I don't think he'll be joining your walks on the beach. Not before breakfast, anyway. Probably not at all. Doesn't care for the sea, does he?'

Gwynneth encouraged people to stay. She missed real conversation. Cousin Haydn was on a visit from Wales. He was a distant cousin she hadn't met before, but she didn't mind. She'd got to know him when she'd started delving into her family history for something to distract her. Years ago, her father had given her an old Bible with a family tree in the front. She'd brought it up to date. Then she had joined a family history society and learned that a good way of tracking down ancestors was to write to local newspapers in the areas where they had lived. She had managed to get a letter published in a Swansea paper.

Haydn had seen it and got in touch. He was an Evans also, and he'd done an immense amount of research. He'd discovered a branch of his family tree that linked up with hers, through Great-Grandfather Hugh Evans of Port Talbot.

Paul shuffled towards the house without even looking up at the drawn curtains.

'Mind you,' Gwynneth continued, 'I'm not surprised Haydn is used to staying indoors, what with the Welsh weather I remember. I expect he reads the Bible a lot, being a man of the cloth.' She checked herself, for she was speaking the obvious again. She pushed open the kitchen door. 'Come on, Paul. Just you and me for breakfast, by the look of it.'

Cousin Haydn eventually appeared in time for mid-morning coffee. On the first day after he'd arrived he'd discarded the black suit and dog-collar in favour of a pink teeshirt. Casual clothes made him look several years younger, say forty-five, but they also revealed what Gwynneth would have called a beer-gut had Haydn not been a minister.

'Feel better for your sleep?' she enquired.

'Infinitely better, thank you, Gwynneth.' You couldn't mistake him for an Australian when he opened his mouth. 'And most agreeably refreshed by a dip in your pool.'

'Oh, you had a swim?'

'Hardly a swim. I was speaking of the small circular pool.'

She smiled. 'The Jacuzzi. Did you find the switch?'

'I was unaware that I needed to find it.'

'It works the pumps that make the whirlpool effect. If you didn't switch it on, you missed something.'

'Then I shall certainly repeat the adventure.'

'Paul used to like it. I'm afraid of him slipping now, so he doesn't get in there.'

'Pity, if he enjoyed it.'

46

'Perhaps I ought to take the risk. The specialist said he may begin to bring other muscles into use that aren't affected by the stroke, isn't that so, my darling?'

Paul gave no sign of comprehension.

'Does he understand much?' Haydn asked.

'I convince myself that he does, even if he's unable to show it. If you don't mind, I don't really care to talk about him in this way, as if he's not one of us.'

Cousin Haydn gave an understanding nod. 'Let's talk about something less depressing, then. A definite prospect of improvement. I have good news for you, Gwynneth.'

She responded with a murmur that didn't convey much enthusiasm. Sermons in church were one thing. Her kitchen was another place altogether.

It emerged that Haydn's good news wasn't of an evangelical character. 'One of my reasons for coming here – apart from following up our fascinating correspondence – is to tell you about a mutual ancestor, Sir Tudor Evans.'

'*Sir* Tudor? We had a title in the family?'

'Back in the seventeenth century, yes.'

'I don't recall seeing him on my family tree.'

Haydn gave the slight smile of one who has a superior grasp of genealogy. 'Yours started in the 1780s, if I recall.'

'Oh, yes.'

'To say that it started then is, of course, misleading. Your eighteenth-century forebears had parents, as did mine, and they, in turn, had parents, and so it goes back, first to Sir Tudor, and ultimately to Adam.'

'Never mind Adam. Tell me about Sir Tudor.' Gwynneth swung round to Paul, who was sucking his thumb. 'Bet you didn't know I came from titled stock, darling.'

Haydn said, 'A direct line. Planter Evans, they called him. He owned half of Barbados once, according to my research. Made himself a fortune in sugar cane.'

'Really? A fortune. What happened to it?'

47

'Most of it went down with the *Gloriana* in 1683. One of the great tragedies of the sea. He'd sold the plantations to come back to the Land of his Fathers. He was almost home when a great storm blew up in the Bristol Channel and the ship was lost with all hands. Sir Tudor and his wife Eleanor were among those on board.'

'How very sad!'

'God rest their souls, yes.'

Gwynneth put her hand to her face. 'I'm trying to remember. Last year was such a nightmare for us. A lot of things passed right over my head. The *Gloriana*. Isn't that the ship they found – those treasure-hunters? I read about this somewhere.'

'It was in all the papers,' Haydn confirmed. 'I have some of the cuttings with me, in my briefcase.'

'I do remember. The divers were bringing up masses of stuff – coins by the bucketful, silverware and the most exquisite jewellery. Oh, how exciting! Can we make a claim?'

Cousin Haydn shook his head. 'Out of the question, my dear. One would need to hire lawyers. Besides, it may be too late.'

'Why?'

'As I understand it, when treasure is recovered from a wreck around the British coasts, it has to be handed over to the local receiver of wrecks or the customs. The lawful owner then has a year and a day to make a claim. After that, the pieces are sold and the proceeds go to the salvager.'

'A year and a day,' said Gwynneth. 'Oh, Haydn, this is too tantalising. When did those treasure-hunters start bringing up the stuff?'

'Last March.'

'Eleven months! There's still time to make a claim. We must do it.'

Haydn sighed heavily. 'These things can be extremely costly.'

'But we'd get it all back if we could prove our right to the treasure.'

He put out his hand in a dissenting gesture. '*Your* right, my dear, not mine. My connection is very tenuous, but yours is undeniable. No, I have no personal interest here. Besides, a man of my calling cannot serve God and Mammon.'

'Do you really believe I have a claim?'

'The treasure-hunters would dispute that, I'm sure.'

'We're talking about millions of pounds, aren't we? Why should I sit back and let them take it all? I need to get hold of some lawyers – and fast.'

Haydn coughed. 'They charge astronomical fees.'

'I know,' said Gwynneth. 'We can afford it, can't we, Paul?'

Paul made a blowing sound with his lips that probably had no bearing on the matter.

Gwynneth assumed so. 'What is it they want – a down payment?'

'A retainer, I think is the expression.'

'I can write a cheque tomorrow, if you want. I look after all our personal finances now. There's more than enough in the deposit account. The thing is, how do I find a reliable lawyer?'

Haydn cupped his chin in his hands and looked thoughtful. 'I wouldn't go to an Australian firm. Better find someone on the spot. Jones, Heap and Jones of Cardiff are the best in Wales. I'm sure they could take on something like this.'

'But is there time? We're almost into March now.'

'It is rather urgent,' Haydn agreed. 'Look, I don't mind cutting my holiday short by a few days. If I got back to Wales at the weekend I could see them on Monday.'

'I couldn't ask you to do that,' said Gwynneth in a tone that betrayed the opposite.

'No trouble,' said Haydn breezily.

'You're an angel. Would they accept a cheque in Australian Pounds?'

'That might be difficult, but it's easily got around. Travellers' cheques are the thing. I use them all the time. In fact, if you're serious about this. . .'

'Oh, yes.'

' . . . you could buy sterling travellers' cheques in my name and I could pay the retainer for you.'

'Would you really do that for me?'

'Anything to be of service.'

She shivered with pleasure. 'And now, if you've got them nearby, I'd love to have ten minutes with those press cuttings.'

He left them with her, and she read them through several times during the afternoon, when she was alone in her room and Paul had gone for one of his walks along the beach. Three pages cut from a colour supplement had stunning pictures of the finds. She so adored the ruby necklace and the gold bracelets that she thought she would refuse to sell them. Cousin Haydn had also given her a much more detailed family tree than she had seen before. It proved beyond doubt that she was the only direct descendant of Sir Tudor Evans.

Was it all too good to be true?

One or two doubts crept into her mind later that afternoon. Presumably the treasure-hunters had invested heavily in ships, divers and equipment. They must have been confident that anything they brought up would belong to them. Maybe her claim wasn't valid under the law. She wondered also whether Cousin Haydn's research was entirely accurate. She didn't question his good faith – how could one in the circumstances? – but knew from her own humble diggings in family history that it was all too easy to confuse one Evans with another.

On the other hand, she told herself, that's what I'm hiring the lawyers to find out. It's their business to establish whether my claim is lawful.

There was an unsettling incident towards evening. She walked down to the beach to collect Paul. The stretch where he liked to wander was never particularly crowded, even at weekends, and she soon spotted him kneeling on the sand. This time he didn't need calling. He got up, collecting his bucket and tottered towards her.

Automatically she held out her hand for the gift he had chosen for her. He peered into the bucket and picked something out and placed it on her open palm.

A dead wasp.

She almost snatched her hand away and let the thing drop. She was glad she didn't, because it was obvious that he'd saved it for her and she would have hated to hurt his feelings.

She said, 'Oh, a little wasp. Thank you, darling. So thoughtful. We'll take it home and put it with all my pretty pebbles and shells, shall we?'

She took a paper tissue from her pocket and folded the tiny corpse carefully between the layers. In the house she unwrapped it and made a space on the shelf among the shells and stones.

'There.' She turned and smiled at Paul.

He put his thumb on the wasp and squashed it.

'Darling!'

The small act of violence shocked Gwynneth. She found herself quite stupidly reacting as if something precious had been destroyed. 'You shouldn't have done that, Paul. You gave it to me. I treasure whatever you give me. You know that.'

He shuffled out of the room.

That evening over the meal she told Cousin Haydn about the incident, once again breaking her own rule and discussing Paul while he was sitting with them. 'I keep wondering if he meant anything by it,' she said. 'It's so unlike him.'

'If you want my opinion,' said Haydn, 'he showed some intelligence. You don't want a wasp in the house, dead or alive. As a matter of fact I've got quite a phobia about them. It's one of the reasons why I avoid the beach. You can't sit for long on any beach without being troubled by them.'

'Perhaps you were stung once?'

'No, I've managed to avoid them, but one of my uncles was killed by one.'

'Killed by a wasp?'

'He was only forty-four at the time. It happened on the front at Aberystwyth. He was stung here, on the right temple. His face went bright red and he fell down on the shingle. My aunt ran for a doctor, but all he could do was confirm that uncle was dead.'

Clearly the tragedy had made a profound impression on Haydn. His account of the incident, spoken in simple language instead of his usual florid style, carried conviction.

'Dreadful. It must have been a rare case.'

'Not so uncommon as you'd think. I tell you, Gwynneth, the wasp is one of God's creatures I studiously avoid at all times.' He turned to Paul and for the first time addressed him directly, trying to end on a less grave note. 'So I say more power to your thumb, boyo.'

Paul looked at him blankly.

Towards the end of the meal Haydn announced that he would be leaving in the morning. 'I telephoned the airport. I am advised I can get something called a standby. They say it's better before the weekend, so I'm leaving tomorrow.'

'*Tomorrow*?' said Gwynneth, her voice pitched high in alarm. 'But you can't. We haven't bought those travellers' cheques.'

'That's all right, my dear. There's a place to purchase them at the airport. All you need to do is write me a cheque. In fact you could write it now in case we forget in the morning.'

'How much?'

'I don't know. I'm not too conversant with the scale of fees lawyers charge these days. Are you sure you want to get involved in expense?'

'Absolutely. If I have no right to make a claim, they'll let me know, won't they?'

'I'll let you know myself, my dear. How much can you spare without running up an overdraft? It's probably better for me to take more, rather than less.'

She wrote him a cheque for ten thousand Australian dollars.

'Then if you will excuse me, I shall go and pack my things and have a quiet hour before bedtime.'

'Would you like an early breakfast tomorrow?'

He smiled. 'Early by my standards, yes. Say about eight? That gives me ample time to do something I promised – try the Jacuzzi with the switch on. Good night and God bless you, my dear. And you, Paul, old fellow.'

Gwynneth slept fitfully. At one stage in the night she noticed that Paul had his eyes open. She found his hand and gripped it tightly and talked to him as if he understood. 'I keep wondering if I've done the right thing, giving Haydn that cheque. It's not as if I don't trust him – I mean, you've got to trust a man of God, haven't you? I just wonder if you would have done what I did, my darling, giving him the cheque, I mean, and somehow I don't think so. In fact I ask myself if you were trying to tell me something when you gave me the wasp. It was such an unusual thing for you to do. Then squashing it like that.'

She must have drifted off soon after because when she next opened her eyes the grey light of dawn was picking out the edges of the curtains. She sighed and turned towards Paul, but his side of the bed was empty. He must have gone down to the beach already.

She showered and dressed soon after, wanting to make an early start on cooking the breakfast. She would get everything ready first, she decided, and then fetch Paul from the beach before she started the cooking. However, this was a morning of surprises.

For some unfathomable reason Paul had already come up from the beach without being called. He was seated in his usual place in the kitchen.

'Paul! You gave me quite a shock,' Gwynneth told him. 'What is it? Are you extra hungry this morning, or something? I'll get it started presently. Would you like some bread while you're waiting? Better give Cousin Haydn a call first and make sure he's awake.'

It crossed her mind as she went to tap on Haydn's door that Paul hadn't brought her anything from the beach. She wondered if she'd hurt his feelings by talking about the wasp as she had.

She didn't like knocking on Haydn's door in case she was interrupting his morning prayers, but it had to be done this morning in case he overslept.

He answered her call. 'Thank you. Is there time for me to sample the Jacuzzi?'

'Of course. Shall we say twenty minutes?'

'That should be ample.'

She returned to the kitchen and made a sandwich for Paul. The bucket he always took to the beach was beside him. Without being too obvious about it, Gwynneth glanced inside to see if the customary gift of a shell or a pebble was there. It was silly, but she was feeling quite neglected.

Empty.

She said nothing about it. Simply busied herself setting the table for breakfast. Presently she started heating the frying pan.

Fifteen minutes later when everything was cooked and waiting in the oven, Haydn had not appeared.

'He's really enjoying that Jacuzzi,' she told Paul. 'We'd better start, I think.'

They finished.

'I'd better go and see,' she said.

When she went to the door, the leg of Paul's chair was jammed against it, preventing her from opening it. 'Do you mind, darling? I can't get out.'

He made no move.

'Maybe you're right,' Gwynneth said, always willing to assume that Paul's behaviour was deliberate and intelligent. 'I shouldn't fuss. It won't spoil for being left a few minutes more.'

She allowed another quarter of an hour to pass. 'Do you think something's happened to him? I'd better go and see, really I had. Come on, dear. Let me through.'

As she took Paul by the arm and helped him to his feet he reached out and drew her towards him, pressing his face against hers. She was surprised and delighted. He hadn't embraced her once since the stroke. She turned her face and kissed him before going to find Cousin Haydn.

Haydn was lying face down on the tile surround of the Jacuzzi, which was churning noisily. He was wearing black swimming-trunks. He didn't move when she spoke his name.

'I think he may be dead,' she told the girl who took the emergency call.

The girl told her to try the kiss of life. An ambulance was on its way.

Gwynneth was still on her knees trying to breathe life into Cousin Haydn when the police arrived. They had come straight round the back of the house.

'Let's have a look, lady.' After a moment the sergeant said, 'He's gone – no question. Who is he – your husband?'

She explained about Cousin Haydn.

'This is where you found him?'

'Well, yes. Was it an electric shock, do you think?'

'You tell me, lady. Was the Jacuzzi on when you found him?'

'Yes.' Gwynneth suddenly realised that it was no longer running. Paul must have switched it off while she was phoning for help. She didn't want Paul brought into this. 'I don't know. I may be mistaken about that.'

'You see, there could be a fault,' the sergeant speculated. 'We'll get it checked. Is your husband about?'

'He was.' She called Paul's name. 'He must have gone down to the beach. That's where he goes.' She told them about the stroke.

More policemen arrived, some in plain clothes. One introduced himself as Detective Inspector Perry. He talked to Gwynneth several times in the next two hours. He went into Cousin Haydn's room and opened the suitcase he had packed for the flight home.

'You say you knew this man as Haydn Evans, your cousin from Wales?'

'That's who he was.'

'A distant cousin?'

Gwynneth didn't care for his grin. 'I can show you the family tree if you like.'

'No need for that, Mrs Molloy. His luggage is stuffed with family trees, all as bogus as his Welsh accent. He wasn't a minister of any church or chapel. His name was Brown. Michael Herbert Brown. An English con man we've been after for months. He was getting too well known to Scotland Yard, so he came out to Queensland this summer. Been stinging people for thousands with the treasure-hunting story. Here's your cheque. Lucky escape, I'd say.'

They finally took the body away in an ambulance.

Detective Inspector Perry phoned late in the afternoon. 'Just thought I'd let you know that your Jacuzzi is safe to use, Mrs Molloy. There's no electrical fault. I have the pathologist's report and I can tell you that Brown was not electrocuted.'

56

'What killed him, then?'

He laughed. 'Sort of appropriate. It was a sting.'

Gwynneth frowned and put her hand to her throat as she recalled what Cousin Haydn had told her. 'A sting from a wasp?'

'In a manner of speaking.' There was amusement in his voice. 'Not the wasp you had in mind.'

'I don't understand.'

'No mystery in it, Mrs Molloy. A sea-wasp got him. You know what a sea-wasp is?'

She knew. Everyone on the coast knew. 'A jellyfish. An extremely poisonous jellyfish.'

'Right, a killer.'

'But Haydn didn't swim in the sea. He kept off the beach.'

'That explains it, then.'

'How?'

'He wouldn't have known about the sea-wasps. That storm washed quite a number on to the beaches. Looks as if Brown decided to take one look at the sea before he left this morning. He'd put on his swimming gear – we know that – and he must have waded in. Didn't need to go far. There were sea-wasps stranded in the shallows. You and I know how deadly they are, but I reckon an Englishman wouldn't. He got bitten, staggered back to the house and collapsed beside the Jacuzzi.'

'I see.' She knew it was nonsense.

'Try and remember, Mrs Morgan. Did you see him walk down to the beach?'

'I was cooking breakfast.'

'Pity. Where was your husband?'

'Paul?' She glanced over at Paul, now sitting in his usual armchair with his arms around his bucket. 'He was with me in the kitchen.' She was about to add that Paul had come up from the beach, but the inspector was already on to other possibilities.

'Maybe someone else saw Brown on the beach. I believe it's pretty deserted at that time.'

'Yes.'

'Be useful to have a witness for the inquest. All right, I heard what you said about him normally keeping off the beach, but it's a fact that he died from a sea-wasp sting. That's been established.'

'I'm not questioning it.'

'I ask you, Mrs Molloy, how else could it have happened? There's only one other possibility I can think of. How could a jellyfish get into a Jacuzzi, for Christ's sake?'

Being of Sound Mind

'ON YOUR FEET.'

'What?'

'They called our numbers.'

Hamish McDinnie, fifty-eight and about to board an airliner for the first time, scanned the departure lounge, dabbing his forehead with pieces of a Kleenex that he had shredded while sitting there. 'Nobody else is moving.'

'They're tourist class.' His brother Alastair waited a second, and then said in a tone that excluded the possibility of defiance, 'Move.'

Fit and forthright from thirty years of teaching what he persisted in calling gym, Alastair had always been the dominant brother, in spite of being two years Hamish's junior. On his fifty-fifth birthday Alastair had taken premature retirement, cannily saving himself from hernias, cartilage problems and the teaching of arithmetic to first years. He had settled for a dignified departure when he could still referee both halves of a football match. Now he was secretly relishing displaying his athletic torso beside the pool at the Nyali Beach Hotel. His only concern was that his blond hair, brushed back like Tarzan's, might acquire a reddish, artifical hue in the merciless African sun.

They passed through to the aircraft. The first-class steward examined their boarding passes, greeted them by name and insisted on stowing away their hand luggage. All this attention made Hamish feel uncomfortable. He wished they had booked as tourists like the other people. He was conscious that the steward's clothes fitted better than his own. Normally he didn't wear a suit at all. He serviced lawnmowers for a living. Being fat, he felt more comfortable in overalls. The pity was that you couldn't wear overalls in the first-class section. The old black pin-stripe he had put on had come in useful for the funeral, but it was tight across the back and the trousers didn't meet at the waist. The gap was bridged by a safety-pin hidden by a belt.

The steward asked if they would care for a glass of champagne. Hamish shook his head, whereupon Alastair said, 'He'll take a glass. We both will.' Then he informed Hamish, 'It's complimentary in the first class.'

'If I may be so bold, gentlemen,' the steward remarked when he returned with individual bottles and tulip-glasses which he proceeded to fill, 'your surname is familiar. Would you by any chance be related to Sir Angus McDinnie, the painter, who died so tragically the other day?'

Alastair managed to convey as he spoke that this was not the first time, nor the tenth, that he had been asked the question. 'His sons.'

'Ah – I wondered, sir. A great loss to the world of art. I was reading his obituary in *The Scotsman* only yesterday. Dreadful.'

'He didna' suffer,' said Hamish.

'I suppose not, sir,' said the steward, and it sounded more like a question than a statement.

'He passed oot from the fumes before the flames reached him,' Hamish went on to explain. 'As, eh . . . as . . .' He looked to his brother to supply the word.

'Asphyxia,' said Alastair. 'However, our father lived to a splendid age.'

'So I saw in the paper, sir.'

'You have to be positive,' Alastair stressed. 'He made the best of his life, enjoyed himself to the end. His whisky, his

60

good food, his smoking – even if it was the smoking that did for him finally.'

'A cigarette-end?'

Alastair nodded. 'Any art studio is a tinder-box, unfortunately.'

'I suppose he was getting absent-minded.'

'Not at all. He was mentally alert. Even in his ninetieth year he was of sound mind.'

'Sound mind, aye,' Hamish affirmed.

'That must be a consolation,' said the steward. 'Well, the circumstances are sad, but I'm honoured to have you aboard, gentlemen.'

'How many hours to Nairobi?' Hamish asked.

'My brother is nervous of flying,' Alastair said with a superior smile, adding, without a trace of Scotland in his accent, 'My wee brother.'

After they were airborne, and a meal had been served, Alastair got up from his seat.

'What are ye doin'?' Hamish asked in alarm.

'Having a stretch. You're allowed to get up, you know. You should try it.'

Hamish grimaced and shook his head.

Upright in the aisle, Alastair spread his arms as if about to lead a gym class. 'I think I should tell you that I intend to make the most of this trip. So should you. The funeral is over. We gave father a decent send-off, and now we're entitled to relax.'

'True,' admitted Hamish.

'He would have wished it,' said Alastair. 'He would have wanted to reward us for our pains.'

'Och aye.'

'I booked a five-day safari to Tsavo National Park.'

Hamish frowned. 'You didna' tell me that.'

'Don't tell me you're scared of animals as well as aeroplanes.'

Hamish was silent.

'You're forever going on about the wild-life films on the television. This is the real thing.'

Somewhere above the Mediterranean, the aircraft gave a lurch and the FASTEN SEATBELTS signs lit up. Over the public address system the captain's voice announced in a benign tone that they were experiencing a small amount of turbulence, and this was quite normal. Without conspicuous haste, Alastair resumed his seat.

Hamish pressed his hands over his knees. He had felt from the outset that this holiday was a mistake. Now he was preparing to meet his Maker. 'We did nothing to be ashamed of,' he said to his brother. 'Did we?'

'It's only turbulence,' said Alastair with his dismissive gym master's air. 'We're simply passing through some high cloud.'

Towards the end of the flight, when the aircraft had started its descent, the steward paused in front of the brothers and delivered a tribute to their father. 'He was certainly the finest Scottish landscapist since the war and perhaps the finest this century. If it doesn't seem insensitive to say so, I just hope none of his major work was lost in the fire.'

'All of the finished work survived,' said Alastair.

'The good stuff was kept in the house,' Hamish put in.

'Wasn't the house destroyed, sir?'

'No. The fire was in the studio.'

Alastair explained, 'The studio was a free-standing workshop in the garden.'

'Ah. I follow you now.'

'The paints and easels were destroyed, and some things he was currently working on, but they weren't of any merit. He hadn't produced anything of merit for ten years or more. He was an old man.'

The steward, who seemed to rate himself as an art

expert, remarked, 'Monet was in his eighties when he painted those vast canvases of water-lilies.'

'Monet was exceptional,' said Alastair.

'Picasso?'

'A con man.'

On recliners under the palms at the Nyali Beach Hotel in Mombasa, the sons of Sir Angus McDinnie sipped chilled drinks and observed the other guests. The air was heavy with the smell of sun-tan lotion.

'All these lassies,' murmured Alastair, who was beginning to acquire a tan.

'What about them?'

No answer came. They lapsed into silence for a time. Above them, sparrows cheeped from invisible places behind the serrations in the bark.

'Father taught me to swim when I was nine,' Hamish reminisced, his thoughts more on the pool than the lassies. 'He took me into Loch Lomond and held me by the back o' m'breeks and made me kick m'legs.'

'I remember. He could have been a fine gym instructor.'

'He was better off painting.'

'You're telling me!'

After a moment, Hamish commented, 'We wouldna' be here but for him.'

'That's a fact.'

'I'm thinkin' o' the will.'

'Mm.' Alastair was less disposed than his brother to think of the will.

'The last will,' persisted Hamish.

Under the next tree, a topless sun-bather jerked up from her recliner as a bird-dropping moistened her back.

Hamish hadn't noticed. 'He came to his senses at the end. The other was a travesty. Isn't that a fact, Ally? A travesty?'

Alastair's attention was elsewhere. 'What are you saying?'

'The will. The first will. I wouldna' begrudge the pictures

63

goin' to the nation,' said Hamish. 'But every last penny of his money to the National Gallery of Scotland? That would have been out of order.'

Under close scrutiny, the woman wiped her back with a tissue and then sank face down again.

That distraction over, Alastair picked up the conversation. 'It's the sort of injustice that can happen under English law. If we'd all remained north of the border instead of moving down to Cornwall, you and I would have been entitled to our *jus relictae*.'

Hamish blinked.

'*Jus relictae*. An automatic one-half share of the estate. It's a right enshrined in Scots law. We'd have got a quarter each, which is less than we finally inherited, but I wouldn't have complained. The English system guarantees nothing for the family.'

'Thank the Lord he listened to you, Al.'

'We are his sons.'

'Aye. We had the right.'

Alastair drew himself up from the sun-bed and leaned towards his brother, speaking in a low voice inaudible to anyone else. 'We need to be clear about this, Hamish. All we did was consult father and get a sense of his intentions. The decision to draw up a new will was his alone. In the wisdom of old age he decided that everything should remain in the family. I phrased it precisely according to his wishes and he signed it. And let this be understood, Hamish – he was of sound mind.'

'So he was, rest his soul. Of sound mind.'

Alastair resumed the preferred tanning position.

After an interval, Hamish said, 'The National Gallery willna' contest it . . . will they?'

'Why should they?'

'It was in *The Scotsman*.'

'What was?'

'About everythin' goin' to the nation.'

'That was years ago. People change their minds. Father did.'

'What about his solicitors?'

'For pity's sake, Hamish. What are you worrying about now?'

'They could make it sticky. They don't know about the new will. They have the old will in their safe.'

'He cancelled it. "*I hereby revoke all wills made by me at any time heretofore.*" '

The safari in Tsavo National Park was hugely enjoyable. Elephants in abundance, zebra, buffalo and rhino stood untroubled by the minibuses that cruised through their domain. Hamish had to admit that it was better than the television. And the safari lodges were infinitely more luxurious than he had imagined. Even the malt whisky was acceptable. Over a glass one evening at Kilaguni Lodge, Hamish was moved to say, 'Da' would have enjoyed this.'

'He would never have travelled so far,' said Alastair. 'The only time he crossed the sea was that trip to Mull in 1954. You and I can be grateful that he was prudent with his money.'

'True.'

'Mind, I could have used some of it years ago, when I was struggling with a mortgage.'

'Our Da' wasn't one to featherbed his sons.' Hamish swirled the whisky in the glass. 'D'ye think we were a disappointment to him, Al?'

'In what way?'

'We didna' have an ounce of art in us.'

This was too sweeping for Alastair. 'Art isn't restricted to painters. Teaching is an art, in my opinion. Besides, I value civilized behaviour higher than any so-called art, and certainly higher than facility with a paintbrush. Loyalty, for instance. You and I devoted ourselves to father's well-being in his last years.'

'You and I?'

'Shall we have another and then retire? It's an early start in the morning.'

Under his mosquito net, Hamish found sleep difficult to achieve. His mind had fixed on his father and the last years. There was nothing, he kept telling himself, to trouble his own conscience. For Father's sake, he had never moved out of the family home. Their mother had died when they were still at school, and father had moved south, as far south as possible, to Cornwall, where the light was supposed to be ideal for painting. Hamish, then fifteen, had left school. Father had needed looking after, insisting that the practicalities of everyday living were inimical to great art. Hamish had supplied his needs, fitting them around a series of part-time jobs. Father's dependence had not lessened as the years passed. And sadly the justification for Hamish's servitude had become less and less apparent.

By the end the painting had amounted to nothing. The old man would take a sheet of watercolour paper and spend the morning soaking it and trying hamfistedly to attach it to a drawing board with gummed paper strips. Watercolour paper had to be stretched, and the process – which in years past had been simple to perform – made such demands on Father's energy and concentration that he would exhaust himself. Unsightly wrinkles would appear in the paper. The gummed strips would attach themselves to his sleeves, his hands, his feet, the floor – everywhere except the board. Because correct preparation was, according to Father, the responsibility of the artist, the stretching could not be entrusted to Hamish. And by the time the task was done, and the paper ready, he didn't paint anything at all. He might make a few pencil marks of no obvious merit or significance. There was never any time left for painting. After lunch he always fitted in a nap on the studio couch. About three in the afternoon he would strip the paper from the board and let it drop on the floor. And when Hamish swept the studio each evening, he would pick up the discarded sheet and stack it on the pile beside the plan-chest under the window.

Finally, depressed by the futility of it all, he had telephoned Alastair, who had his own house on the other side of town. Truth to tell, Alastair had not been the devoted son he claimed; he had been an infrequent visitor since the public announcement that the National Gallery of Scotland was to inherit the entire estate. However, on learning that Father was exhibiting obvious signs of senility, he had cycled over. Hamish had shown him the studio and the ever-mounting pile of discarded paper.

'It occurs to me,' Alastair had said after some thought, 'that this may be a symptom of something else.'

'What's that?'

'When did he last have his eyes tested?'

'I couldna' say. You know what he's like about anything like that. He's always too busy, he says.'

'To my recollection he's been wearing the same glasses for a quarter of a century. The reason he can't paint is that he can't see out of them.'

'He'll nae have them changed.'

'You're right,' Alastair had said. 'You're definitely right about that.'

The safari was over, but they still had another week under the palms at the Nyali Beach Hotel. The Kenyan staff flitted among the recliners delivering milk-shakes and chilled drinks to the basking guests. Alastair's hair, as he had feared, was acquiring russet streaks, so he wore his safari hat except at meal times. Three gold chains now adorned his deep-bronzed chest.

'Admit it – you've enjoyed all this,' he challenged Hamish.

67

'All right, I have.'

'You'll be back next year.'

'I'll have to think about that.'

'Don't be so wimpish, Ham. You can afford it. You could afford to stay here permanently if you wanted, for the rest of your life.'

'I wouldna' say that.'

'Of course you could. We're millionaires now, even after the taxes have been paid. Be realistic, man. There are forty-seven pictures to sell if we want. The galleries are queuing up to buy them.'

'We couldna' sell the pictures, Al.'

'Why not?' demanded Alastair on a soaring note of disbelief. 'We own them.'

'It's his work. It shouldna' be split up. Da' wouldna' like that.'

'Da' wouldna' like that,' Alastair mimicked him. 'Snap out of it, man – you're grown-up now. You can do as you want. I tell you, I'm going to sell my share of the pictures, so they'll be split up anyway.'

'We owe it to Da' to keep them together,' Hamish tried to insist.

'We owe nothing to Dad. He would have seen us starve.'

Hamish was deeply shocked. 'How can ye say that?'

'It's true. You slaved for the whole of your life to give him the freedom to paint. Yes, slaved. He paid you nothing and he would have left you nothing.'

'He left us everything, Al.'

'Only because I insisted on it. I brought the will form and filled it in and put the pen in his hand and called in the postman and the gardener to be witnesses.'

Hamish reached for his shirt. His skin was out in goose-bumps, as if a breeze had sprung up. 'But Da' knew what he was signing . . . did he not?'

'He signed. Just look at those lassies standing beside the pool. They might as well not be wearing anything.' Alastair sat up and slipped his feet into his flip-flops. 'See you presently.'

Dinner that evening was a buffet outdoors on the terrace, but in no way a night off for the chef. A feast that must have been hours in the preparation, as spectacular as anything the McDinnies had ever seen, was ranged on long tables, brilliantly lit, for the darkness around them was total. And no mosquitoes threatened.

The brothers had a table on the opposite side of the terrace. Alastair's white Christian Dior shirt, open at the neck to display the chains, enhanced his tan. He had purchased it that afternoon in one of the hotel boutiques. The light-blue canvas trousers and white espadrilles were from the same source.

Hamish was in the pin-stripe he had worn for the flight.

'That thing *again*?' said Alastair.

'What's wrong with it?'

'You're no better than Dad.'

'What do you mean?'

'You'll never break out. You're locked into yourself.'

Later, when they were drinking coffee and waiting for the tribal dancers to perform, Hamish said, 'You ought to show more respect for our Da'.' By his standard it was a strong rebuke, and he immediately softened it. 'Lord knows, he wasna' easy to understand. When you bought him that magnifier, he ought to have shown some gratitude.'

'I've never given that another thought,' said Alastair, smiling at two unaccompanied women on the next table.

'Aye, but you gave it plenty of thought at the time, about Dad's eyesight, and you went to all the trouble of finding the thing.'

'It was only a magnifying lens on a stand,' Alastair said dismissively. 'I got it secondhand from a jeweller. It looked as if it would come in useful.'

69

'Did I tell you he never used it? He ignored it. He left it on the plan-chest where you placed it.'

Alastair was quick to make a correction. 'What do you mean – I *placed it*? I don't recall placing it anywhere. Anyway I've dismissed it from my mind, and so should you.'

Hamish didn't dismiss it. Alastair's attitude troubled him. It was unlike his brother to shrug off the credit for a generous act. The magnifier had been a handsome present, a five-inch diameter lens mounted on an angle-poise stand which would certainly have enabled father to have got a better view of his painting if he had used it. Father? That old stick-in-the-mud? Fat chance! Curious, really, that Alastair should ever have supposed it would be used.

Whatever Alastair claimed, he it was who had positioned the magnifier on the plan-chest under the window. Father had never touched it, and nor had Hamish. Hamish had been under firm instructions never to tamper with anything in the studio. He'd been allowed to sweep the floor. Cigarette-ends and discarded sheets of paper he was permitted to touch. Nothing above floor-level.

Like Father, he had ignored the magnifier's existence. In fact one afternoon some months before – it must have been March or April, when the winter was turning to spring – the thing had succeeded in deceiving him. Father had quit the studio early, leaving his litter of cigarette-butts, crumpled tissues and paper. Outside, the sun lingered, and when Hamish as usual had picked up the discarded sheet of watercolour paper to place it on the pile beside the plan-chest, he had noticed what he thought was a paint-mark on the surface of the top sheet, a blue-edged oval. Amazing. Father hadn't got so far as using paint for months, if not years. It was quickly obvious that the effect was caused by sunlight through the lens. The blue of the spectrum. Stupid. Hamish had laughed out loud at his own mistake.

70

They flew home at the end of the week, Hamish in his suit, nervous as before, Alastair laden with duty-free. In the first-class section they were greeted by the steward they had met on the flight out.

'What a coincidence!' Hamish said.

'Not in the least,' Alastair informed him. 'They work in a roster. He'll have done this each Saturday since we left. This is the turn-round of the flight out.'

As if to confirm this, they were brought the morning papers from England. 'We haven't seen a paper or watched television for three weeks,' Alastair told the steward.

'You haven't missed much,' the steward replied. 'Petrol prices are up again and the West Indians won the cricket. Ah.' He snapped his fingers. 'But there was an item in the week about your father, or rather the fire that killed him. What was it now? The investigation team discovered how the fire started, and it wasn't a cigarette as everyone had supposed. Apparently a pile of drawing paper caught fire.'

'That must have been a cigarette,' said Alastair.

'No.'

'It's obvious.'

'No. Let me get this right. The paper was underneath a window. It was something to do with a magnifying lens that your father used in his work. The sun shone through and set light to the paper. One of those freakish accidents that no one could guard against.'

'But I don't see how . . .' Hamish started to say, and then on a long, despairing note, he said, 'Oh, no . . .'

Alastair, more in control, commented, 'Really it makes no difference how the fire started. It could have been an electrical fault or anything. It doesn't bring Father back.'

Hamish covered his eyes and vented his grief in a high moan of distress that was covered by the sound of the aircraft engines. At first he hadn't been able to fathom how the faint oval of blue light he had seen on the watercolour paper all those months ago could have intensified to the pinpoint beam sufficient to start a fire. Then, agonized, he understood. He had created the conditions himself by stacking up the paper, a sheet at a time, day after day, for months on end. The higher the stack, the smaller and brighter the pool of light. He just hadn't registered how dangerous it was. Some days there hadn't been any sunlight at all. On the others, he had ignored it. Having once mistaken the blue outline for a paint-mark, he'd resolved not to be caught again. But one day in summer the stack had reached the focal point, the level at which it ignited.

Alastair muttered, 'Drink your champagne and shut up. It's not the end of the world.'

'It was murder,' Hamish said.

'Keep your voice down. Murder with a magnifying glass? That's a laugh.'

'You meant to kill him and you did.'

'Correction. We did.'

'*You* brought the thing into the studio. *You* stood it beside the paper-stack.'

'And you raised the level of the stack, little by little, day by day,' said Alastair, 'so let's have no pointing of the finger.'

'I had no idea.'

'You mean you didn't think. As I told you before, you're a slave of routine. Just like Father.' He switched off the reading light. 'Better get some sleep while we can. We're going to be busy when we get back.'

'Why?'

'For God's sake, Ham! We're the executors. We have to administer the will. We'll get nothing until we're granted probate.'

That, at any rate, was true. They had paid for the holiday on spec, out of their own savings.

Hamish didn't sleep. He closed his eyes and remembered

72

his father, not the shambling figure in carpet slippers struggling with gummed paper, but the man he had been in his prime, reading the riot act to the Royal Academy on the subject of abstract art, which he had likened in its blandness to Muzak. A tyrant in public and private life. Easier to respect than to love.

It seemed only a short interval before the steward slid the blinds from the windows, admitted the morning sun and handed out the breakfast menus.

'Get home and get a few hours' rest,' Alastair ordered as if Hamish were the school football team. 'We'll meet tonight and start sorting out Dad's papers.'

The train had reached Penzance.

Soon after getting home, Hamish phoned Alastair. 'I wanted to catch you before you got to bed.'

'What now?'

'The will.'

'What about the will?'

'I mean the one you got him to sign. Did ye happen to keep a copy?'

'Yes, of course.'

'That's all right, then.'

After some hesitation, Alastair said, 'Is there a problem?'

'No problem,' Hamish said evenly. 'So long as the copy you have is legal.'

'*Legal?* Of course it isn't legal. The only legal copy is the original, the actual document he signed and the witnesses signed. That's the one we need for the Probate Office. That's among his papers.'

'If it is, I havena' found it.'

'It must be. In the writing desk where he kept his bank statements and everything. I put it there myself less than a month ago. Have another look. I'll wait.'

After a sufficient pause, Hamish said, 'It isna' there.'

'For crying out loud! Where else could it be?'

'I'm trying to think, Al. I'm just a little afeared . . . Och, no, it couldna' be.'

'What are you saying, you gibbering idiot?'

'You know what he was like, Al. He may have been slower in his old age, but he was of sound mind. We agreed on that.'

'Come to the point, man!'

'I'm trying to, Al. It isn't so easy to remember. Is that the jetlag? Da' kept the things he valued in his pocket. His wallet and his cigarettes. Sometimes he asked for his cheque-book and his bank statements. I'm just wondering if I handed him the will together with the bank statements.'

'He took the will to the studio?'

'He didna' know there would be a fire, Al.'

The voice became hysterical. 'God, I don't believe this.' In the shocked silence, Hamish fancied he could hear the thought process in his brother's brain. The second will was destroyed, so the previous will would take effect. The entire estate would go to the National Gallery of Scotland. The pictures, the house, the money, everything. 'I'm coming over. This can't be true.'

The phone clicked as Alastair rang off.

Hamish sat back in father's chair. 'It isna' true,' he said to himself, 'but it's right.'

He picked up the will he had found among father's papers, the second will that Alastair was so exercised about, the top copy, signed and witnessed. He ripped it in half and then into quarters. Continuing to tear it into smaller pieces, he took them to the toilet, dropped them in and flushed them away.

74

Shock Visit

JUST AS MRS BLOOMFIELD WAS reaching for the phone a shaft of sunlight dazzled her. Out in the street someone had opened a car door. She had no idea whose car it was. It had drawn up plumb in front of the house.

A man in tinted glasses climbed out, stared straight at the house as if making up his mind and then dipped to remove a briefcase from the car's interior. Mrs Bloomfield let out a troubled breath. She had never seen the man before, but from the look of him he was from one of those religious sects that knocked on doors. They always wore dark suits and white shirts and carried cases containing their literature. And they invariably looked as if they hadn't eaten a good meal in weeks. They usually came in twos, however. She couldn't see a second man yet. She retreated to the far side of the living room where she couldn't possibly be spotted from outside.

The click of the front gate was so long in coming that she was encouraged to hope that the man had decided to try another house further up the street. She inched forward, curiosity overcoming caution, and peered out. The same man was still out there on the other side of the privet hedge. He had his hands up to his face. Did they offer up prayers before they knocked? Mrs Bloomfield asked herself.

She said aloud on a note of despair, 'Oh, no – why me?' and backed away from the window.

Now the gate definitely clicked and steps came up the path. Mrs Bloomfield fingered the silver crucifix at her throat. She didn't propose to discuss her beliefs with anybody, let alone a stranger. She would not go to the door. Let him give up and go away, whatever he wanted.

The doorbell chimed its two disarming notes.

There was nothing to show she was at home. The car was in the garage with the door closed.

The chimes sounded again. And again, several times over.

The caller's persistence undermined Mrs Bloomfield's resolve a little. She had a safety chain on the door. She could always ask what he wanted and tell him to go away. That was the reasonable thing to do. First, she needed another look at him to make absolutely sure it was nobody she knew. If it turned out to be a friend who had come on an unexpected visit she couldn't very well slam the door in his face.

The curve of the bow window gave a narrow view of the porch. All she had to do was make a space between the edge of the curtain and the window frame.

She sidled closer and eased the curtain aside with a fingertip. The man wasn't at the door any longer. In her agitated state she had failed to notice that the chimes had stopped. Had he given up? She bit her lip and shut her eyes and willed him to get in his car and drive off. Her strength of will must have been less than his, for when she opened her eyes she was looking straight into his face. He was only a yard away from her, standing right up to the window, gesturing, jabbing his finger towards the door. Mrs Bloomfield rocked back in a paroxysm of alarm, her hand to her heart. She backed right against the wall, beside the piano, where she couldn't possibly be seen from outside.

It was a monstrous intrusion, staring in at someone's window like that. No one had any right. She tried to slow down her breathing and get control of her nerves. Outrageous behaviour. He must have been standing on the flowerbed to have got so near. Well, she simply had to wait for him to go away. They always give up in the end, however persistent they seem, she told herself as if she were thoroughly accustomed to getting rid of unwanted callers. She had an inner voice that sometimes surprised her by coming to her rescue in moments of stress, a firm, decisive voice that quite overrode the weaker tendencies of her personality. It was telling her to dismiss the visitor from her thoughts. Unclenching her hands, she moved into the hall and stood in front of the thermometer hanging on the wall above her husband's collection of miniature ceramic houses. It was mounted on wood and shaped like a guitar, with the glass tube along the narrow part. She didn't actually study the temperature so much as the painted scene on the guitar, of whitewashed buildings with red roofs and wooden balconies. There were palms and poinsettias and a strip of green-blue sea.

Feeling more calm, she turned towards the kitchen. She would put on the kettle. Forget all about him. Make herself a cup of hot, sweet tea.

She pushed open the kitchen door and went rigid. The man was standing by the draining-board. He had come in by the back door.

'How are you, Mrs Bloomfield?'

The blood rushed from her head. She felt as if her body wasn't her own. She heard herself say in a whisper, 'What on earth . . .?'

He took a step towards her and extended his hand. He was bone-thin and as tall as the fridge-freezer. 'I came round the back when I guessed you were having trouble with the front door. Is it jammed? I expect you had the catch down. It's easily done.'

'Get out! You have no right!'

He grinned oddly – inanely, Mrs Bloomfield thought –

making a jerky little movement with his head. 'At first I thought you were hard of hearing.'

'Who are you?' she managed to say.

He fished in his pocket and handed a visiting card to her. 'David Tolpuddle. This won't take long, madam, I assure you.'

Mrs Bloomfield possessed two pairs of glasses. She called them her doing glasses and her seeing glasses. Unfortunately she happened to be wearing her seeing glasses which were no good for seeing anything so small as a visiting card.

She dropped the card on the table. She had found her forceful voice. 'Kindly leave my house at once.'

David Tolpuddle said, 'But we have an appointment.'

'Oh, no, we do not.'

'Two p.m. on Tuesday. It *is* Tuesday.'

'I don't know anything about this.'

'Pardon me, you *are* Mrs Bloomfield?'

'Well, yes.' Despite her sense of outrage, she found herself responding to his deferential tone.

'So we have an appointment.'

'Not to my knowledge.'

'Then I dare say your husband arranged it.'

'My husband?'

'Is Mr Bloomfield at home today?'

This is a try-on, she thought. Somehow he has chanced on our name, perhaps in the phone book, or one of those lists the credit-card companies sell to people. 'You had better tell me what this is about.'

Tolpuddle spread his hands as if to show how reasonable his business was. 'The valuation.'

'It's transparently obvious that you have made a mistake.'

He shook his head. Then he took a step towards Mrs Bloomfield that made her sway back. 'I hope you haven't already come to terms with one of my competitors, Mrs

78

Bloomfield. That wouldn't be very ethical, would it, before I had an opportunity to quote?'

She stood her ground and said, 'Will you leave my house this instant or do I have to call the police?'

That patently shook him. His face twitched again. 'There's no need for that. I'm here in a professional capacity.'

'Do you call this professional, frightening me out of my wits, forcing your way into my house by the back door?'

He reddened. 'I wouldn't describe it as forcing. The door was unlocked. I was out of order to let myself in, I admit. I can only say in my defence that in my line of business one becomes accustomed to letting oneself into other people's houses.'

She wondered for a moment if he was confessing to being a housebreaker. She had never pictured a burglar in a pin-stripe suit, but the newspapers every day were full of peculiar things that wouldn't have happened thirty years ago. A burglar with a visiting card?

As if he read her mind, he picked up the card from where she had dropped it on the kitchen table and held it out to her. 'I'm a valuer. You see? David Tolpuddle, estate agent and valuer.'

'Estate agent?'

'And valuer. I stress the word valuer because that is my purpose in being here, to make the valuation. People don't always think kindly of estate agents. It's a much maligned profession, Mrs Bloomfield. Let's admit it, the way you just spoke the words lacked the respect automatically accorded to a solicitor, say, or a bank manager. But I would argue that I am serving the public in a responsible capacity, just the same.'

Mrs Bloomfield's mystification grew as her panic diminished. 'Who sent you here?'

He cleared his throat. 'I wasn't *sent*, madam, I engaged to come. I am the chairman.'

'I don't know you.'

'My name is on the boards. Surely you have noticed our boards? Thomas and Tolpuddle, Estate Agents and Valuers. Sold!' He snapped his fingers and made Mrs Bloomfield start. 'My partner Archie Thomas retired six years ago. The decisions are mine alone. You must have seen the boards all over town. Red lettering on a blue background. Very eye-catching. As to why I'm here, I presume you invited me to come, or your husband did. You must have spoken to Angela in the office, the black girl with the endearing smile.'

'I most certainly did not – and my husband didn't ask you to come, I'm sure of that.'

'Oh, but somebody did, emphatically. Yesterday afternoon. Angela wrote it on the card. Wait a minute. We can check.' He put his briefcase on the table, opened it, took out a camera, a calculator and a couple of instruments Mrs Bloomfield had never seen before and leafed through the documents underneath. 'Got it! *Valuation, 38, Bandmaster Street, 2 p.m., Tuesday, 30th September. Mr B. Bloomfield.* It was your husband who came to the office.'

Mrs Bloomfield shook her head. 'It's a mistake.' Then she added, 'Basil didn't mention it to me.' Immediately the inner voice told her that she shouldn't have spoken, for what she had said had weakened her case. 'Well, whatever the explanation may be, this house is not for sale.'

'Not yet. I always say no obligation and no fee. And now with your permission I'll just walk around and form an impression, make a few measurements.'

'You will not!'

'I would offer to come back some other time . . .'

'You'd be wasting your time.'

'. . . but that won't be possible,' said Tolpuddle, articulating his words in a slow, unstoppable rhythm. 'I'm in competition with four other agents, Mrs Bloomfield.

This is a cut-throat business. If I delay the inspection I've no guarantee that you won't place your property with one of my competitors. For all I know, your husband may have invited them all to make valuations. That's the common practice. So I'd be a prize chump if I let this slip through my fingers. Let me show you how painless it is. I'll begin here. Switch on my tape-recorder, like so – that's for Angela to work from. 38, Bandmaster Street, Angela. Superior detached residence within a few minutes walk of the local shopping parade, schools and railway station. In the kitchen we have Wrighton kitchen units, stainless steel double sink with mixer tap, Vent-Axia extractor fan, ceramic hob, Zanussi electric cooker – is the cooker to be included, Mrs Bloomfield? It's advisable when they're built in like this.'

Mrs Bloomfield was shaking. She couldn't reply.

'It's marginal to the final valuation, anyway,' said Tolpuddle. 'More of a selling-point really. Ceramic hob with four burners, Potterton gas-fired boiler. Cork-O-Plast floor tiles. Recessed lighting. Five power units. Double-glazed window and steel-framed door and I think we're ready to measure up.' He pressed a button on the recorder, pocketed it and picked another instrument off the table. 'This is a clever little gadget. Did you, by any chance, watch the Olympic Games on television? If so, you may have seen the long jump in progress.'

He isn't a housebreaker or an estate agent, Mrs Bloomfield thought. He's escaped from a mental home. She said, more indulgently, 'I think you'd better leave now, don't you?'

He continued as if he hadn't heard, 'The way they measure the jumps may have caught your attention. The International Olympic Committee don't use tape-measures these days and nor do Thomas and Tolpuddle. It's all done with a gadget like this. You take a sighting of the two points you are measuring and read it off.

Seventeen foot six. Splendid size for a kitchen but it wouldn't win a gold medal at the Olympics.' Smiling, he bundled everything into his suitcase and marched into the hall.

Mrs Bloomfield called out, 'You're wasting your time. I spoke to my husband as recently as Sunday evening and he told me he would never agree to move from here. Never.'

Tolpuddle turned and gave her a look of extraordinary intensity, like a horse disturbed in its grazing. 'You talked about moving?'

'Yes, and he was adamant.'

'Nevertheless you did discuss it?'

'Yes, but that doesn't mean—'

He stepped closer. 'How about you, Mrs Bloomfield? What are your wishes on the matter? Do I detect that you would like to move away from here?'

'That isn't the point.'

Tolpuddle smiled. 'Pardon me. It *is* the point. It is precisely the point. Where did you tell Mr Bloomfield you would like to live – somewhere abroad? Somewhere in the sun?' His eyes lingered on the souvenir thermometer. 'Tenerife. Am I right?'

She said as dismissively as she was able, 'It doesn't arise.'

'Doesn't it?' said Tolpuddle, holding a finger in the air. 'I wouldn't be quite so dogmatic if I were you. Tenerife. I don't blame you for thinking of Tenerife. Plenty of people retire to Tenerife. That's a very shrewd move with the market as it is. You'll get an extremely well-appointed villa over there for the price a superior property like this will fetch. As a matter of fact, one of the agencies I deal with recently sent me details of a particularly fine development in Tenerife. Los Gigantes. Do you know it? Handsome two-bedroom villas with a marvellous view across the water to the most spectacular cliffs. Perhaps your husband inspected the brochure when he called at the office yesterday. If he didn't, I'll send you one. No obligation.'

'He would have told me,' insisted Mrs Bloomfield.

'He must have wanted to surprise you. Pretended he wouldn't leave in a thousand years and then came straight to our office to arrange the valuation. What a charming surprise for you! We men may have tough exteriors, but underneath we're as soft as you are, softer even.'

She remained unconvinced. 'When Basil's mind is made up, there's no shaking him. If you really want to know, he reduced me to tears – that's how charming it was. This is all a mistake – or someone is playing a dreadfully cruel joke on me.'

'No shaking him, you say, but you're speaking of workaday matters,' said Tolpuddle. 'This was something else: one of the great decisions of your lives. How will the Bloomfields spend their retirement? Battling against the English climate for the rest of their days or basking in unending sunshine in the Canaries? I'm not surprised your Basil had second thoughts. But this isn't getting the valuation completed. Shall we look at the reception room?'

'No.'

Tolpuddle brushed the objection aside. 'I know exactly what you're going to say – you haven't had a chance to tidy up. I understand, Mrs Bloomfield. But *you* must understand that it doesn't make a jot of difference to me. I'm oblivious of ashtrays and newspapers. The state of your house is a matter of supreme indifference to me. No, that's badly phrased. Let me put it another way. I'm so impressed by its structural features and the state of repair, which is immaculate so far as I can see, that I have no eyes for the little things that make it a home. However, if you want to tidy up the reception room I'll take a look upstairs first.'

Mrs Bloomfield said, 'I'm going to call the police.'

She hadn't said it with conviction. The announcement was no deterrent to her visitor. He was already mounting the stairs. Halfway up, he leaned over the banisters and said, 'There's no need to come up unless you wish. Three bedrooms, is it, and the bathroom and separate WC? I won't take long. And if the bed isn't made yet, don't trouble yourself in the least.'

She didn't follow him upstairs. Neither did she call the police. She remained downstairs in the kitchen, unhappy and confused. It was unthinkable after that bitter argument on Sunday that Basil had changed his mind. He had never been one to relent. Anyway, he would have mentioned it. Surely he would have mentioned it yesterday or this morning, knowing that Mr Tolpuddle would call?

Faintly, she heard the movement of the footsteps upstairs and Tolpuddle's voice speaking into the tape-recorder as he passed from bedroom to bedroom. She went back to the kitchen and poured herself a brandy from the bottle she kept for emergencies. She was less concerned about Tolpuddle than she had been when he arrived.

He talked animatedly as he came downstairs. 'Immaculate, Mrs Bloomfield. We'll have no trouble finding a purchaser, assuming, of course, that you and your husband place the property in our hands. And you'll find that my commission is very competitive. I just need to look at the reception room – a through-room, I believe I noticed from the outside when I was taking photographs. Very much in demand just now.'

'You took photographs?' She recalled seeing him with his hands to his face when she had assumed he had been saying prayers.

He was so far on with his sales patter that he seemed not to be listening any more. 'As a matter of fact I have a young couple on my books who are desperate to find a house like yours. Quite desperate. Wedding coming up in two months. And what is more, they have cash in hand. Do you know what that means, Mrs Bloomfield? No chain.

He'll pay the asking price in good old Bank of England notes if you wish, and you can exchange contracts within a matter of days. Don't ask me how he got the money, but it's got a copper-bottom guarantee. I practise absolute discretion with my clients, buyers and vendors alike. Everything is treated in the strictest confidence. I could tell some secrets about the people in this town, but my lips are sealed.'

All of this made no impression on Mrs Bloomfield. She was trying to account for Basil's erratic behaviour. The invasion by Mr Tolpuddle had paled into insignificance.

Perhaps her preoccupations were transmitted in some way to Tolpuddle, because he suddenly said, 'Do you know what I think? It's love, that's what it is. True love.'

She snapped out of her reverie. 'What?'

'Love, Mrs Bloomfield. An act of love as beautiful as a poem. After the difference of opinion you had on Saturday your husband thought the matter over and saw how much it meant to you to retire to the Canaries. He's a proud man, not easily swayed once his mind is made up, but this decision came from the heart. He decided to put your happiness before his pride and he came to my office and arranged the valuation. He couldn't have signalled more clearly to you that he's ready to change his mind.' Tolpuddle beamed.

Mrs Bloomfield fingered her wedding ring, turning it on her finger. 'I can't believe a word of what you're saying.'

'Ah, but you must. You can't ignore a beautiful gesture like this. Accept it for what it is. When he comes in, tell him that you'd like to put your house on the market as soon as possible.'

That other voice of hers said acidly, 'You don't give up easily, do you?'

'Certainly not, my dear, because I'm pinning my confidence on you now. You and I are not really at cross purposes at all. Our interests coincide.' He flushed at the good sense of what he had said. 'I'll finish the inspection now and you can have my valuation before I go.' He opened the door of what Mrs Bloomfield called her living-room and marched in, saying into the tape-recorder, 'The reception room, Angela. Attractive through room with bow window and glazed patio door to paved terrace. Natural stone hearth with gas fire. Two double radiators. Telephone point.'

Mrs Bloomfield stood in the hall staring at the souvenir thermometer from Tenerife.

Tolpuddle didn't spend long in the living-room. In fact he stopped dictating rather abruptly. Mrs Bloomfield was in the kitchen when he emerged. She said, 'Are you satisfied now?'

He opened his mouth as if to speak and nothing came out.

Mrs Bloomfield swirled the brandy in her glass and swallowed the contents at a gulp. Then she told Tolpuddle, 'You shouldn't have forced your way in as you did.'

'You weren't locked at the back,' he pointed out.

'People usually come to the front door.'

'People usually answer the doorbell.'

'That doesn't excuse it, Mr Tolpuddle.' She took the glass to the sink and ran some water over it. 'Are you still certain that my husband called at your office yesterday afternoon?'

He looked shocked. 'It's on record. I showed you.'

'With a view to selling this house?'

'I assume so.'

She stared out of the window at the apples on the trees. 'He ought to have told me. Don't you think he ought to have told me?'

'I can't comment. That's personal, Mrs Bloomfield.'

'Just now you were commenting freely enough, telling me it was love that made him do it.'

'I suppose I got carried away.'

She sensed that he would leave soon. He needed an exit-line, that was all.

He wound himself up. 'My usual practice is to give an on-the-spot valuation and write to you later to confirm it.'

'I keep telling you I'm not interested. Isn't that clear to you by now?'

'Even so.'

'Goodbye, Mr Tolpuddle.'

'I'll get it in the post tonight. Just in case.'

He seemed to want to keep this fiction going to the very end. She sighed. 'If you wish.'

He fastened his briefcase. 'I won't press you for a decision. You have my card.'

'Yes.'

'One other thing. If you don't want any more agents to bother you, I should lock up at the back.'

Mrs Bloomfield rolled her eyes upwards. She had never met anyone so persistent. When she had closed the front door she walked into the living-room and watched him get into his car and drive away. The car fairly raced up the street.

She turned from the window, picked up the phone and dialled a number. 'Is that the police? I think you had better come and see me. I was going to call you an hour ago, but somebody called.'

They asked for her name and address.

While she was speaking she let her gaze travel slowly around the room, over the furniture she had dusted and polished for years, the table, chairs, piano, sideboard and china cabinet. This was her home, her address, and how she hated the place! Finally she allowed herself to look down at the carpet, at Basil's body, and beside it the candlestick she had used an hour ago to batter him to death.

The Haunted Crescent

A GHOST WAS SEEN LAST Christmas in a certain house in the Royal Crescent. Believe me, this is true. I speak from personal experience, as a resident of the City of Bath and something of an authority on psychic phenomena. I readily admit that ninety-nine per cent of so-called hauntings turn out to have been hallucinations of some sort or another, but this is the exception, a genuine haunted house. Out of consideration for the present owners (who for obvious reasons wish to preserve their privacy), I shall not disclose the exact address, but if you doubt me, read what happened to me last Christmas Eve, 1988.

The couple who own the house had gone to Norfolk for the festive season, leaving on the Friday, December 23rd. Good planning. The ghost was reputed to walk on Christmas Eve. Knowing of my interest, they had generously placed their house at my disposal. I am an ex-policeman, by the way, and it takes a lot to frighten me.

For those who like a ghost story with all the trimmings – deep snow and howling winds outside – I am sorry. I must disappoint you. Christmas, 1988, was not a white one in Bath. It was unseasonably warm. There wasn't even any fog. All I can offer in the way of atmospheric effects are a full moon that night and an owl that hooted periodically in the trees at the far side of the sloping lawn that fronts the Crescent. It has to be admitted that this was not a spooky-looking barn owl, but a tawny owl, which on this night was making more of a high-pitched 'kee-wik' call than a hoot, quite cheery, in fact. Do not despair, however. The things that happened in the house that night more than compensated for the absence of werewolves and banshees outside.

It is vital to the story that you are sufficiently informed about the building in which the events occurred. Whether you realised it or not, you have probably seen the Royal Crescent, if not as a resident, or a tourist, in one of the numerous films in which it has appeared as a backdrop to the action. It is in a quiet location north-west of the city and comprises thirty houses in a semi-elliptical terrace completed in 1774 to the specification of John Wood the Younger. It stands comparison with any domestic building in Europe. I defy anyone not to respond to its uncomplicated grandeur, the majestic panorama of one hundred and fourteen Ionic columns topped by a portico and balustrade; and the roadway at the front where Jane Austen and Charles Dickens trod the cobbles. But you want me to come to the ghost.

My first intimation of something unaccountable came at about twenty past eleven that Christmas Eve. I was in the drawing-room on the first floor. I had stationed myself there a couple of hours before. The door was ajar and the house was in darkness. No, that isn't quite accurate. I should have said simply that none of the lights were switched on; actually the moonlight gave a certain amount of illumination, silver-blue rectangles projected across the carpet and over the base of the Christmas tree, producing an effect infinitely prettier than fairylights. The furniture was easily visible, too, armchairs, table and grand piano. One's eyes adjust. It didn't strike me as eerie to be alone in that unlit house. Anyone knows that a spirit of the departed is unlikely to manifest itself in electric light.

No house is totally silent, certainly no centrally-heated

house. The sounds produced by expanding floorboards in so-called haunted houses up and down the land must have fooled ghost-hunters by the hundred. In this case as a precaution against a sudden freeze, the owners had left the system switched on. It was timed to turn off at eleven, so the knocks and creaks I was hearing now ought to have been the last of the night.

As events turned out, it wasn't a sound that alerted me first. It was a sudden draught against my face and a flutter of white across the room. I tensed. The house had gone silent. I crossed the room to investigate.

The disturbance had been caused by a Christmas card falling off the mantelpiece into the grate. Nothing more alarming than that. Cards are always falling down. That's why some people prefer to suspend them on strings. I stooped, picked up the card and replaced it, smiling at my overactive imagination.

Yet I had definitely noticed a draught. The house was supposed to be free of draughts. All the doors and windows were closed and meticulously sealed against the elements. Strange. I listened, holding my breath. The drawing-room where I was standing was well placed for picking up any unexplained sound in the house. It was at the centre of the building. Below me were the ground floor and the cellar, above me the second floor and the attic.

Hearing nothing, I decided to venture out to the landing and listen there. I was mystified, yet unwilling at this stage to countenance a supernatural explanation. I was inclined to wonder whether the cut-out of the central heating had resulted in some trick of convection that gave the impression or the reality of a disturbance in the air. The falling card was not significant in itself. The draught required an explanation. My state of mind, you see, was calm and analytical.

Ten or fifteen seconds passed. I leaned over the

banisters and looked down the stairwell to make sure that the front door was firmly shut, and so it proved to be. Then I heard a rustle from the room where I had been. I knew what it was – the card falling into the grate again – for another distinct movement of air had stirred the curtain on the landing window, causing a shift in the moonlight across the stairs. I was in no doubt any more that this was worth investigating. My only uncertainty was whether to start with the floors above me, or below.

I chose the latter, reasoning that if, as I suspected, someone had opened a window, it was likely to be at the ground or basement levels. My assumption was wrong. I shall not draw out the suspense. I merely wish to record that I checked the cellar, kitchen, scullery, dining-room and study and found every window and external door secure and bolted from inside. No one could have entered after me.

So I began to work my way upstairs again, methodically visiting each room. And on the staircase to the second floor, I heard a sigh.

Occasionally in Victorian novels, a character would 'heave' a sigh. Somehow the phrase has always irritated me. In real life I never heard a sigh so weighty that it seemed to involve muscular effort – until this moment. This was a sound hauled up from the depths of somebody's inner being, or so I deduced. Whether it really originated with somebody or some *thing* was open to speculation.

The sound had definitely come from above me. Unable by now to suppress my excitement, I moved up to the second floor landing, where I found three doors, all closed. I moved from one to the other, opening them rapidly and glancing briefly inside. Two bedrooms and a bathroom. I hesitated. A bathroom. Had the 'sigh', I wondered, been caused by some aberration of the plumbing? Air locks are endemic in the complicated

91

systems installed in these old Georgian buildings. The houses were not built with valves and cisterns. The efficiency of the pipework depended on the variable skill of generations of plumbers.

The sound must have been caused by trapped air.

Rationality reasserted itself. I would finish my inspection and prove to my total satisfaction that what I had heard was neither human nor spectral in origin. I closed the bathroom door behind me and crossed the landing to the last flight of stairs, more narrow than those I had used so far. In times past they had been the means of access to the servants' quarters in the attic. I glanced up at the white-painted door at the head of these stairs and observed that it was slightly ajar.

My foot was on the first stair and my hand on the rail when I stiffened. That door moved.

It was being drawn inwards. The movement was slow and deliberate. As the gap increased, a faint glow of moonlight was cast from the interior on to the panelling to my right. I stared up and watched the figure of a woman appear in the doorway.

She was in a white gown or robe that reached to her feet. Her hair hung loose to the level of her chest – fine, gently shifting hair so pale in colour that it appeared to merge with the dress. Her skin, too, appeared bloodless. The eyes were flint-black, however. They widened as they took me in. Her right hand crept to her throat and I heard her give a gasp.

The sensations I experienced in that moment of confrontation are difficult to convey. I was convinced that nothing of flesh and blood had entered that house in the hours I had been there. All the entrances were bolted – I had checked. I could not account for the phenomenon, or whatever it was, that had manifested itself, yet I refused to be convinced. I was unwilling to accept what my eyes were seeing and my rational faculties could not explain. She could not be a ghost.

I said, 'Who are you?'

The figure swayed back as if startled. For a moment I thought she was going to close the attic door, but she remained staring at me, her hand still pressed to her throat. It was the face and form of a young woman, not more than twenty.

I asked, 'Can you speak?'

She appeared to nod.

I said, 'What are you doing here?'

She caught her breath. In a strange, half-whispered utterance she said, as if echoing my words, 'Who are you?'

I took a step upwards towards her. It evidently frightened her, for she backed away and became almost invisible in the shadowy interior of the attic room. I tried to dredge up some reassuring words. 'It's all right. Believe me, it's all right.'

Then I twitched in surprise. Downstairs, the doorbell chimed. After eleven on Christmas Eve!

I said, 'What on earth . . .?'

The woman in white whimpered something I couldn't hear.

I tried to make light of it. 'Santa, I expect.'

She didn't react.

The bell rang a second time.

'He ought to be using the chimney,' I said. I had already decided to ignore the visitor, whoever it was. One unexpected caller was all I could cope with.

The young woman spoke up, and the words sprang clearly from her. 'For God's sake, send him away!'

'You know who it is?'

'Please! I beg you.'

'If you know who it is,' I said reasonably, 'wouldn't you like to answer it?'

'I can't.'

The chimes rang out again.

I said, 'Is it someone you know?'

'Please. Tell him to go away. If you answer the door he'll go away.'

I was letting myself be persuaded. I needed her co-operation. I wanted to know about her. 'All right,' I relented. 'But will you be here when I come back?'

'I won't leave.'

Instinctively I trusted her. I turned and descended the two flights of stairs to the hall. The bell rang again. Even though the house was in darkness, the caller had no intention of giving up.

I drew back the bolts, opened the front door a fraction and looked out. A man was on the doorstep, leaning on the iron railing. A young man in a leather jacket glittering with studs and chains. His head was shaven. He, at any rate, looked like flesh and blood. He said, 'What kept you?'

I said, 'What do you want?'

He glared. 'For crying out loud – who the hell are you?' His eyes slid sideways, checking the number on the wall.

I said with frigid courtesy, 'I think you must have made a mistake.'

'No,' he said. 'This is the house all right. What's your game, mate? What are you doing here with the lights off?'

I told him that I was an observer of psychic phenomena.

'Come again?'

'Ghosts,' I said. 'This house has the reputation of being haunted. The owners have kindly allowed me to keep watch tonight.'

'Oh, yes?' he said with heavy scepticism. 'Spooks, is it? I'll have a gander at them meself.' With that, he gave the door a shove. There was no security chain and I was unable to resist the pressure. He stepped across the threshold. 'Ghost-buster, are you, mate? You wouldn't, by any chance, be lifting the family silver at the same time? Anyone else in here?'

I said, 'I take exception to that. You've no right to force

your way in here.'

'No more right than you,' he said, stepping past me. 'Were you upstairs when I rang?'

I said, 'I'm going to call the police.'

He flapped his hand dismissively. 'Be my guest. I'm going upstairs, right?'

Sheer panic inspired me to say, 'If you do, you'll be on film.'

'What?'

'The cameras are ready to roll,' I lied. 'The place is riddled with mikes and tripwires.'

He said, 'I don't believe you,' but the tone of his voice said the opposite.

'This ghost is supposed to walk on Christmas Eve,' I told him. 'I want to capture it on film.' I gave a special resonance to the word *capture*.

He said, 'You're round the twist.' And with as much dignity as he could muster he sidled back towards the door, which still stood open. Apparently he was leaving. 'You ought to be locked up. You're a nutcase.'

As he stepped out of the door I said, 'Shall I tell the owners you called? What name shall I give?'

He swore and turned away. I closed the door and slid the bolts back into place. I was shaking. It had been an ugly, potentially dangerous incident. I'm not so capable of tackling an intruder as I once was and I was thankful that my powers of invention had served me so well.

I started up the stairs again and as I reached the top of the first flight, the young woman in white was waiting for me. She must have come down two floors to overhear what was being said. This area of the house was better illuminated than the attic stairs, so I got a better look at her. She appeared less ethereal now. Her dress was silk or satin, I observed. It was an evening gown. Her make-up was as pale as a mime-artist's, except for the black liner around her eyes.

She said, 'How can I thank you enough?'

I answered flatly, 'What I want from you, young lady, is an explanation.'

She crossed her arms, rubbing at her sleeves. 'I feel shivery here. Do you mind if we go in there?'

As we moved into the drawing-room I noticed that she made no attempt to switch on the light. She pointed to some cigarettes on the table. 'Do you mind?'

I found some matches by the fireplace and gave her a light. 'Who was that at the door?'

She inhaled hard. 'Some guy I met at a party. I was supposed to be with someone else, but we got separated. You know how it is. Next thing I knew, this bloke in the leather jacket was chatting me up. He was all right at first. I didn't know he was going to come on so strong. I mean I didn't encourage him. I was trying to cool it. He offered me these tablets, but I refused. He said they would make me relax. By then I was really scared. I moved off fast. The stupid thing was that I moved upstairs. There were plenty of people about, and it seemed the easiest way to go. The bloke followed. He kept on following. I went right to the top of the house and shut myself in a room. I pushed a cupboard against the door. He was beating his fist on the door, saying what he was going to do to me. I was scared out of my skull. All I could think of doing was get through the window, so I did. I climbed out and found myself up there behind the little stone wall.'

'Of this building? The balustrade at the top?'

'Didn't I make that clear? The party was in a house a couple of doors away from you. I ran along this narrow passageway between the roof and the wall trying all the windows. The one upstairs was the first one I could shift.'

'The attic window. Now I understand.' The sudden draught was explained, and the gasp as she had caught her breath after the effort.

She said, 'I'm really grateful.'

'Grateful?'

'Grateful to you for getting rid of him.'

I said, 'It would be sensible now to call a taxi. Where do you live?'

'Not far. I can walk.'

'It wouldn't be advisable, would it, after what happened? He's persistent. He may be waiting.'

'I didn't think.' She stubbed the cigarette into an ashtray. After a moment's reflection she said, 'All right. Where's the phone?'

There was one in the study. While she was occupied, I gave some thought to what she had said. I didn't believe a word of it, but I had something vastly more important on my mind.

She came back into the room. 'Ten minutes, they reckon. Was it true what you said downstairs, about this house being haunted?'

'Mm?' I was still preoccupied.

'The spook. All that stuff about hidden cameras. Did you mean it?'

'There aren't any cameras. I'm useless with machinery of any sort. I reckoned he'd think twice about coming in if he knew he was going to be on film. It was just a bluff.'

'And the bit about the ghost?'

'That was true.'

'Would you mind telling me about it?'

'Aren't you afraid of the supernatural?'

'It's scary, yes. Not so scary as what happened already. I want to know the story. Christmas Eve is a great night for a ghost story.'

I said, 'It's more than just a story.'

'Please.'

'On one condition. Before you get into that taxi, you tell me the truth about yourself – why you really came into this house tonight.'

She hesitated.

97

I said, 'It needn't go any further.'

'All right. Tell me about the ghost.' She reached for another cigarette and perched on the arm of a chair.

I crossed to the window and looked away over the lawn towards the trees silhouetted against the city lights. 'It can be traced back, as all ghost stories can, to a story of death and an unquiet spirit. About a hundred and fifty years ago this house was owned by an army officer, a retired colonel by the name of Davenport. He had a daughter called Rosamund, and it was believed in the city that he doted on her. She was dressed fashionably and given a good education, which in those days was beyond the expectation of most young women. Rosamund was a lively, intelligent and attractive girl. Her hair when she wore it long was very like yours, fine and extremely fair. Not surprisingly, she had admirers. The one she favoured most was a young man from Bristol, Luke Robertson, who at that time was an architect. In the conventions of the time they formed an attachment which amounted to little more than a few chaperoned meetings, some letters, poems and so on. They were lovers in a very old-fashioned sense which you may find difficult to credit. In physical terms it amounted to no more than a few stolen kisses, if that. Somewhere in this house there is supposed to be carved into the woodwork the letters L and R linked. I can't show you. I haven't found it.'

Outside, a taxi trundled over the cobbles. I watched it draw up at a house some doors down. Two couples came out of the building laughing and climbed into the cab. It was obvious that they were leaving a party. The heavy beat of music carried up to me.

I said, 'I wonder if it's turned midnight. It might be Christmas Day already.'

She said, 'Please go on with the story.'

'Colonel Davenport – the father of this girl – was a lonely man. His wife had died some years before. Lately he had become friendly with a neighbour, another resident of the Crescent, a widow approaching fifty years of age by the name of Mrs Crandley, who lived in one of the houses at the far end of the building. She was a musician, a pianist, and she gave lessons. One of her pupils was Rosamund. So far as one can tell, Mrs Crandley was a good teacher and the girl a promising pupil. Do you play?'

'What?'

I turned to face her. 'I said do you play the piano?'

'Oh. Just a bit,' said the girl.

'You didn't tell me your name.'

'I'd rather not, if you don't mind. What happened between the Colonel and Mrs Crandley?'

'Their friendship blossomed. He wanted her to marry him. Mrs Crandley was not willing. In fact, she agreed, subject to one condition. She had a son of twenty-seven called Justinian.'

'What was that?'

'Justinian. There was a vogue for calling your children after emperors. This Justinian was a dull fellow without much to recommend him. He was lazy and overweight. He rarely ventured out of the house. Mrs Crandley despaired of him.'

'She wanted him off her hands?'

'That is what it amounted to. She wanted him married and she saw the perfect partner for him in Rosamund. Surely such a charming, talented girl would bring out some positive qualities in her lumpish son. Mrs Crandley applied herself diligently to the plan, insisting that Justinian answered the doorbell each time Rosamund came for her music lesson. Then he would be told to sit in the room and listen to her playing. Everything Mrs Crandley could do to promote the match was done. For his part, Justinian was content to go along with the plan. He was promised that if he married the girl he would be given his mother's house, so the pattern of his life would alter

99

little, except that a pretty wife would keep him company rather than a discontented, nagging mother. He began to eye Rosamund with increasing favour. So when the Colonel proposed marriage to Mrs Crandley she assented on the understanding that Justinian would be married to Rosamund at the same time.'

'How about Rosamund? Was she given any choice?'

'You have to be aware that marriages were commonly arranged by the parents in those days.'

'But you said she already had a lover. He was perfectly respectable, wasn't he?'

I nodded. 'Absolutely. But Luke Robertson didn't feature in Mrs Crandley's plan. He was ignored. Rosamund bowed under the pressure and became engaged to Justinian in the autumn of 1838. The double marriage was to take place in the Abbey on Christmas Eve.'

'Oh, dear – I think I can guess the rest of the story.'

'It may not be quite as you expect. As the day of the wedding approached, Rosamund began to dread the prospect. She pleaded with her father to allow her to break off the engagement. He wouldn't hear of it. He loved Mrs Crandley and his thoughts were all of her. In despair, Rosamund sent the maidservant with a message to Luke, asking him to meet her secretly on the basement steps. She had a romantic notion that Luke would elope with her.'

My listener was enthralled. 'And did he come?'

'He came. Rosamund poured out her story. Luke listened with sympathy, but he was cautious. He didn't see elopement as the solution. Rather bravely, he volunteered to speak to the Colonel and appeal to him to allow Rosamund to marry the man of her choice. If that failed, he would remind the Colonel that Rosamund could not be forced to take the sacred vows. Her consent had to be freely given in church, and she was entitled to withhold it. So this uncomfortable interview took place a day or two later. The Colonel, naturally, was outraged. Luke was banished from the house and forbidden to speak with Rosamund again. The unfortunate girl was summoned by her father and accused of wickedly consorting with her former lover when she was promised to another. The story of the secret note and the meeting on the stairs was dragged from her. She was told that she wished to destroy her father's marriage. She was said to be selfish and disloyal. Worse, she might be taken to court by Justinian for breach of promise.'

'Poor little soul! Did it break her?'

'No. Amazingly, she stood her ground. Luke's support had given her courage. She would not marry Justinian. It was the Colonel who backed down. He went to see Mrs Crandley. When he returned, it was to tell Rosamund that his marriage would not, after all, take place. Mrs Crandley had insisted on a double wedding, or nothing.'

'I wouldn't have been in Rosamund's shoes for a million pounds.'

'She was told by her father that she had behaved no better than a servant, secretly meeting her lover on the basement steps and trifling with another man's affections, so in future he would treat her as a servant. And he did. He dismissed the housemaid. He ordered Rosamund to move her things to the maid's room in the attic, and he gave her a list of duties that kept her busy from five-thirty each morning until late at night.'

'Cruel.'

'All his bitterness was heaped on her.'

'Did she kill herself?'

'No.' I said with only the slightest pause, 'She was murdered.'

'*Murdered*?'

'On Christmas Eve, the day that the wedding would have taken place, she was suffocated in her bed.'

'Horrible!'

'A pillow was held against her face until she ceased to

breathe. She was found dead in bed by the cook on Christmas morning after she failed to report for duty. The Colonel was informed and the police were sent for.'

'Who killed her?'

'The inspector on the case, a local man without much experience of violent crimes, was in no doubt that Colonel Davenport was the murderer. He had a powerful motive. The animus he felt towards his daughter had been demonstrated by the way he treated her. It seemed that his anger had only increased as the days passed. On the date he was due to have married, it became insupportable.'

'Was it true? Did he confess to killing her?'

'He refused to make any statement. But the evidence against him was overwhelming. Three inches of snow fell on Christmas Eve. It stopped about eight-thirty that evening. The time of death was estimated at about eleven p.m. When the inspector and his men arrived next morning no footsteps were visible on the path leading to the front door except those of the cook, who had gone for the police. The only other person in the house was Colonel Davenport. So he was charged with murdering his own daughter. The trial was short, for he refused to plead. He remained silent to the end. He was found guilty and hanged at Bristol in February, 1839.'

She put out the cigarette. 'Grim.'

'Yes.'

'There's more to the story, isn't there? The ghost. You said something about an unquiet spirit.'

I said, 'There was a feeling of unease about the fact that the Colonel wouldn't admit to the crime. After he was convicted and condemned, they tried to persuade him to confess, to lay his sins before his Maker. A murderer often would confess in the last days remaining to him, even after protesting innocence all through the trial. They all did their utmost to persuade him – the prison governor, the warders, the priest and the hangman himself. Those people had harrowing duties to perform. It would have helped them to know that the man going to the gallows was truly guilty of the crime. Not one word would that proud old man speak.'

'You sound almost sorry for him. There wasn't really any doubt, was there?'

I said, 'There's a continuous history of supernatural happenings in this house for a century and a half. Think about it. Suppose, for example, someone else committed the murder.'

'But who else could have?'

'Justinian Crandley.'

'That's impossible. He didn't live there. His footprints would have shown up in the snow.'

'Not if he entered the house as you did tonight – along the roof and through the attic window. He could have murdered Rosamund and returned to his own house by the same route.'

'It's possible, I suppose, but why – what was his motive?'

'Revenge. He would have been master in his own house if the marriage had not been called off. Instead, he faced an indefinite future with his domineering and now embittered mother. He blamed Rosamund. He decided that if he was not to have her as his wife, no one else should.'

'Is that what you believe?'

'It is now,' said I.

'Why didn't the Colonel tell them he was innocent?'

'He blamed himself. He felt a deep sense of guilt for the way he had treated his own daughter. But for his selfishness the murder would never have taken place.'

'Do you think he knew the truth?'

'He must have worked it out. He loved Mrs Crandley too much to cause her further unhappiness.'

There was an interval of silence, broken finally by the sound of car-tyres on the cobbles below.

She stood up. 'Tonight when you saw me at the attic door you thought I was Rosamund's ghost.'

I said, 'No. Rosamund doesn't haunt this place. Her spirit is at rest. I didn't take you for a real ghost any more than I believed your story of escaping from the fellow in the leather jacket.'

She walked to the window. 'It is my taxi.'

I wasn't going to let her leave without admitting the truth. 'You went to the party two doors along with the idea of breaking into this house. You climbed out on to the roof and forced your way in upstairs, meaning to let your friend in by the front door. You were going to burgle the place.'

She gasped and swung around. 'How do you know that?'

'When I opened the door he was expecting you. He said, "*What kept you?*" He knew which house to call at, so it must have been planned. If your story had been true, he wouldn't have known where to come.'

She stared down at the waiting cab.

I said, 'Until I suggested the taxi, you were quite prepared to go out into the street where this man who had allegedly threatened you was waiting.'

'I'm leaving.'

'And I noticed that you didn't want the lights turned on.'

Her tone altered. 'You're not one of the fuzz, are you? You wouldn't turn me in? Give me a break, will you? It's the first time. I'll never try it again.'

'How can I know that?'

'I'll give you my name and address, if you want. Then you can check.'

It is sufficient to state here that she supplied the information. I shall keep it to myself. I'm no longer in the business of exposing petty criminals. I saw her to her taxi. She promised to stop seeing her boyfriend. Perhaps you think I let her off too lightly. Her misdemeanour was minor compared with the discovery I had made – and I owed that discovery to her.

It released me from my obligation, you see. I told you I was once a policeman. An inspector, actually. I made a fatal mistake. I have had a hundred and fifty years to search for the truth and now that I have found it I can rest. The haunting of the Royal Crescent is at an end.

Curl Up and Dye

'HOW WOULD YOU LIKE IT today, sir? Amazing how fast it grows, isn't it? A quick trim all round, perhaps, just to tidy you up? You wouldn't want too much off. Not like the old days. This dates me, I know, but I go back to the wartime, shearing the rookies as they joined up. RAF basic training camp. I was the next in line after the recruitment interview and the medical. If they got as far as me, there was definitely no escape. Fifteen heads an hour, I cut in those days. It was the war effort, you see. All done with scissors and hand-clippers. We weren't on electric. Yet I swear I never drew blood, and if I did I had my styptic pencil ready.

'You don't mind me talking as I work? I told them when I offered myself for this, don't expect me to do it in silence. I'm a compulsive talker, and none of your regulations are going to stop me. I shall fraternise. People don't want a silent barber, do they? Talking is part of the experience. I've had customers – clients, I ought to call them these days – who tell me they come for the conversation. It's a bit one-way with me, I know, but you'd be surprised how much you can learn by listening. Politics, sport, last night's television, travel. I haven't actually been abroad myself, but the wife is an authority. You know the way some women sit up in bed reading those romantic novels? Well, my Brenda reads travel brochures. She has them stacked by the bed. Hundreds. She can tell you the temperature in Torremolinos, or how to approach an African bull elephant or haggle with a gondolier. I'm always learning something new from Brenda. She's sixty-five and never been further than Clacton, but you could take her anywhere. The place she really wants to see is China. I say to her wouldn't you settle for the Costa Brava and a Chinese takeaway, but no, she's set her heart on seeing the Great Wall and the pandas. So I saved up for years, and last summer, we almost got there. It makes me hopping mad to think about it. I booked the China tour as a surprise. Paid the deposit without letting her know. The first Brenda knew of it was when I told her casually she'd be needing some injections. She was on to it in a flash. I've never seen her so excited. Then what do you think happened? A bolt from the blue. Disaster.

'How does the front look to you, sir? A little more to come off, would you say? We could train it across, or let it fall over the forehead in the modern style. If you ask me, it wants another half-inch off. All right?

'My disaster. You just wouldn't believe what happened. I must tell you that I'd worked in the same shop in Battersea since I was demobbed in 1945. A real, old-fashioned barber's shop with the striped pole outside, and three adjustable leather chairs, the sort with head-rests. A bench behind, where the customers waited and read *Picture Post* and *Everybody's*. The smell of Brylcreem in the air. This is before your time, sir. Two assistants and a boy to do the sweeping. Scores of regular customers. Men I'd known since their mothers brought them in as nippers and perched them on a piece of wood across the arms of the chair. I had the monopoly, you see. The only barber in Battersea High Street. There was Sally Anne's, the ladies' salon, across the street, and between us we had the hair-cutting business wrapped up. Not that I took advantage, mind. I always charged the going rate. There aren't many overheads in barbering, if you'll excuse the pun. If people wanted to be generous with tips, that was another thing.

'Old Smithy, my boss, retired in 1962, and I bought the business. Put in some nice chrome fittings and a few more electric points, but kept the character of the establishment, if you know what I mean. I was proud of what I'd achieved. Barbering is an honourable trade, mentioned more than once in Shakespeare. '*I must to the barber's, monsieur, for methinks I am marvellous hairy about the face.*' *A Midsummer Night's Dream*. You didn't take me for a connoisseur of the stage, did you? Appearances can be deceptive. Take yourself, for example. No offence, but who'd expect to find a man of class like you in a place like this?

'To come back to last year, I was standing by the shop window in a quiet moment between customers one morning last July, when I noticed something going on across the road. Well, not exactly going on. *Coming off* is what I ought to say, and what was coming off was the sign over Sally Anne's salon. Nobody had told me the place was changing hands, but in my time that particular business has been bought and sold seven times over. There isn't the continuity in ladies' hairdressing that you find in the gents' side of the business.

'Forward slightly, if you would, sir. Perfect.

'In the course of that day and the next, I kept an eye on the progress of the workmen. The entire shop front was taken out and tarted up. Smoked glass with white gloves and top hats painted on it. A tiled surround. Even a ruddy door that opened automatically. A trifle over the top for Battersea, I thought, but maybe I'm old-fashioned. The real shock was yet to come.

'I don't have to tell you that ladies' hairdressing is a growth industry – if you'll pardon another pun. Anyone with half an eye can see that new salons have opened all over the country in the last ten years. I should think

108

they've trebled in number. It's cut-throat competition. Look at some of the names they dream up. You've got to laugh. *The Friendly Wave. Beyond the Fringe.* How they think of them, I can't imagine. There's a salon down Bermondsey way called *Shear Genius.* But the one that really creases me is *Curl Up and Dye.* How about that?

'Quite still, sir. Wouldn't want to nick your ear, would I?

'This one across the street from me was called *Toppers.* Don't stop me now, will you? I'd like to finish the story if you've got the time, and I reckon you have. As I was saying, I saw the sign go up over the shop. Watched the fellows screwing it in place. Very upmarket lettering, it was. Black on silver, all glittering, like. Fair enough, I thought, *Toppers* might have more going for it than *Sally Anne's.* Best of luck. I hope for your sakes the ladies of Battersea go for it. Then I happened to notice there was another word under it, in smaller letters. I had to step outside my shop to see it properly. It was *Unisex.*

'I tell you, I practically blew a gasket when I saw it. Unisex. They were moving in on my trade. Right there across the street from me, without so much as a by your leave, chum. After almost forty years. I marched across and asked them just what the hell was going on. The young blokes said the sign was going on, and that was all they knew about it. They were just the shop outfitters. If I had any complaints, I'd better address them to the management when the shop opened on Monday.

'Management! Do you know who they put in charge of that shop? Some young girl of seventeen. Maybe eighteen. No older. She looked as if she was taking a day off school. She had five others working with her. The only way of telling who was in charge was that this one chewed gum. Naturally, she wasn't the owner. She couldn't tell me who was. She took her instructions from a fellow called Stan who was coming to collect the takings at the end of the day. I told her I'd like a word with him, but of course I got nowhere. Stan sensed some aggro, and he wasn't staying to cop it.

'I tried several times to catch up with him, and then I thought, blow me, why bother? I'll take it up with the Chamber of Commerce. So I did. And what good did it do? Sweet F.A. "*We all have to face competition, you know,*" they told me. "*It's a free market. You've had a good run. The day of the one-sex salon is numbered. Have you thought of expanding into ladies' hairdressing?*" I won't tell you what I answered to that. No disrespect, but I'm a barber and I'll die a barber, not a blinking teazy-weazy.

'So there was no support from that quarter. It was pretty obvious that I just had to get on, or get out. My prices were competitive, and I did a good job. Nothing fancy, but who wants his hair shampooed and dried with a blower? All right, I lost a few of my younger customers. I expected to. If you ask me, it wasn't the styling they went for, it was the chance to chat up the talent over there.

'After a couple of months, I was feeling more happy about it. I won't say I didn't feel the draught a bit, but I told myself it was worth sitting it out to see the competition off. I was kidding myself.

'One evening at six-thirty, when the *closed* notice is up and I'm locking up, some big fellow steps out of a Cortina and approaches me. "Sorry," I tell him, "I'm closing," but I can see at a glance that he doesn't actually need a haircut. He's as bald as a baby. He says, "Smart thinking, squire. I can see you've got it all weighed up." I say, "What do you mean?" and he says, "Like you just said, you're closing. Congratulations on your retirement. Shall we say next Saturday?" He steps past me into the shop and says, "Not a bad place. A bit run down, but in a good position. You ought to get a fair price." I don't like the sound of this at all, but I manage to smile, and say, "I think you're misinformed. I've got no intention of retiring." To which he says in a low voice, "It's been decided. Better put up a notice tomorrow. Let your regular customers know. And call in at the agent's by the station. They'll soon flog this for you." I say, "Who sent you?" But he won't tell me, so I say, "What if I don't want to sell?" He just gives a shrug and says, "It isn't a question of what you want, squire." Then he walks out, gets into his car and drives away. I've never seen him since.

'I suppose you're wondering what I did about it. Can't expect you to have heard about my little drama. I ignored it. Carried on as usual. Saturday came and nothing happened. Brenda wasn't feeling too good on Sunday. She'd just had her injections for the China trip. So we stayed in. No, that's a lie. I slipped out to the pub for a pint at lunchtime and met Humphrey Lawson, the fellow who runs the record shop next door to mine. He asked me something about the alterations I was having done to the shop. I said, "What alterations?" He told me he'd been past the back of the shops on his way to church and seen one of those cement-mixing lorries backing up towards my place. I said it must have been a mistake. I wasn't having any work done.

'I forgot about it until Monday morning. Turned up at the shop and couldn't open the door. There was a two-foot layer of rock-hard cement right through the shop and the room behind. That's what the bastards did to my business. Forced open a window at the back and spread a ton of wet cement across the floor. I had to get the fire brigade to smash through the door, and then it was like stepping on to a platform. My head was touching the ceiling. All my stuff was ruined. Chairs, cupboards, plumbing, even the plate glass windows. I was ruined. I mean, I faced a massive bill just to get the place into a state fit to sell to someone else.

'We cancelled the China trip and gave up the shop. Brenda was heartbroken. She'll never get that holiday now. The shop became a launderette. My customers had to change the habits of a lifetime. It was a cut-and-blow-dry at Topper's for twice the price after that. All by appointment only and how about some of our special conditioner for sixty pence extra? When I found out what had happened, and why, I felt sick to the back teeth. It wasn't just my business that folded. This was happening all over London. One of the East End mobs had set up a chain of unisex hairdressers. They went under all sorts of fancy names, but the form was the same: move into a prime position in the high street, tart up the shop front, hire a handful of teenage girls for peanuts and put the frighteners on the competition. Anyone who didn't agree to close got a weekend visit like mine.

'How are we doing, sir? I'll just run the razor up the back of your neck. This is one of the few things I managed to save from the shop. This, and my scissors and comb and the old-fashioned cut-throat I use for trimming the sideboards. That's a service you wouldn't get in those unisex salons. A cut-throat razor gives an unbeatable finish. Funny, I've become very possessive about my equipment since the shop went. I carry everything in this case. Won't let it out of my sight.

'You're probably wondering what all this did to my life. It's not *my* life I'm bothered about, sir. I had a good run. I don't care what happens to me. It was Brenda who took the biggest knock. She really wanted that trip to China. You've got to understand that it was the great ambition of her life. She's not the same person at all now. Shattered. No interest in anything. Just sits and stares all day. She's been to doctors, psychiatrists . . . She'd be better off in a mental ward, poor duck.

'As for me, I've adjusted pretty well. There's always work for a barber, and if the customers can't come to you, the obvious thing is to go to them. I thought of hospital work at first, but there aren't the openings that you'd think. Round here, it's all carved up between a couple of barbers who were forced out of business before I lost mine.

'You know, there are ex-barbers all over London who were clobbered by the same mob. All right, the law caught up with the bullyboys eventually. But we lost our livelihoods. We can't start up again. Most of us haven't got the capital.

'Don't ever talk to me about justice. What happened when the case came to court? Topper's was forced to close, and now there isn't a barber in Battersea High Street. My old customers have a two-mile bus-ride if they want a haircut. Crazy.

'Anyway, not to be beaten, I applied to the prison service. I thought prisoners need haircuts the same as anyone else, and I was right. They took me on. So here I am. I've built it up to four days a week in the last six months. That's three prisons, including this one. I don't mind the work. No tips, of course. They expect *me* to bring in cigarettes. No, don't ask me, sir. I've none left today.

'You have to be responsible working in prison, mind. It's all a matter of trust. They used to search me as I came through the gate, but they never found anything except a packet of fags which I said was my own, and my barbering implements. I'd be a fool to try anything, wouldn't I? I mean, trying to smuggle in a gun or drugs, or something. I find the vast majority of your prisoners very co-operative, as a matter of fact. Given a chance – and I am a compulsive talker, I admit – most prisoners talk quite freely to me. It's a sort of escape, I suppose, spending twenty minutes with a barber. Like a link with the world outside.

'That's what I tell myself. I'm performing a social service. I keep it as civilized as conditions allow. Just you and me in here and the screw outside. I said at the outset I'll take one man at a time. I don't want anyone behind my back, not when there's scissors in my hand. The next man comes in when I'm ready, and not before.

113

'Have a squint in the mirror, now, and see what you think. Nice job? And the back? Good. Don't get up, sir. I want to tidy you up with my cut-throat. Sideboards are just a little ragged, aren't they? A man like you is used to being decently turned out. Oh, yes, I know a bit about you, sir. Quite a lot. Picked it up here and there from my clients in the prisons. I know what you're in for. Six months, isn't it, for demanding money with menaces?

'Took me a while to track you down. I mean, I didn't know your face, and you wouldn't know me. I don't suppose you even heard of me, a big-shot like yourself. The man who came to my shop that Saturday night was just one of your bullyboys, one of dozens. You wouldn't know who he was if I asked you now. But I wasn't interested in him. I wanted to find the man who gave the orders. Barbering has its uses. Snip-snip. Snippets of information. I can listen, as well as talk. You pleaded guilty, shopped a few of your mates, and the police didn't press the charges of violence that would have put you away for much longer.

'What I say is that prison isn't bad enough for the likes of you, ruining people's lives. Easy, sir. I don't want to strangle you. That wouldn't be a barber's way. I'm just pulling the strings of the cape nice and tight to get a grip. You won't feel much. I sharpened it specially this morning. Like I said, it gives an unbeatable finish.'

Friendly Yachtsman, 39

RACHEL SHOUTED ACROSS THE ROOM: 'Mother, you're pathetic! Mentally you're still in Noddy-land.'

Carla felt pathetic. She was on the point of tears. Until this moment she had coped rather well as a single parent – better than others who talked of the teenage rebellion as if World War III had broken out in their homes. Her only daughter, Rachel, had got to fifteen and never thrown a tantrum.

It wasn't that Rachel was repressed. She was a lively, articulate girl with firm opinions. She hadn't needed to vent any frustration because, ever since the divorce, Carla had put her energy and imagination into creating a close, loving relationship between them. They were more like sisters, really, calling each other by first names, sharing experiences. They went to aerobics, played squash, and listened to pop records together.

Of course there was an age gap – Carla was thirty-six – but they conspired to ignore it. If you'd put a gun to Carla's head, she would have admitted that she really preferred Bob Dylan to Madonna, but Rachel never inquired. They made allowances for each other like the best of friends.

Until now. The way Rachel was talking, she plainly wanted to goad Carla into a reaction.

'I don't know why you're staring at me like that.'

'Rachel, this isn't like you.'

'What do you know about me, anyway?'

'Darling, we've always been open with each other.'

'So what's different? I've told you my plans. I'm not deceitful.'

'I didn't say you were,' answered Carla, telling herself to stay calm. This was it – the bottled-up aggression they had warned her to expect. She found it hard to believe the defiance in her daughter's eyes.

'You're jealous,' Rachel said, touching a raw nerve. 'Just because you never had the offer of a trip like this, you want to stop me.'

'That isn't fair, Rachel.'

'Then I can go? Well, I'm going anyway. Try and stop me.'

'I haven't even met this boy.'

'It isn't just him. There's Cindy, and the other guy, Simon, and it's not the Gobi Desert, for crying out loud. It's only a week in Cornwall.'

Carla was silent, more hurt than she wanted to show. She was being forced into the role of the heavy-handed parent while Rachel treated her like a betrayer. And she couldn't deny that there was some envy mingled in with her concern about the wisdom of the trip.

At fifteen, she wouldn't have dared propose such an adventure. Her mother would have had hysterics and her father would have telephoned the school. Her elderly, overprotective parents had practically locked her away until she was nineteen. As a result, when she started work she had married the first man who gave her a kiss and the promise of escape. The marriage had been a disaster.

Well, a disaster in every respect but one. She had Rachel. She didn't want to lose her now.

'All right,' she said with a sigh. 'I shall have to trust you, won't I?'

Rachel embraced her. 'I'm sorry about those mean things I said. You've been a wonderful mother, Carla, and a good mate, too.'

That last remark, phrased as it was, like a summing-up, pained Carla more than anything else that had been said. She felt a wrench, and then an ache. She and Rachel would never be as close again.

Over the next week, the ache turned insidiously to something else. Carla resented being left behind. And she resented her own daughter having the freedom that she herself had been denied. Rachel had called her jealous, and she was.

She tried telling herself that Rachel was entitled to have her independence. A young girl needed friends of her own age. A trip like this was an important stage in the process of growing into a well adjusted modern woman.

All that was true, but where did it leave Carla? What about *her* future, *her* prospect of friends? She'd given her best years to Rachel. At this moment they seemed like lost years. She wished she could have them back.

Envy is a cancerous emotion. It lodged in Carla and spread destructively. She found herself looking at Rachel's fresh skin and the sheen on her young hair and thinking: I was like that, and look at me now.

In the three weeks before Rachel left for the holiday, the tension increased between mother and daughter. And it was all on Carla's side. She knew it was selfish and immature. *She* was behaving like the frustrated teenager. She had to find some way of distracting herself.

She fantasized. If I can't go to Cornwall with Rachel, there's no reason why I shouldn't go on holiday with someone else. Well – it does no harm to think about it.

The envy receded a little. To feed her fantasy, she bought one of those magazines in which lonely people advertise for friends. That night, in the privacy of her room, she poured herself a cherry brandy. Then she opened the magazine and worked her way down the columns, looking first at the ages of the men who advertised and then, more closely, at the descriptions of any between thirty-five and forty-five. Telling herself she was only playing a game of make-believe, Carla rejected each of the men who struck her as pushy or fast and eventually penciled a ring around one:

FRIENDLY YACHTSMAN, 39, six foot and successful, but shy, seeks blonde, intelligent lady of similar age for weekend sailing trip. Photo appreciated. Box No. 5059.

Carla's mouth had gone dry. She poured another drink and opened the drawer where she kept her photos.

In the next few days, her feelings about Rachel's holiday underwent a change. 'I'm starting to get excited for you,' she remarked when they went out together to buy a sleeping-bag.

'So long as you don't get depressed when I'm gone,' said Rachel.

'I don't think I will now,' answered Carla.

Friendly yachtsman, 39, had replied by return mail. His name was Herb and he was American. He was just amazed that so many charming ladies had responded to his advert, but he liked Carla's letter and photo best and looked forward to meeting her.

Would she allow him to take her to lunch at the Savoy – a chance to meet and talk about the sailing and where they would go, with no commitment yet on either side?

No commitment be damned. Carla bought a tapered black skirt and a snappy black-and-white-check jacket to wear at lunch. She was surprising herself by her single-mindedness. Why not? she thought. Aren't I entitled to some excitement, too?

'Take a long look at me,' Herb offered immediately after they met. 'See if I measure up to my ad.'

Carla smiled, and thought to herself that thirty-nine was a slight underestimate, but he was just as tall as he'd claimed, and tanned as a sailor should be. He had glittering blue eyes, too, and that was an added bonus. She said: 'Do I look as if I'm disappointed?'

He said in his soft American accent: 'Carla, you look terrific. You know, I had over eighty letters, yet when I saw your picture I said to myself, this is the one.'

For most of the lunch he talked about his yacht, a cruising boat harboured at St Mawes.

'Where's St Mawes?' asked Carla.

'Cornwall.'

Her pulse quickened.

He showed her pictures of the boat's interior, the saloon, and the galley. She'd never set foot inside a yacht, but she could see that this one was luxuriously equipped.

'About the sleeping quarters,' said Herb. 'You got your own, okay? Just because we happen to be alone on a boat together, I'm not going to be pressing for a heavy relationship or anything.'

She liked that. It was the sort of reassurance you got from a mature man. So different from the adolescent pestering that Rachel would have to cope with.

'What should I wear – if you decide to invite me?' asked Carla. 'I haven't done this before, you know.'

'I'd like to take care of that, if you don't mind,' said Herb. 'You'll need some special gear. Would you give me some idea of the size you take?'

She presumed he was talking about oilskins, but she hadn't realized that they had to be fitted. She wrote down her measurements.

'One other thing, Carla. You have beautiful hair. Do you ever wear it loose?'

It was drawn back from her face, coiled, and held in

place with a slide. 'Sometimes, when I'm indoors. But not when I go out.'

'You should. You definitely should.'

'It's rather long.'

'Have it cut to the level of the shoulders. Say about here.' He showed her, and with such obvious interest and concern that she felt amused – and pleased.

She agreed to a short cruise along the Cornish coast the weekend before Rachel returned. Herb explained that he would already be in the West Country on business, so if she drove down he'd meet her on the Friday evening in the public car park at St Mawes.

'Is it a large car park?' Carla asked.

'Relax. It's as quiet as a morgue in the evenings. I'll be the only guy in sight.'

She didn't tell Rachel about Herb. When she drove her to the station the following week and left her on the platform with Cindy and the boys, she was able to say 'Enjoy yourself ' without a twinge of envy.

The same afternoon she went to the hairdresser's.

While the stylist was finishing someone else, Carla picked up a magazine filled with pictures and reports of hunt balls and cocktail parties. She didn't have much interest in the social set, but there was nothing else to read. She'd flicked through as far as the adverts at the back before she had an idea that she'd glimpsed a familiar face in one of the pictures. She took a deep breath and turned back the pages for a second look.

It was one of a set of photos taken at a preview of an art exhibition. Two couples stood holding champagne glasses. The caption read: *Sir Roger and Lady Harkness with Mr and Mrs Jack Pearman of New York. Wendy Pearman is managing director of the Trendy Wendy chain of fashion stores.*

It wasn't Trendy Wendy who had caught Carla's attention. It was the tall, suntanned man beside her. Jack

Pearman of New York? He was *her* American, Herb. There could be no doubt about it.

Carla closed her eyes and tried to calm herself. Was it so surprising that Herb should have used another name when he advertised? What bothered her more was that he was a married man. To be fair, he hadn't deceived her about that – she simply hadn't liked to ask.

What now? Her weekend in Cornwall was slipping out of sight. She ought to forget it.

God help me, she thought, I'll be back where I started, pathetically envious of my fifteen-year-old daughter. If I hadn't picked up this magazine, I would never have known. Could I be mistaken about the photograph?

She took another look. It was impossible to imagine him as anyone else but the Herb she knew.

She looked at the wife's picture. Besides being a successful businesswoman, Trendy Wendy was quite good-looking – blonde, with shoulder-length hair. She didn't have the look of a wife who was being deceived.

Strangely, there was something else in her look, something about the proportions of the face, the wide eyes and high cheekbones. Carla stared at the picture. The features were hers! The woman was strikingly like herself.

Was it so remarkable, she rationalized? Presumably Herb was attracted to her cast of face. He'd picked it out from his eighty applications.

The stylist spoke over Carla's shoulder: 'How would you like your hair cut today, madam?'

Carla pointed to the picture. 'Like this. Shoulder length.'

To hell with her doubts. She'd answered the advert in good faith. The prospect of a weekend on the yacht had quite banished her negative feelings towards Rachel. She was going to be positive. After so many years, she was entitled to some high living.

*

The car park at St Mawes was deserted except for two trucks and about a dozen cars. Herb stepped into the beam of her headlights. 'You can park it there, beside mine.'

His was a Rolls-Royce Silver Spirit.

'I thought we'd eat on the boat,' he told her. 'Carla, I love your hair like that.'

The yacht was the equivalent in sailing craft of the Rolls-Royce. Carla had her own sleeping berth as promised, a cosy cabin with white leather upholstery and crimson woodwork. Better than a sleeping-bag in a tent. She opened the wardrobe.

'Herb, this is stacked with clothes.'

'Sure,' he called from the galley. 'They're for you. Try the jacket and white pants. See if they fit.'

They fitted perfectly. They were brand new. They had the Trendy Wendy label.

Dinner consisted of steak fillet with tomatoes and asparagus tips accompanied by Châteauneuf du Pape, 1979.

'You're a terrific cook,' said Carla when they had finished.

'No,' said Herb. 'Efficient, that's all. To be a terrific cook, you need to be creative. When it comes to creativity, I'm way down the field.' He carried the plates to the galley. 'And now you'd better get some sleep,' he suggested. 'The forecast is good, and I'd like to set off on the morning tide.'

'Isn't this terrific?' Herb called to Carla when she appeared on deck next morning. The gulls were swooping and wheeling over the shimmering water. 'Why don't you sit on the cabin roof and get the feel of the sun on your skin? Did you find that green costume?'

'I'm wearing it,' answered Carla, as she slipped the

bathrobe from her shoulders.

'Wave to the guys in the fishing boat. They appreciate good looks.'

She waved and got an old-fashioned wolf-whistle in return. She felt slightly foolish.

Herb started the engine. He drew Carla's attention to several other spectators as the yacht cruised out of the harbour. 'Wave to them.'

She had an uneasy feeling that she was being exhibited as the blonde on his boat, so she said: 'I'm going below now, to get some breakfast. Can I cook for you?'

Herb said quite sharply: 'No. Stay where you are. I have other plans. See the coastguard up there? He's got his glasses on you.'

She turned over and lay face down, brooding about the sharpness in his tone of voice. Presently she asked, 'Where are we going?'

'Across the Narrows to Falmouth.'

'Why?'

'I like it there.'

'Aren't we going out to sea?'

'Maybe later.'

It seemed to Carla that they'd hardly gone any distance when he anchored in Falmouth, some way off shore, but among other sailing boats. He said: 'Now we'll have brunch. No, don't get up. We'll eat on deck.'

She said: 'If you don't mind, I'd rather sit at a table to eat.'

He said casually: 'Dangle your legs over the side. Same thing.'

His offhanded manner stung her into remarking: 'Is this how you treat your wife?'

He gave her a sharp look. 'I didn't say I had a wife.'

She said: 'You didn't tell me your name is Jack Pearman, either.'

The colour drained from his face. 'How did you know that?'

She told him about the picture in the magazine. 'She must be a very able woman, your wife.'

'Wendy is the most brilliant lady I've ever met,' he said without warmth or pride. 'I married her before she was famous, when we were both in art school. She had a genius for design and a cool head for business. I was smart enough to see it.'

'Are you in the same business?'

'I turn out a few designs, but I don't have Wendy's talent.' There was a hard edge to the words, which he made an effort to soften by adding with a sly grin: 'What do I have? I have her Rolls-Royce and her yacht.'

'This is *hers*?' Carla said in a shocked voice.

'Don't look so guilty. She's never set foot on it. Won't come near it. She gets seasick.'

Carla felt pretty sick herself. She didn't want to stay aboard Wendy Pearman's boat with Wendy Pearman's husband, wearing clothes designed by Wendy Pearman. She demanded to be taken back to St Mawes.

'No problem,' said Herb indifferently. 'We'll go back this evening.'

'I'd like to go now.'

He shook his head. 'The tide is wrong.'

Carla knew nothing about tides. She had to accept his explanation. He took the yacht out to sea for the afternoon, but it was no pleasure. She was thinking only of getting home.

It was after dark when he finally set her down in St Mawes. 'Too bad it didn't work out,' he said. 'Are you sure you wouldn't like to sleep on board tonight?'

She put up at a St Mawes hotel and left early on Sunday morning, still angry with herself for getting involved in such a humiliating experience.

The house was depressingly silent when she let herself in. She turned on the television news while she waited for

124

the kettle to boil. Presently she heard a familiar name and turned and saw a face remarkably like her own on the screen, the blonde hair cut to shoulder-length. Even the jacket and blouse resembled those she had worn aboard the yacht.

The newsman said: 'Wendy Pearman, founder of the multi-million-pound Trendy Wendy fashion empire, is missing, believed drowned, after an ocean trip off the south coast of Cornwall in her luxury yacht today. Her husband, Jack Pearman, left her sunbathing on deck while he was at the helm. When he realized she had disappeared, he alerted the coastguard by radio and a search of the area was made, using helicopters and emergency vessels, but nothing was found. Mrs Pearman was a non-swimmer.'

'She also hated boats,' said Carla aloud. She switched off the television and poured herself a drink, trying to make sense of the tragedy – if it *were* a tragedy, for she doubted very much whether Wendy Pearman had taken that trip.

She decided not to get involved. If the woman was really dead, nothing could bring her back. But it was a puzzle.

Carla went to bed.

Sometime in the night she woke to the sound of a door being closed and knew someone was in the house! The stairs creaked. Footsteps crossed the landing.

Carla's heart was pounding. The bedroom door opened.

'Are you awake?'

Carla felt for the light switch. 'Rachel! What's happened? Why are you here?'

Rachel reached out and clasped her mother, pressing her face into her shoulder. Her eyes were moist. 'It was horrible. I'm so glad to find you here.'

'Darling, what is it? Tell me.'

'I left the others and came home.'

'Oh, Rachel – why?'

'Something really hateful happened. Someone came to the camp-site and told us that some pot-holers had found a

125

dead body in an old mineshaft. The two boys wanted to see it brought to the surface. I told them I didn't want to go, but – it was a woman. She was blonde. The blanket slipped off her face and I saw her and, oh, Carla, she looked like you. They said she must have fallen down there some time before the weekend. They don't know who she is.'

'But I do,' said Carla. She reached for the phone and began dialling for the emergency-services operator.

'Carla, why did you cut your hair?'

She didn't answer. She was already talking to the operator . . .

After Carla had spent the morning at the police station making a statement, she met Rachel and told her why she had cut her hair. She told her everything.

Rachel was silent for a long time. Then she said: 'So the dead woman I saw was Wendy Pearman?'

'Yes.'

'And her husband pushed her down the mineshaft?'

Carla nodded. 'Some days ago. He'd planned it for a long time. He advertised for a blonde, knowing he could take his pick from all the photos. I must have been the closest to her in looks, so after he'd murdered Wendy he dressed me in her clothes and paraded me on his yacht to convince people that she was still alive. Thanks to that picture in the hairdresser's I knew who he was. After I left, he faked the accident at sea to account for her disappearance.'

Rachel frowned. 'Why did he kill her?'

'She had all the talent.'

'Exactly! He needed her. He could have carried on living like a king. What made him do it?'

'Envy.'

'But that's unreasonable.'

'Yes,' said Carla. 'And deadly.'

The Pomeranian Poisoning

ROSEBUD BOOKS
VOLUMES OF ROMANCE
Battersea Bridge Road
London SW11

12th May

Dearest Honeypot,

Have you gone into hiding? My telephonist has a sore finger from trying your number, and your Grizzly Bear is going spare. Can't work, can't think of anything else. Horrid fears that his Honeypot has been stolen by some other bear and taken to another part of the forest.

Put him out of his misery, won't you, and tell him it isn't true? The weekend in Brighton wasn't so disappointing as all that, was it? The trouble with this bear is that he's too excitable when he gets the chance of Honey, but he remains huggingly affectionate. He passionately wants another chance to prove it.

Do pick up the blower and comfort your fretful

Grizzly

P.S. Are you writing anything at present? A brilliant opportunity has cropped up. Couldn't possibly make Honeypot any sweeter, but could guarantee to make her infinitely richer.

Garden Flat
310 Arch Street
Earls Court
SW5
Sunday afternoon

Dear Frank (I'd rather drop the nursery names, if you don't mind),

As you see, I've moved from Fulham. Your letter was sent on. Take a deep breath and pour yourself a double scotch, Frank. I'm living with a guy called Tristram. He's my age and could pass for my twin brother and we have so much in common that I can hardly believe it's true. We both adore Status Quo, Martin Amis, Chinese takeaways, Steve Bell, Porsches, Spielberg, Daley Thompson, goosedown duvets and so much else it would take the rest of today and next week to list it. Tristram went to public school (Radley) and Sussex University. He has a degree in American Studies and he's terribly high-powered. He knows Milton Friedman and James Baldwin and masses of people who come up on the box. I know you'll understand when I say that I'm totally committed to Tristram now.

Pause, for you to top up the scotch.

Frank, I want you to know that this has nothing to do with what happened, or didn't quite happen, that Saturday night in Brighton. I blame that bottle of Asti. We should have stayed on g. and t. Whatever, no hard feelings, OK?

I'm not sure if you still feel the same about the business opportunity you mentioned, but I *am* quite intrigued, as a matter of fact. Yes, I've been doing some writing – tinkering away at a novel about the women's movement, the first of a five-book saga, actually – but Tristram and I are both on Social Security so I wouldn't mind putting the novel on one side if there's cash on tap now. But I must make it clear that it's my writing talent, such as it is, that's up for grabs, and nothing else. Putting it another way, Frank darling, I'm open to advances in pounds sterling.

We don't have a phone yet, and it gets expensive using pay-phones, so be a darling and write by return.

Be kind to me.

Luv,

Felicity

ROSEBUD BOOKS
VOLUMES OF ROMANCE

23 May

Dear Felicity,

You may wonder why it took me so long to answer your letter; on the other hand, you may wonder that I bothered to answer it at all. I need hardly say that I am deeply hurt. For me, the age-difference between us was never an impediment, and I rashly imagined you felt the same way. You gave me no reason to suppose there was anyone else in your life. You appeared to enjoy our evenings together. True, I caught you closing your eyes at the proms from time to time, but I took it that you were transported by the music. You always seemed to revive in time for our suppers in the Trattoria. I find myself putting a cynical construction on everything now.

I suppose I must accept that I was just a meal-ticket, or a sugar-daddy, or whatever cruel phrase is currently in vogue for it.

As to that literary project I happened to mention, I shall obviously look elsewhere. The work required is unde-manding and I dare say I shall have no difficulty finding an author willing to make a six-figure sum for a short children's book.

You may keep my LP of the Enigma Variations. To listen to it ever again would be too distressful.

Your former friend,
     Franklin

Garden Flat,
310 Arch Street,
SW5
Wednesday morning

Grizzly Darling!

What a wild, ferocious bear you were last night. Honeypot has never felt so stirred.

When I arrived with the Elgar and the Mateus Rosé, I honestly meant to say sorry and a civilized goodbye. You're so masterful!

If you still mean what you said (and if you don't I shall throw myself under a train) could you come with the van some time between six-thirty and seven on Friday evening? Tristram will be at his Karate class and it will avoid a scene that might otherwise be too hairy for us all. I haven't much stuff to move out, darling. One trip will be enough, I'm sure.

Hugs and kisses,
    Your
        Felicity

My own dearest Tristram,

Please, darling, before you do anything else, read this to the end. It's terribly important to our relationship that you understand what I have done, and why.

I've moved out. I'm going to stay with Frank, that

130

doddery old publisher guy I told you about. Before you blow your top, Tris, hear me out. I've agonized over this for days. Darling, you know I wouldn't walk out on you without a copper-bottomed reason. Frank means nothing to me. He's a dingbat: pathetic, ugly, flabby, but – and this is the point – he knows a way to make me fabulously rich. I mean stinking rich, Tris. We're talking telephone numbers. And for what? For some book he wants me to write. He hasn't given me all the details yet. He's boxing clever until I move in with him, which is part of the deal, but I understand it's only a children's book he wants. I can finish it in a matter of days if I pull out all the stops, and then I'll be off like a bunny, sweetheart.

He insisted that I go and live in his house in the backwoods of Surrey while I'm writing the thing. Isn't it a bore? I'm not giving you the address because I know what you'll do. You'll be down there kicking in the door, and who could blame you? But just pause to think.

If I pass up this opportunity, what sort of future do you and I have? I mean, I *know* it's terrific being together, but what prospect is there of ever getting out of this damp slum? I've had enough, Tris, and so have you. Admit it.

I can almost hear you say I'm selling myself, and I suppose I am if I'm honest, but let's face it, I spent a weekend with Frank in Brighton before I met you. It's not as if he's a total stranger. And if I am selling myself, what a price!

Which is why I'm asking you to keep your cool and try to understand that this is the best chance we've got. Just a short interval, darling, and then we can really start to live.

There won't be a minute when you're out of my thoughts, lover.

I'll write again soon.

Be patient, darling!

Ever your
      Felicity

This dreary pad in Surrey
Saturday night

Dearest Tristram,

Has it been only a week? It feels like *months*. A life sentence with hard labour, and I've been doing plenty of that. Writing, I mean. Non-stop. The reason I can do so much is that I know every word, every letter, I write is worth pounds and pounds. Guaranteed. It's crazy, but it's true. I'm on to a winner, Tris. You see, Frank – he's my publisher-friend – has told me exactly how this is going to work, and he's right. It can't miss. He and I are going to split – wait for it – half a million dollars!

For a kids' book?

Yes!

Scrape yourself off the floor and I'll tell you how this miracle works.

You know that Frank is the chairman of Rosebud Books, who publish romance fiction, and before you knock it, remember that my only published work, *Desire Me Do*, paid for our new telly, among other things. Frank's outfit isn't exactly Mills & Boon, but he helps beginners like me to get started and I dare say it makes life more tolerable for a few thousand readers of the things.

One of Frank's regular writers was an eccentric old biddy called Zenobia Hatt. That was her real name, believe it or not. I'm using the past tense because she died four or five years ago, before I got to know Frank. Apparently she was prolific. Her books didn't sell all that well, but she kept producing them. And she expected to see them in the shops. Every time she walked into a supermarket and spotted a display of paperbacks, she checked to see if her latest was among them. If it wasn't, she made a beeline for Rosebud Books to tear a strip off Frank. She was always

132

tearing strips off Frank. Even if the book was in the shop, something about it would upset her, like the cover design, or the quality of paper they were using. I don't know why he continued to publish her, but he did. She always appeared with her two dogs in tow. They were Pomeranians. If you think I'm rabbiting on about nothing important, you're making a big mistake. This *is* important.

Do you know about Pomeranians? They're toy dogs. Funny little beggars with enormous ruffs, neat faces and tiny legs. They come in most colours. You know how some old ladies are with dogs? Zenobia doted on hers.

Well, like I said, she died, and this is the important bit, Tristy. In her will, she left the house and everything she had to be divided between her relatives. That is, except any future income from her books. You get royalties trickling in long after a book is published, you see. Zenobia decreed that the future profits for her writing should go into a trust fund to pay for her dogs to be kept in style in some rip-off place in Hampstead that caters for pampered pets who have come into money. The residue was to be awarded annually as a literary prize: the Zenobia Hatt prize.

Nice idea, right? The snag was that Zenobia wasn't really in the Barbara Cartland class as a best-selling writer. The royalties paid the fees at the dogs' home for a couple of years and the Pommies were put down. There was never any residue, so the prize was never awarded.

End of story? Not quite. Cop this, love.

A couple of months ago, Frank had a phone call from California. Some film producer was asking about the rights to a Rosebud book called *Michaela and the Mount*, by – you guessed – Zenobia Hatt! It was a cheap romance she published years ago, so long ago, in fact, that it was out of print, so Frank wouldn't make a penny out of any deal. Don't ask me why, but this book is reckoned to be the perfect vehicle for some busty starlet they reckon is the next Madonna.

Tris darling, they bought it for half a million bucks! The money goes into the trust and by the terms of Zenobia's will it has to be offered as the prize for 1987. The lot. The doggies aren't on the payroll anymore, so every silver dollar is up for grabs. And who do you think is going to win?

Shall I tell you how? The point is that Zenobia didn't offer her money for any common or garden novel. She had very clear ideas about the sort of book she wanted to encourage. She had it written into her will that the prize should go to the best published work of fiction that featured a Pomeranian dog as one of the main characters. As you can imagine, that limits the competition somewhat.

When Frank cottoned on to this, he did some quick thinking. Animal stories don't usually feature on the Rosebud list, but he reckoned he could stretch a point and commission a book for kids featuring Tom the Pom that he'd rush through before the end of the year to scoop the prize. He'd go fifty-fifty with the writer, and that's me, sweetheart. I've signed an agreement and pay-day will be some time in January, when the trustees award the prize. It's as simple as that. No-one else has time to get a book out, because the news hasn't broken yet, and won't until the film deal is finalized. You know what American lawyers are like. Well, perhaps you don't, but the trustees expect to sign the contract in October or November. *Tom the Pom* will hit the shops in time for Christmas and it doesn't matter a brass farthing how many it sells, because it's certain to clean up half a million bucks.

That's the story so far, my love. Naturally I can't wait to finish *my* story and hand it over. Then there'll be nothing to keep me here. I hope to see you Friday at the latest, and what a reunion that will be . . .

Luv you,
      Felicity

Same Place, Unfortunately
Thursday

Tris darling,

I'm not going to make it by tomorrow. I showed Frank
what I've written so far and he wants some changes, some
of them pretty drastic. I tried pointing out that it didn't
really matter if the writing was sloppy in places, so long as
I finished the flaming book and it got into print before the
end of the year, but he came over all high and mighty and
sounded off about standards and the reputation of his
house. I wondered what on earth his house had to do with
it until I discovered he was talking about Rosebud Books,
his publishing house. He says he doesn't want an inferior
book to carry his imprint, especially as *Tom the Pom* is
certain to get a lot of attention when it wins. I suppose he
has a point.

So it's back to the keyboard to hammer out some
revisions. What a drag!

I suppose Monday or Tuesday would be a realistic
estimate.

Impatiently,
Luv,
        Felicity

Wednesday

Oh, Tris,

I'm so depressed! I've had the mother and father of a
row with Frank. I finished the book yesterday, with all the
changes he wanted. He read it last night. He wasn't exactly
over the moon, but he agreed it couldn't wait any longer,
so he would hand it over to his sub-editor. I said fine, and

would he kindly drop me and my baggage at the flat on his way to the office. Tris, he looked at me as if I was crazy. He said we had an agreement. I said certainly we had, and I'd fulfilled my side of it by finishing the book. Now I was ready to go home.

Whereupon he deluged me with a load of gush about how it was much more than a publishing agreement to him. He wouldn't have asked me to write the book if he hadn't believed I was willing to move in with him. I meant more to him than all the money and if I walked out on him now he would drop the typescript in the Thames.

Tris, I'm sure he means it. He knows I need the money and he's going to keep me here like a hostage until the book is in the shops. He could cancel it at any stage up to then. I'll be here for *months*.

There's no way out that I can see. You and I are just going to have to be patient. The day the book is published, I'll be free. And ready to collect my share of the prize. Let's go ski-ing in February, shall we? And what sort of car shall we buy? We can have that Porsche. One each, if we want. If we both look forward to next year, perhaps we can get through. We *must* get through.

Tris, don't try and trace me here, darling. It would be too painful for us both.

I'm thinking of you constantly.

Your soon-to-be-rich, but sorry-to-be-here
    Felicity

As Before
1 August.

Tris my love,

Did you wonder if I was ever going to write again? Are you starting to doubt my existence? Dear God, I hope not. The reason it has been so long is that I get dreadfully

136

depressed. I've written any number of letters and destroyed them when I read them through a second time. It's no good for me to wallow in self-pity, and it certainly won't do much for you.

So this time, I'll be positive. Another month begins today. For me, another milestone. I've endured ten weeks now, and I'm still looking at my watch all day long.

I expect you'd like to know how I pass my days. I get up around nine, after he's left for work. Breakfast (half a grapefruit, coffee and toast), then a walk if it's fine. Without giving anything away – and I won't, so don't look for clues – there are some beautiful walks through the woods here. I see squirrels every day and sometimes deer. Often I collect enough mushrooms to have on toast for lunch, or if I'm really energetic I might put them into a quiche. The rest of the morning and most of the afternoon is devoted to my writing. The novel, I mean. It's slow work, but it's good stuff, Tris, a sight better than *Tom the Pom*, which is going to make so much more money. Crazy. (*T. the P.* was in proof four weeks ago, by the way, and this is the good news: LIBERATION DAY is earlier than I dared to hope – September 30th). Later in the afternoon I might do some reading. The trouble is that the only books here are Rosebud Romances, which depress me, even if they're sufficiently well-written to be readable, and boring non-fiction on hunting, shooting and fishing that he only keeps for the leather bindings.

Around 6, I get something out of the freezer for the evening meal. He comes home about 7 and that's all I'm going to say about my day. I stop living then.

Perhaps you wonder why I don't slip away to London during the day to see you. Tris, I've often thought of it. I know that I couldn't bear to come back here if I did. He'd stop publication of the book and you and I would have endured all this for nothing. No, I must hold out here.

Please be strong for me.

Less than two months to go!
Love
        Felicity

                    The Same
                    19th August

Tris darling

I have a horrid feeling that Frank suspects something. It's like this. Ever since he moved me here, he's assumed that it's for keeps. He constantly talks about his future as if I'm part of it. Like he talks about the two of us (him and me) taking trips on Concorde or the Orient Express when we've got our hands on the Zenobia Hatt prize. Naturally I go along with this, letting him think I can't imagine anything more blissful than sharing the rest of my life with him and half a million bucks.

Up to now, I'm sure he's believed me. Up to last night, anyway. Then, out of the blue, he mentioned you, Tris. I don't think either of us have spoken your name since he brought me here. He asked me if I'd been in touch with you, and of course I denied it. Just to sound more convincing, I went a bit further and said I'd forgotten all about you.

Frank went on to say that he only happened to speak of you because by chance he was driving along Arch Street at lunchtime yesterday and he saw a tall, dark guy in leathers coming out of number 310 with his arm around a strikingly good-looking redhead. I must admit he caught me off guard for a moment. I must have looked concerned, because he took me up on it at once and asked why I'd gone so pale.

I see now that it was a shabby, underhand trick to test my reactions. I can't fathom how he knows that you go in for leathers, because I've never told him, but I'm sure of one thing, and that's that you wouldn't cheat on me while I'm in purgatory here.

If Frank wants a battle of wits, he'll find I'm more than a match for him. I think last night was just a try-on, but I'm taking no chances. I'll make sure no one sees me posting this.

I've discovered a way of making my walks more interesting. Among those boring old books on blood sports in the library I found an illustrated guide on the fungi of Great Britain. I take it with me and try and identify the different species along the paths. I'm doing quite well so far, with four different sorts of toadstools as well as the mushrooms I have for lunch.

Six weeks today and we'll be together, Tris. For keeps.

I'll write when I can.

Miss you so much.

       Felicity

Still Holed-Up Here
September 10th

Well, Tris, my darling,

It's a day for celebration. I've actually had a copy of *Tom the Pom* in my hands! The printers have delivered it on time. But before you uncork the champagne, let me explain that this still isn't publication day. That remains the same, September 30th. They send the books out to the shops ready for the big day, but no-one is supposed to sell them before then. In theory, Frank could cancel the publication, call them back and burn them all, and I actually believe he would if he knew I was planning to give him the elbow once I've qualified for the prize.

The book strikes me as pretty abysmal now that I've had a chance to read it again. However, they've dressed it up in a shiny laminated cover with cute illustrations by some artist (who won't have any claim on the prize, incidentally, because it's awarded to the writer) and I expect they'll sell a few hundred.

I'm glad to have something to give me a boost, because Frank has been driving me mad. He keeps wanting assurances that I'm committed to him for life, and he constantly paws me. I think he senses that I find it disagreeable, and that makes him even more persistent. He often mentions you now, and that redhead he is supposed to have seen you with. It's as if he senses what's in my mind and wants me to break down and admit it.

Sometimes I feel so angry that I'd like to stop him getting *any* of the prize, like the poms that were put down before they could come into a fortune. You and I would be twice as well off then.

I do my best to divert myself on my walks, which I'm now taking morning and afternoon, in all weathers. I'm becoming quite an expert on fungi. I've found and identified several more species, including *Amanita Phalloides*, known commonly as the Death Cap or the Destroying Angel. Not to be confused with the mushroom, as it is fatal if eaten. There's a small crop of them under an oak only five minutes from here.

Only three weeks now, my love!
     Felicity

Here, but not for much longer
One day to Liberation

Darling Tristram,

By the time you get this, it will be Publication Day and I will have freed myself from Frank for ever. He has become quite insufferable.

I've come to a momentous decision. It's been forced on me partly because I'm desperately frightened to tell him

140

that I'm leaving him. I don't want the confrontation, and I know that if I just walk out, he'll track me down. I don't ever want to see him again. He gives me the creeps. And I feel bitter that he's due to collect such a large share of the prize. It's supposed to go to the writer, Tris, and I was the one who slogged it out for days inventing a story. Frank didn't do a damn thing except hand it to the printer.

I want you to do something for me, Tris. Please, darling, burn every one of the letters I wrote you. I don't want anyone to know I was ever here. *Make sure you do this.*

Trust me, whatever happens, because I love you.

> Felicity

Grizzly,
> Quiche in the oven.
>> Honeypot.

Sydney, Australia
30 March

Dear Felicity,

I'm not sure whether you're permitted to receive letters in Holloway, particularly letters from former boyfriends. Maybe you don't want to hear from me anyway, but I think I owe you some kind of explanation. If it upsets you, well, you've got thirty years to get over it.

I followed your trial in the Aussie papers. They covered it quite fully in the tabloids. Apparently murder by poisoning is still a good paper-seller. They don't have death-cap toadstools here, but there are other kinds of poisonous fungi that I suppose one could disguise in a quiche. The reports I read suggested that you didn't know it would take up to a week for Frank to die. Books on fungi don't always go into that sort of detail. I wondered why they couldn't save him by washing out his stomach or something, but apparently the toxins are absorbed before the first effects appear. Looking at it from his point of view, at least he lived long enough to tell his suspicions to the police.

You'll notice I haven't given an address above. That isn't from secrecy. It's because I'm on a cruise around the world. Some months ago I met this gorgeous redhead called Imogen. To be brutally honest, she moved in with me at Earls Court after you went to live with Frank. I got lonely, Fel, and I figured you had company, so why shouldn't I?

Imogen is one of those quiet girls who are capable of surprising you. I didn't know she found a bunch of your letters to me and secretly read them. I didn't know she had any talent as a children's writer until last January, when she was announced as the winner of the Zenobia Hatt prize. I don't suppose you had a chance to see the press reports. The trustees received only two entries. Imogen's *One Hundred and Two Pomeranians*, which she published privately at her own expense in December, was judged to be closest to the spirit of the award.

No hard feelings? The cash wouldn't have been much use to you, would it?

Cheers, love.
                                    Tristram

Ginger's Waterloo

[This story was drafted by my son, Phil, who commutes by train to London, and I'd like to record my thanks to him. P.L.]

AND THIS IS HOW BAD things can happen.

I stood on the new station, in the new suit for the new job, with no idea whose ground I was invading. The regular commuters were streaming along the platform for the eight-sixteen to Waterloo.

A glance at the flipping metal digital clock told me I had eight minutes before the train pulled in. Bad news. I would have preferred to get straight on to a waiting one without having to negotiate this minefield.

Grey clouds hung indolently over Shipley. Rain was threatening. Only threatening. A pity, this. Even a light drizzle would have forced a hasty rearrangement under Shipley's station canopy. The two uncovered ends of the platform would then have been given up except by the few willing to unfurl their tightly rolled umbrellas.

But the rain held off. Since Joyce and I had moved to 19, Winter Gardens three weeks previously, the sun had not once broken through. The weather here was as implacable as the inhabitants. Still, I tried telling myself, this was October, a time of the year when it was unfair to judge the potential of any town. Joyce, an unfailing optimist, was sure our small square of rear garden would be a sun-trap in summers to come.

I'd ventured along the platform to the less populated end and found a space. Enough room here to swing a cat, I thought. Yes, that insensitive phrase truly came into my head that Monday morning just minutes before I met Colin.

This end was where the singles hung out. Or loners, if you like; anyway, the people who preferred their own company to anyone else's. Executive briefcases, broadsheet newspapers and definitely no eye contact. Naked without a *Times* of my own, I positioned myself the requisite eighteen inches from the platform edge, pretending to be completely absorbed in the billboard opposite, an advert for cigarettes.

At the edge of my field of vision I noticed another minute flip down on the station clock. Five more to go. The man on my left saw my eyes move. He flinched and closed his paper a little in case I sneaked a glimpse of the headlines. Probably he was relishing the arrival of whoever it was who usually stood where I had taken up position. The space had asked to be filled – a sure sign it already had an owner. I expected hot breath on the back of my neck any second.

I actually felt homesick for Barton Vales Station. The tree-lined car park, Joe punching tickets and apologizing to every passenger for late-running trains. The sound of birds, not buses. But that was gone now. I couldn't even imagine it existing any longer. Surely Barton Vales had ceased to be, out of respect, the minute I left?

I'd exchanged that rustic idyll for a City job with the biggest insurance company in Europe. In no time at all, I'd promised Joyce, we'd reap the benefits.

Four minutes. I read the health warning on the cigarette ad. Didn't smoke myself.

Then Colin came into my life.

'I shouldn't stand there if I were you.'

Ignore. Ignore. Read the health warning again.

'You're in the wrong place, mate.'

Jesus, he's definitely talking to me, I thought. And this was worse than I'd imagined. I'm no snob, but the accent wasn't the sort you expected on the eight-sixteen to London.

'I can always spot a new face.'

His face, and a gust of garlic breath, invaded me from my right. I stared ahead like a guardsman. No paper to hide behind. I cursed myself for walking past the newsstand.

'I mean you, mate.'

A note of aggression in the voice. Because I'm a coward, I responded by sliding my eyes a fraction his way.

Fatal.

Eye contact. He was in.

'This is a gap, see?'

I didn't need telling.

The others around me relaxed and started to read the share prices again. They weren't being spoken to. I was.

'The carriages all stop at certain places, right?' The stocky, scruffy figure pointed a denimed arm at the sign '6' which hung directly above my head. 'There won't be no door here when it comes. You'll be stood facing the gap between the carriages.'

I nodded and tried to appear grateful for the information.

He stabbed a finger at several of the people around me and said, embarrassingly in the circumstances, 'These clever buggers here, see, they've got it sorted. They're stood ready by the doors, ain't they? You won't get a look in, mate.'

I remained as deadpan as I could, allowing how acutely uncomfortable I felt. Just go away now, please.

'Straight up,' he said. 'I tell no lies. They've got it down to inches here, mate. Worst station on the line. Cut-throat. You're new to the game, I can see – a butterboy.'

Brilliant. New job, my first day on the eight-sixteen, and

145

I'd found the loudmouth.

'Don't take offence, squire. I like your style.'

Perhaps it was the compliment that did it. Or just relief that he wasn't about to turn nasty.

Stupidly, I felt compelled to respond. 'It's coming, I think.'

'Bang on time, for once.'

'Unusual, is it?'

'Unheard of, these days. Better expect a hold-up at Clapham Junction.'

A joke. I rewarded it with a grin.

The eight-sixteen cruised in, brakes squealing, and the mêlée started. Doors opened and released a few sleepy-eyed shop assistants and schoolteachers to a day's work in Shipley, while the London-bound lot plunged in and planted cold-trousered rears on still-warm seats.

'This way, mate,' my new-found friend bawled in my right ear, grabbing my sleeve. 'Always space in a smoker.'

Now, I have never smoked in my life – nor do I intend to. I had until that day avoided smoking compartments in restaurants and trains. I travel on the lower decks of buses, avoiding any contact with the noxious weed. But that day, that Monday, because I was too weak to antagonize the loudmouth, I clambered in with him.

Tobacco stung my nostrils. We sat opposite each other, squeezed on the ends of seats of three.

'Good to get some cloth under your bum, eh? Never failed to find a seat in a smoker before it pulls out. Standing-room only in the other carriages. By the way,' he continued, offering a muscular hand, 'mine's Colin. What's yours?'

My cynical old Dad once told me that friends are like fish. Kept too long, they begin to smell. Three weeks after our first encounter, Colin stank.

That may sound mean, but I hadn't sought him out in

146

the first place. We had, by now, become regulars. I deeply regretted my initial wish to blend into Shipley's status quo. I was discovering it had unforeseen consequences. I just couldn't fend Colin off. Every morning I endured him for the twenty-seven minutes from Shipley to Waterloo. I'd arrive at the terminus with my paper unread and tightly curled, my hands black from the newsprint, my face aching from the polite smile as he talked at me.

You see, there was no escape from his conversation. He enjoyed a chat, he told me. There wasn't much chatting in his work as a contract-plumber on the new Nomura building in the City. He must have been the only tradesman on the train. I've nothing against plumbers, but Colin was redefining my limits of tolerance. My new suit reeked of stale tobacco. The smoke clung to my hair. My eyeballs, soft from sleep, stung from the exhaled poison from Colin's roll-ups.

As the days passed, my frustration increased. Frankly it was becoming intolerable. Colin's outspokenness was acutely embarrassing. At the beginning, I'd been willing to put up with it just to avoid a scene, even tried to persuade myself that it was amusing. By now it was confirmed as uncouth and insupportable. My fellow travellers, well-bred to the core, said nothing, but rolled their eyes at each other and rustled their papers during particularly unpleasant harangues.

So what held me back? What prevented me from avoiding him? Why didn't I step smartly into a different carriage – a non-smoker – to enjoy some privacy and my paper?

Cowardice. I didn't dare provoke him. My dread of an ugly outburst grew daily in me like a cancer, stronger than the rage I felt at the daily imposition.

'Take women, for instance. Take my wife. Are you listening, Davey?'

How I loathed his distortion of my name. Why didn't I

147

correct him? I suppose it was better he called me that, than David, which I reserved for friends who were, frankly, more my type. Oh God, not again! He was about to come out with it once more.

'I said take my wife, and I wish you would.' Followed by the quick look round to see who was smiling. 'No, wouldn't wish that on Adolf Hitler. I mean, I don't know about your missus, Davey boy, and believe me I don't want to pry, but, like, it's different once they get that ring on their finger. Your sex bomb turns into a couch potato, know what I mean?'

I just nodded, aware that every woman in the carriage expected me to put a stop to his boorish talk. As I didn't, they could only assume I was another bigot. If only the voice weren't so loud, so coarse.

'Take Louise, right? She's got her life to lead, the same as you or me. She's out all day and comes back knackered. We're both knackered, right? Now, I'm no chauvinist.'

You could have fooled me, I thought – and so, no doubt, thought everyone else in the carriage.

'No, very liberated I am. I do my share. I don't mind washing up. And I'll open a tin for the cat. It was my cat in the first place. I just think, as a bloke, I'm entitled to some sort of dinner on the table. Nothing fancy, just meat and two veg, maybe. I mean, marriage is supposed to be a partnership, am I right?'

Here it came again, as familiar now as Vauxhall Bridge flying by. The wife and cat diatribe. Colin felt left out. Couldn't stand the wife all woosey over the cat.

'Don't get me wrong, Davey. I've nothing against cats. I grew up with cats. And Ginger, well, she's affectionate. It's her nature. She's looking for attention, like they do. She wants fussing up, but there are limits. I get home, like, and all I see is Louise and Ginger all over each other. Okay, so Louise hasn't seen her all day, but I need my dinner. The cat gets fed. I see to that. And I'm bloody starving.'

148

A silence. Time for my lines. Wearily, like an actor in a long run, I said, 'Why not make yourself a sandwich?'

'Ain't the food for a hungry fella, is it, Davey, eh? Ain't the food to send vigour coursing through these veins, is it? No, not a pesky sandwich.'

A pause. I hadn't been listening. Missed my cue. Fortunately the script was unchanging.

'I always enjoy a takeaway myself,' I said too late and too flatly, watching the silver rails collide and cross in rhythmical patterns beneath me.

'Ah, now you *are* talking, Davey. Don't mind a bit of foreign myself. Louise, God bless her, just laps up that Chinky grub. Ever tried that chicken chop-suey thing? Hey, it's no wonder they're all walking round like this . . . I say, Davey, like this, eh?'

Dreading this, I looked up to see his fingers at the outer corners of his eyes, pulling the skin sideways. A goofy mouth, bottom lip pulled under top teeth, completed the hideous parody.

'Fu Manchu, ain't I? Numburrhh flifty-two wi plawn balls and flied ri. Ginger likes a bite of the old sweet and sour, you know. They're canny creatures, females, whatever bloody species they are. Listen to this. I reckon Ginger has twigged that if she plays with Louise for half an hour when she comes in, then there's no meal for me. So it's off down the takeaway. I bring back the sweet and sour, and Ginger gets her portion, see?'

'I see.'

But I didn't want to see. I sincerely hoped the mental images of Colin's crass domestic life, his apathetic wife and his manipulative cat, would be erased from my mind, replaced by something more uplifting.

The airbrakes swished and hissed under our feet, the points clattering repeatedly, a sombre drumming into Waterloo, and work. Very likely I was the only passenger arriving there with a sense of release. Each day I longed to leave that train, to step into anonymity, knowing that our captive audience was dispersing. The appalling Colin would disappear, too, bound for his plumbing contract.

And now I have to explain something, and it's not easy, so bear with me.

Between the train and the ticket-barrier, I talked to Colin each morning. I felt the pressure to respond to the diatribe he'd given me all the way from Shipley. I'd said very little in the train. Now, with no one else eavesdropping, I could humour the man. I didn't want to part on bad terms. I've already admitted to being a coward. I'm also a humbug. So I pretended to share his opinions.

'I couldn't agree with you more, old man,' I'd find myself saying as I eyed the approach of the ticket collector's gate.

'Yeah?' he'd say.

'Women. And cats. They need training. They don't like it, but it's got to be done.'

'Just what I said, Davey. You and me, we think alike. Not like these wimps, eh?'

'Absolutely not, Colin.'

'Your meal always on the table, then?'

'Every day, Colin – or else.' An absolute lie, but strangely exhilarating to plant a fictional seed of my own chauvinistic home life in his head.

'You got it well sussed, Davey.' He put a comradely hand on my shoulder. 'So what would you do, then, about Louise and Ginger?'

'Well, Colin,' I said, raising my voice to compete with the Tannoy. 'It's a matter of priorities. Who wears the trousers?' We had reached the gate. That morning I paused to finish the conversation. 'Just talk to Louise. Tell her you expect certain standards. She has to know you're boss. You'll be fine after that.'

'Talk to her? You reckon?'

150

'They love it, Colin, they love it.'

'Yeah?'

'See you, then.'

He looked grateful, if doubtful. 'Yeah, Davey. Tomorrow, eh?'

And I left him and stepped out briskly to the sanctuary of the Underground, where nobody talked. There was just the drone of the trains that whisked me away from the station, and my shame.

In those few weeks I had made a good start with my insurance giant. I rose to the challenges my new post offered. Moving from small claims to the juicier stuff proved stimulating. I had my own office, too – a distinct improvement on the ghastly impersonality of the open-plan system I had endured before. The others in my group proved a lively lot and were quick to invite me to join them for pub lunches in shoulder-to-shoulder London bars, where the outrages of previous claims (mostly apocryphal, I'm sure) were cheerfully discussed.

My Group Head, Mr Law, was less approachable, a bit of a stickler for procedures (we speculated over lunch one day that he was probably into bondage in his sex life), but scrupulously fair. He dispensed advice without ever knocking my small-claims background. He even referred to it as a useful training ground that had developed my attention to detail, a definite asset in my present post.

'You see, Walters,' he told me in confidence, 'we all have to start somewhere. I've studied every one of your reports. You don't miss anything. The others here . . . well, there's a tendency to rush things. Successful broking, Walters, begins with a sharp eye. You seem to have it. Indeed, I have a feeling you could go far.'

Naturally, this conversation sent my confidence soaring, with its hint that I was ahead of the others in the group. I cast myself as the young hopeful, sure of promotion. That four years in the sticks sorting small claims was bearing fruit. So I had nothing to fear, one evening when I had volunteered to work late, when Mr Law called me into his office.

'Ah, Walters. Still enjoying the work here?'

'Tremendously, Mr Law.'

'Good, good. Sit down, please. Just an informal chat. I see from the records you reside in Shipley, yes?'

'Yes, sir,' I replied, a trifle uncertain what bearing this might have on my promotion prospects.

'Never been to Shipley myself,' he continued, his back to me as he stared at the lighted cityscape eighteen floors below.

Feeling the need to contribute something, I volunteered, 'It suits me, Mr Law. Suits me fine. At this stage in my career. Good amenities. Convenient for London.' I was slipping smoothly into the staccato-style speech Mr Law himself used, the businesslike delivery that fitted me for the role of Deputy Group Head.

He continued to survey the trail of ant-like humanity on its way home. 'My sister moved there not long ago. She's an artist. Abstract stuff. I don't understand it at all. It sells, I'm told. I haven't seen much of her lately. Don't care much for the man she married. We're not a marrying family.'

He turned from the window quite suddenly and looked at me. 'Walters, I need help.'

Christ. Now I was out of my depth. I had a hideous feeling it was going to be personal. Was he, perhaps, infatuated with one of the secretaries? I could see myself as a go-between pandering to Mr Law's perverted tastes.

What relief, then, as he continued, without mention of whips and handcuffs, 'I'm down your way at sissie's next week. Tuesday. Duty visit. Her first exhibition. The preview. Sure to run late. The last train leaves at eleven-ten – too early for me. Have to use their sofa-bed.

Inevitably I shall travel up by train on Wednesday. You're a good timekeeper, Walters. Always in by nine-thirty. Tell me, which train do you catch from Shipley?'

'The eight-sixteen,' I told him.

'In that case I'll look out for you in Shipley Station on Wednesday morning.'

'Splendid.'

'Shall we say ten past, just to be sure?'

'Fine, Mr Law,' I said, without a thought of Colin.

But I was sharply reminded the next time I saw him, on the Monday.

'Cha, mate.'

'Hello, Colin.'

'Didn't do no good, what you told me last week,' he announced, attaching the verbal tow-rope that would drag me once again up the cat-and-wife alley.

'Really?' I responded without interest.

'Louise has taken it bad. I gave her a rollicking like you said, and she walked out.'

'Left you?' I said, more concerned. I didn't want to be responsible for a broken marriage.

'Not for keeps. She's not that daft. Just pushed off, God knows where. She did the same Friday, Saturday and Sunday. She's got a pal, I reckon.'

'Maybe.' I tried to sound casual, as he had. From his tone, it hadn't dawned on him yet that the 'pal' might be a boyfriend.

Then he added, 'Doesn't come home until after I've gone to bed.'

'What do you do?'

'Sit around all evening with Ginger for company.'

The train was approaching. I had something more urgent on my mind than Colin's domestic crisis. Wednesday was too close.

'You, er, working all this week, Colin?'

'Sure thing, mate.'

'Wednesday?'

'Same as ever.'

We were seated in the smoker as usual. I wondered frantically how I might disentangle myself from the routine for one day. In a perfect world, I would just ignore Colin on Wednesday and travel up with Mr Law. But our arrangement was too entrenched for that. Colin regarded me as a soulmate. I'd got in too deep, particularly in our conversations between train and ticket barrier at Waterloo.

What if the two met? I shuddered at the prospect of Mr Law being subjected to Colin's inane monologue all the way to London. In my mind's eye I could see my Group Head grimly enduring the barrage, and later adding a note to my personal file: *Showed early promise, but betrayed a lack of discrimination in the company he keeps. Might be better employed, after all, in some limited capacity. Small claims, perhaps?*

The nightmare was interrupted.

'Louise and I, we go back years. Then wallop. Ginger's on the scene. Don't ask me how. She sort of adopted us both. Mind you, I didn't object at first. It was good company for Louise. Me, too. Let's be honest. But now Louise ignores me. It's hurtful, Davey, and I'm getting flaming mad with her. I blame the cat. I shouldn't, but I do.'

'Well, yes.'

'She could be jealous of Ginger. Is it possible? Do you think she's jealous of Ginger?'

I caught eyes observing me, peering over the tops of *The Times* like snipers in the trenches at the Somme. 'I wouldn't know.'

Then, unexpectedly, came an impassioned plea, made all the more ludicrous by the presence of the other passengers: 'I couldn't bear to lose Louise. I want her back. I want my Louise back, Davey. That's all.' He was on the verge of tears.

I looked at the thickset plumber and mentally commanded him to snap out of this. Pitiful though he was, my major concern was my own predicament. For God's sake, he was just someone I met in the train each morning.

'Help me, Davey. You have an answer, don't you?'

Oh, this was great entertainment for the others. A highlight in the saga, like the murder of a well-known soap-opera character to push up the ratings at Christmas.

Vauxhall came up. We were just a few minutes from Waterloo. I had to settle this today. It couldn't be allowed to run on, not into Wednesday.

'I'll need to think,' I told him. 'Take it easy while I consider the matter.'

Believe me, my brain worked overtime.

Colin watched me, mercifully silent until we reached the terminus.

On the platform, away from the eavesdroppers, I gave him the advice he'd begged for. I tried to sound calm. 'From all you've told me, it's obvious that Ginger is a problem. She came between you and Louise, and now you want to get back on the old footing with your wife and you can't. It won't work. The solution to me, an outsider, is this. Get rid of Ginger.'

His eyes widened. 'But how, Davey, how?'

For once we were walking quite slowly along the platform, and anyone who travelled with us must have got far ahead, out of earshot.

Speaking as if to a child, I said, 'Any way you choose. In a sack, isn't that the way it's done? Tie the top and drop it in a river. No more Ginger.'

'But what about Louise? She's not going to like this.'

'She's out every evening, isn't she?'

'Well, yes, but . . .'

'How will she know? Cats run away, Colin.'

'True, but it seems kind of –'

I lost my patience with him. 'Do what you bloody want.

155

You asked for advice and I gave it to you.'

I heard him say, 'I'll think about it, Davey,' as I marched on and gave up my ticket.

Colin wasn't on the train next morning and my hopes were raised for Wednesday. I got to the station early, really early. I had a dozen possible strategies in mind and just one purpose: to keep Colin and Mr Law apart. I bought a copy of the *Financial Times*, to impress my boss, and stood by the station entrance. Mr Law, being tall, would be easy to spot.

'What you doing here, Davey?'

God, no! Colin had caught me on the blind side.

'Er, Colin, I er . . .' But I didn't have to fumble long for an excuse.

He was keen to tell me something. 'Done it, mate. Like you said. Monday night. Louise and me, it's all made up, at least for now, anyway.'

'Ah.'

'Look,' he went on, 'Don't take offence, Davey, but I'm going to sit by myself this morning, okay?'

'Fine,' I said, trying to sound just a little despondent as the tidal wave of relief crashed over me.

'Ah, there you are, Walters.'

The worst possible outcome. Mr Law, bang on eight-ten, and just ten seconds too early for me. Colin was lingering.

'You're not offended, are you, Davey? Listen, why don't you come round for a drink tonight? I'll be fine by then. You can meet Louise. You know, put some names to faces, mate?'

My toes curled. I was caught between two conversations.

'Is it always so crowded?' from Law.

'Just for an hour, eh?' from Colin.

'Eight-sixteen on schedule, I hope?' Law.

'Forty-seven, Cramer Way. The green door. About seven.' Colin.

'Yes, Colin. I'll do my best.'

'Champion!' And Colin was away.

My toes uncurled.

'A friend?' enquired Law.

'I wouldn't put it so strongly as that, Mr Law. Actually he's a local plumber. The fellow gave me some advice about installing central heating. Seems to think I want to get to know him better, which I don't.'

'Ah, I know the sort.'

The eight-sixteen arrived dead on time. It hadn't let me down. Moreover, Mr Law and I stepped into a non-smoking carriage and found two empty seats. I glowed with satisfaction.

I was so relieved at how the day had turned out that I decided that evening to take up Colin's invitation. I needed a drink. And Colin's decision to travel alone had given me the break I needed. I was willing to show some gratitude. We would drink to our futures.

I might even get to like travelling in Colin's company now that the cat and wife saga had come to an end. We'd have something different to talk about. Football, perhaps. Or television. But I would avoid any more marriage counselling.

47, Cramer Way was fronted by the green door Colin had mentioned. A council-built house with a carport and a white van standing there. I pushed the doorbell.

'Davey – come in, mate.' Colin reached out and grasped my arm. He was towel-drying his hair. 'Just had a shower. The brick-dust gets everywhere. Come through to the kitchen.'

The kitchen was a tip. I stood, conspicuous in my coat, surveying unwashed pans and piles of tinfoil takeaway trays. And he'd brought me in here from choice.

A beer was offered. 'You don't mind drinking from the can? I don't have a glass handy. Give us your coat, Davey.

Louise'll be through that door any minute.'

I took a sip of beer, grateful that it came from a sealed container. My eyes travelled around the cramped room and spotted a grease-spattered photograph standing on the fridge. Colin's wedding. The couple stood on what I recognized as Shipley Library's steps, confetti scattered over an ill-fitting suit and summer dress and jacket. She looked attractive, face vibrant with the occasion. Colin's remark about the couch potato came back to me. I felt uncomfortable knowing so much about Louise before I met her.

'The wedding snap,' said Colin, opening a can. 'Don't times bleeding change, eh?'

I passed no comment.

'Hey up,' he said. 'Here she comes now, bang on cue.'

I turned to face the front door, first placing my can on the kitchen table. It didn't seem right to be drinking when the lady of the house arrived.

But nothing happened. The door didn't open. I looked towards Colin and saw that he was watching the back door. That, also, remained closed – apart from one small section. The bottom left-hand panel. The cat-flap.

It opened.

'Louise, my little beauty!' Colin cried as he swept the creature into his arms, a small, white cat. 'Look, we've got a visitor. Remember I told you about Davey, the man on the train?'

I froze.

'Davey told me what to do with Ginger.'

Louise purred approvingly in Colin's arms.

Stroking her head, Colin said to me, 'Honestly, Davey, I could cheerfully have killed you as well the other night. Do you know how difficult it is tying a live woman into a sack?'

A Case of Butterflies

BEFORE CALLING THE POLICE, HE had found a butterfly in the summerhouse. It had unsettled him. The wings had been purple, a rich, velvety purple. Soaring and swooping, it had intermittently come to rest on the wood floor. His assumption that it was trapped had proved to be false, because two of the windows had been wide open and it had made no move towards the open door. He knew what it was, a Purple Emperor, for there was one made of paper mounted in a perspex case in his wife Ann's study. As a staunch conservationist, Ann wouldn't have wanted to possess a real specimen. She had told him often enough that she preferred to see them flying free. She had always insisted that Purple Emperors were in the oak wood that surrounded the house. He had never spotted one until this morning, and it seemed like a sign from her.

'You did the right thing, sir.'

'The right thing?'

'Calling us in as soon as you knew about this. It takes courage.'

'I don't want your approval, Commander. I want my wife back.'

'We all want that, sir.'

Sir Milroy Shenton made it plain that he didn't care for the remark, mildly as it was put. He rotated his chair to turn his back on the two police officers and face the view along King's Reach where the City skyline rises above Waterloo Bridge. He stared at it superficially. The image of the butterfly refused to leave his mind, just as it had lingered in the summerhouse. Less than an hour ago he had called the emergency number from his house in Sussex. The police had suggested meeting in London in case the house was being observed, and he had nominated the Broad Wall Complex. He had the choice of dozens of company boardrooms across London and the Home Counties that belonged in his high-tech empire. The advantage of using Broad Wall was the proximity of the heliport.

He swung around again. 'You'll have to bear with me. I'm short of sleep. It was a night flight from New York.'

'Let's get down to basics, then. Did you bring the ransom note?'

Commander Jerry Glazier was primed for this. He headed the Special Branch team that was always on stand-by to deal with kidnapping incidents. International terrorism was so often involved in extortion that a decision had been taken to involve Special Branch from the beginning in major kidnap inquiries. Captains of industry like Shenton were obvious targets. They knew the dangers, and often employed private bodyguards. Not Shenton: such precautions would not square with his reputation in the city as a devil-may-care dealer in the stock market, known and feared for his dawn raids.

Glazier was assessing him with a professional eye, aware how vital in kidnap cases is the attitude and resolve of the 'mark'.

First impressions suggested that this was a man in his forties trying to pass for twenty-five, with a hairstyle that would once have been called short back and sides and was now trendy and expensive. A jacket of crumpled silk was hanging off his shoulders. The accent was Oxford turned cockney, a curious inversion Glazier had noted lately in the business world. Scarcely ten minutes ago he had read in *Who's Who* that Shenton's background was a rectory in Norfolk, followed by Winchester and Magdalen. He had married twice. The second wife, the lady now abducted, was Ann, the only daughter of Dr Hamilton Porter, deceased. Under *Recreations*, Shenton had entered *Exercising the wife*. It must have seemed witty when he thought of it.

Now he took a package from his pocket. 'Wrapped in a freezer bag, as your people suggested. My sweaty prints are all over it, of course. I didn't know it was going to be evidence until I'd read the bloody thing, did I?'

'It isn't just the prints.' Glazier glanced at the wording on the note. It read, IF YOU WANT HER BACK ALIVE GET ONE MILLION READY. INSTRUCTIONS FOLLOW. 'There's modern technology for you,' he commented. 'They do the old thing of cutting words from the papers, but now they dispense with paste. They use a photocopier.' He turned it over to look at the envelope. 'Indistinct postmark, wouldn't you know.'

'The bastards could have sent it any time in the last six days, couldn't they?' said Shenton. 'For all I know, they may have tried to phone me. She could be dead.'

Glazier wasn't there to speculate. 'So you flew in from New York this morning, returned to your house and found this on the mat?'

'And my wife missing.'

'You've been away from the house for how long, sir?'

'I told you – six days. Ann had been away as well, but she should have been back by now.'

'Then I dare say there was a stack of mail waiting.'

'Is that relevant?'

The pattern of the interview was taking shape. Shenton was using every opportunity to assert his status as top dog.

'It may be,' Glazier commented, 'if you can remember what was above or below it in the stack.' He wasn't to be intimidated.

'I just picked everything up, flipped through what was there and extracted the interesting mail from the junk.'

'*This* looked interesting?'

'It's got a stamp, hasn't it?'

'Fair enough. You opened it, read the note, and phoned us. Did you call anyone else?'

'Cressie.'

'Cressie?'

'Cressida Concannon, Ann's college friend. The two of them were touring.'

'Touring where, sir?'

'The Ring of Kerry.'

'*Ireland*?' Glazier glanced towards his assistant, then back at Shenton. 'That was taking a chance, wasn't it?'

'With hindsight, yes. I told Ann to use her maiden name over there.'

'Which is . . .?'

'Porter.'

'So what have you learned from her friend?'

'Cressie's still over there, visiting her sister. She last saw Ann on Wednesday at the end of their holiday, going in to Cork airport.'

'Have you called the airline to see if she was on the flight?'

Shenton shook his head. 'Tracing Cressie took the best part of half an hour. I flew straight up from Sussex after that.'

'Flew?'

'Chopper.'

'I see. Did your wife have a reservation?'

'Aer Lingus. The two-fifteen flight to Heathrow.'

Glazier nodded to his assistant, who left the room to check. 'This holiday in Ireland – when was it planned?'

'A month ago, when New York came up. She said she deserved a trip of her own.'

'So she got in touch with her friend. I shall need to know

more about Miss Concannon, sir. She's an old and trusted friend, I take it?'

'Cressie? She's twenty-four carat. We've known her for twelve years, easily.'

'Well enough to know her political views?'

'Hold on.' Shenton folded his arms in a challenging way. 'Cressie isn't one of that lot.'

'But does she guard her tongue?'

'She's far too smart to mouth off to the micks.'

'They met at college, you say. What were they studying?'

'You think I'm going to say politics?' Shenton said as if he were scoring points at a board meeting. 'It was bugs. Ann and Cressie's idea of a holiday is kneeling in cowpats communing with dung-beetles.'

'Entomology,' said Glazier.

'Sorry, I was forgetting some of the fuzz can read without moving their lips.'

'Do you carry a picture of your wife, sir?'

'For the press, do you mean? She's been kidnapped. She isn't a missing person.'

'For our use, Sir Milroy.'

He felt for his wallet. 'I dare say there's one I can let you have.'

'If you're bothered about the media, sir, we intend to keep them off your back until this is resolved. The Press Office at the Yard will get their co-operation.'

'You mean an embargo?' He started to remove a photo from his wallet and then pushed it back into its slot. Second thoughts, apparently.

Glazier had glimpsed enough of the print to make out a woman in a see-through blouse. She seemed to be dancing. 'I mean a voluntary agreement to withhold the news until you've got your wife back. After that, of course . . .'

'If I get her back unharmed I'll speak to anyone.'

'Until that happens, you talk only to us, sir. These people, whoever they are, will contact you again. Do you have an answerphone at your house?'

'Of course.'

'Have you played it back?'

'Didn't have time.' Shenton folded the wallet and returned it to his pocket. 'I don't, after all, happen to have a suitable picture of Ann on me. I'll arrange to send you one.'

'Listen to your messages as soon as you get back, sir, and let me know if there's anything.'

'What do you do in these cases – tap my phone?'

'Is that what you'd recommend?'

'Commander Glazier, don't patronise me. I called you in. I have a right to know what to expect.'

'You can expect us to do everything within our powers to find your wife, sir.'

'You don't trust me, for God's sake?'

'I didn't say that. What matters is that you put your trust in us. Do you happen to have a card with your Sussex address?'

Shenton felt for the wallet again and opened it.

Glazier said at once, 'Isn't that a picture of your wife, sir, the one you put back just now?'

'That wasn't suitable. I told you.'

'If it's the way she's dressed that bothers you, that's no problem. I need the shot of her face, that's all. May I take it?'

Shenton shook his head.

'What's the problem?' asked Glazier.

'As it happens, that isn't Ann. It's her friend Cressida.'

Between traffic signals along the Embankment, Glazier told his assistant, Inspector Tom Salt, about the photograph.

'You think he's cheating with his wife's best friend?'

'It's a fair bet.'

'Does it have any bearing on the kidnap?'

'Too soon to tell. His reactions are strange. He seems more fussed about how we intend to conduct the case than what is happening to his wife.'

'High-flyers like him operate on a different level from you and me, sir. Life is all about flow-charts and decision-making.'

'They're not all like that. Did you get anything from the airline?'

'Everything he told us checks. There was a first class reservation in the name of Ann Porter. She wasn't aboard that Heathrow flight or any other.'

The next morning Glazier flew to Ireland for a meeting with senior officers in the *gardai*. Cork airport shimmered in the August heat. At headquarters they were served iced lemonade in preference to coffee. A full-scale inquiry was authorized.

He visited Cressida Concannon at her sister's, an estate house on the northern outskirts of Cork, and they talked outside, seated on patio chairs. She presented a picture distinctly different from the photo in Shenton's wallet; she was in a cream-coloured linen suit and brown shirt buttoned to the top. Her long brown hair was drawn back and secured with combs. Like Lady Ann, she was at least ten years younger than Shenton. She had made an itinerary of the tour around the Ring of Kerry. She handed Glazier a sheaf of hotel receipts.

He flicked through them. 'I notice you paid all of these yourself, Miss Concannon.'

'Yes. Ann said she would settle up with me later. She couldn't write cheques because she was using her maiden name.'

'Of course. Porter, isn't it? So the hotel staff addressed her as Mrs Porter?'

'Yes.'

'And was there any time in your trip when she was recognized as Lady Shenton?'

'Not to my knowledge.'

'You remember nothing suspicious, nothing that might help us to find her?'

'I've been over it many times in my mind, and I can't think of anything, I honestly can't.'

'What was her frame of mind? Did she seem concerned at any stage of the tour?'

'Not once that I recall. She seemed to relish every moment. You can ask at any of the hotels. She was full of high spirits right up to the minute we parted.'

'Which was . . .?'

'Wednesday, about twelve-thirty. I drove her to the airport and put her down where the cars pull in. She went through the doors and that was the last I saw of her. Surely they won't harm her, will they?'

Glazier said as if he hadn't listened to the question, 'Tell me about your relationship with Sir Milroy Shenton.'

She drew herself up. 'What do you mean?'

'You're a close friend, close enough to spend some time alone with him, I believe.'

'They are both my friends. I've known them for years.'

'But you do meet him, don't you?'

'I don't see what this has to do with it.'

'I'll tell you,' said Glazier. 'I'm just surprised that she went on holiday with you and relished every moment, as you expressed it. She's an intelligent woman. He carries your picture fairly openly in his wallet. He doesn't carry one of Lady Ann. Her behaviour strikes me as untypical, that's all.'

She said coolly, 'When you rescue her from the kidnappers, you'll be able to question her about it, won't you?'

Before leaving Ireland, Glazier had those hotels checked. Without exception the inquiries confirmed that the two women had stayed there on the dates in question. Moreover, they had given every appearance of getting on well together. One hotel waiter in Killarney recalled that they had laughed the evenings away together.

Within an hour of Glazier's return to London, there was a development. Sir Milroy Shenton called on the phone. His voice was strained. 'I've heard from them. She's dead. They've killed her, the bastards, and I hold you responsible.'

'Dead? You're sure?'

'*They're* sure.'

'Tell me precisely how you heard about this.'

'They just phoned me, didn't they? Irish accent.'

'A man?'

'Yes. Said they had to abort the operation because I got in touch with the filth. That's you. They said she's at the bottom of the Irish Sea. This is going to be on your conscience for the rest of your bloody life.'

'I need to see you,' said Glazier. 'Where are you now?'

'Manchester.'

'How do they know you're up there?'

'It was in the papers. One of my companies has a shareholders' meeting. Look, I can't tell you any more than I just did.'

'You want the killers to get away with it, sir?'

'What?'

'I'll be at Midhurst. Your house.'

'Why Midhurst?'

'Get there as soon as you can, Sir Milroy.' Glazier put an end to the call and stabbed out Tom Salt's number. 'Can you lay on a chopper, Tom?'

'What's this about?' Salt shouted over the engine noise after they were airborne.

'Shenton. His wife is dead.'

'Why would they kill her? While she was alive she was worth a million.'

'My thought exactly.'

Salt wrestled with that remark as they followed the

167

ribbon of the Thames southwards, flying over Richmond and Kingston. 'Don't you believe what Shenton told you?'

'She's dead. I believe that much.'

'No kidnap?'

'No kidnap.'

'We're talking old-fashioned murder, then.'

'That's my reading of it.'

There was a break in the conversation that brought them across the rest of Surrey before Salt shouted, 'It's got to be Cressie Concannon, hasn't it?'

'Why?'

'She wasn't satisfied with her status as the mistress, so she snuffed her rival and sent the ransom note to cover up the crime.'

Glazier shook his head. 'Cressie is in Ireland.'

'What's wrong with that? Lady Shenton was last seen in Ireland. We know she didn't make the flight home.'

'Cressie didn't send the ransom note. The postage stamp was British.'

The pilot turned his head. 'The place should be coming up any minute, sir. Those are the South Downs ahead.'

Without much difficulty they located Shenton's house, a stone-built Victorian mansion in a clearing in an oak wood. The helicopter wheeled around it once before touching down on the forecourt, churning up dust and gravel.

'We've got at least an hour before he gets here,' Glazier said.

'Is there a pub?' asked Salt, and got a look from his superior that put him off drinking for a week.

Rather less than the estimated hour had passed when the clatter of a second helicopter disturbed the sylvan peace. Glazier crossed the drive to meet it.

'No more news, I suppose?' Sir Milroy Shenton asked as he climbed out. He spoke in a more reasonable tone than he'd used on the phone. He'd had time to compose himself.

'Not yet, sir.'

'Found your way in?'

'No, we've been out here in the garden.'

'Not much of a garden. Ann and I preferred to keep it uncultivated except for the lawns.'

'She must have wanted to study the insect life in its natural habitat.'

Shenton frowned slightly, as if he'd already forgotten about his wife's field of study. 'Shall we go indoors?'

A fine curved staircase faced them as they entered. The hall was open to three floors. 'Your wife had a study, I'm sure,' said Glazier. 'I'd like to see it, please.'

'To your left – but there's nothing in there to help you,' said Shenton.

'We'll see.' Glazier entered the room and moved around the desk to the bookshelves. 'Whilst we were waiting for you I saw a couple of butterflies I'd never spotted before. I used to collect them when I was a kid, little horror, before they were protected. Did you know you had Purple Emperors here?'

Shenton twitched and swayed slightly. Then he put his hand to his face and said distractedly, 'What?'

'Purple Emperors. There were two in the summerhouse just now. The windows were open, but they had no desire to leave. They settled on the floor in the joints between the boards.' Glazier picked a book off the shelf and thumbed through the pages, finally turning them open for Shenton's inspection. 'How about that? Isn't it superb? The colour on those wings! I'd have sold my electric train-set for one of these in my collection.' He continued to study the page.

'You must have lived in the wrong area,' said Shenton, with an effort to sound reasonable.

'I wouldn't say that,' said Glazier. 'There were oaks in the park where I played. They live high up in the canopy of the wood. You never see them normally, but they are

169

probably more common than most of us realised then.'

'This isn't exactly helping to find my wife,' said Shenton.

'You couldn't be more wrong,' said Glazier. 'How long ago did you kill her, Sir Milroy?'

Shenton tensed. He didn't respond.

'She's been dead a few weeks, hasn't she, long before your trip to New York. She didn't visit Ireland at all. That was some friend of Cressida Concannon's, using the name of Ann Porter. A free trip around the Ring of Kerry. No wonder the woman was laughing. She must have thought the joke was on you, just as the expenses were. I don't suppose she knew that the real Lady Ann was dead.'

'I don't have to listen to this slanderous rubbish,' said Shenton. He'd recovered his voice, but he was ashen.

'You'd better. I'm going to charge you presently. Miss Concannon will also be charged as an accessory. The kidnapping was a fabrication. You wrote the ransom note yourself some time ago. You posted envelopes to this address until one arrived in the condition you required – with the indistinct date-stamp. Then all you had to do was slip the ransom note inside and hand it to me when you got back from New York and alerted us to your wife's so-called abduction. How long has she been dead – four or five weeks?'

Shenton said with contempt, 'What am I supposed to have done with her?'

'Buried her – or tried to. You weren't the first murderer to discover that digging a grave isn't so easy if the ground is unhelpful. It's always a shallow grave in the newspaper reports, isn't it? But you didn't let that defeat you. You jacked up the summerhouse and wedged her under the floorboards – which I suppose was easier than digging six feet down. The butterflies led me to her.'

Shenton latched on to this at once. Turning to Tom Salt he said, 'Is he all right in the head?'

Salt gave his boss a troubled glance.

Shenton flapped his hand in derision. 'Crazy.'

'You don't believe me?' said Glazier. 'Why else would a Purple Emperor come down from the trees? Listen to this.' He started reading from the book. ' *"They remain in the treetops feeding on sap and honeydew unless attracted to the ground by the juices of dung or decaying flesh. They seldom visit flowers."* ' He looked up, straight into Shenton's stricken eyes. 'Not so crazy after all, is it?'

Youdunnit

YOU.

Yes, you, reading this.

How would you like to be a character in this story? Take a deep breath. It's a murder mystery. If you suffer from nightmares, nervous rashes, or have a dicky heart, better turn to something less dangerous. But if you think you can take it, read on.

Now step into the story.

Someone speaks your name.

Cautiously you answer, 'Yes?'

You find yourself in an office furnished simply with a desk and two chairs, the sort of room universally used for interviewing purposes. It might seem totally impersonal were it not for the glass-fronted case mounted on the wall in front of you. Inside is a large stuffed fish.

'You may sit down. This will take a little time.' Although the bearded man behind the desk isn't wearing a uniform, authority is implicit in his voice and manner. He is broad-shouldered, with a thick neck. His head is bald at the crown, with a crop of grizzled hair at the sides and back as compensation. His age would be difficult to estimate, but he is obviously a long-serving officer who gives the impression that he knows everything about you and is interested only in having it confirmed. He spends a moment looking at the papers in front of him. You are not deceived by the humorous sparkle in his brown eyes. You sense that it may shortly turn into an accusing gleam. But at the beginning he doesn't threaten. He starts on a quiet, disarming monotone, his eyes on his notes.

'Have you any idea why you are here?'

'Well,' you say, 'I was reading this crime story –'

He looks up with more interest. 'So you read crime stories?'

'Sometimes, yes.'

'Do you ever get ideas from what you read?'

This sounds like a question to duck. 'I'm not sure what you mean.'

'It's obvious what I mean,' he tells you sharply. 'So-called ingenious methods of murder. Anyone who reads crime stories knows how devious they are. Writers have been concocting murder mysteries for at least a hundred and fifty years, ever since Edgar Allan Poe. What was that one of his in which an orang-utan turned out to be the killer?'

'*The Murders in the Rue Morgue*?'

'Right. I don't get much time for reading in this job, but I know the plots. Years ago in those country house murders it was sufficient surprise for the butler to have done it. Most of them are a sight more ingenious than that, of course. There was the mad wife in the attic. There was the postman nobody noticed, who actually carried the corpse away in his sack. Did you read that one?'

'I may have done.'

'Chesterton. I met him once, many years ago. I've met them all. It dates me, doesn't it? Dorothy L. Sayers. Agatha Christie. She was a fiendish plotter. Sweet lady, though. Rather shy, in fact.'

Not only does it date him, you think to yourself; it takes some believing. G.K. Chesterton must have died fifty years ago, at least. Theoretically it's possible that they met, but it seems more likely that he is making it up.

'You sound like a real enthusiast,' you venture, still unsure where all this is leading. Is he doing this to make

173

you feel inferior?

'The Agatha Christie story that impressed me most,' he says, 'was the murder that turned out to have been committed by the narrator of the story.'

'Yes, clever.'

'I came across one in which the detective did it. There's no end to the twists in these stories. One of these days I fully expect to find out that the reader did it. Not so much a whodunnit as a youdunnit.'

You smile nervously. 'That would be stretching it.'

'Oh, I don't know.' He eyes you speculatively. 'You didn't answer my question just now. Do you get ideas from crime stories?'

'Not that I'm aware of,' you say. 'I don't know what use I could make of them.'

He fingers his beard. 'That remains to be discovered. Let's talk about you. Shall I lay out the essential facts? I want to ask you about a Saturday evening towards the end of last summer.'

'Last summer?' Your hand finds the edge of your chair and grips it. This isn't going to be easy. Last summer was a long time ago. You have sometimes wondered how reliable a witness you would be if you were ever called to testify to something you saw the same day. But last summer . . .

'To be precise, the last Saturday in August. You were expecting a visitor, a rather special visitor, so special that you'd put a bottle of champagne on ice and . . .' He looks up and arches his eyebrows, plainly inviting you to continue.

You frown and say, 'There's obviously some mistake.'

He stares back. 'What's your difficulty?'

'What you just said. It has nothing to do with me.'

'Are you certain?'

'Absolutely.'

He folds his arms. 'What exactly is your difficulty? Remembering the day? It was an unusually warm, still

174

evening. Still as the grave. Days like that deserve to be remembered. You *do* remember it?'

'The day?'

'The last Saturday in August.'

'It isn't so simple. I suppose I could if something were to jog my memory.'

He says with faintly sinister sarcasm, 'If necessary I can arrange that. Let's get to the bubbly, then – the champagne. More up your street than trying to remember which day it was, I dare say.'

'What do you mean? I'm not in the habit—'

'I didn't say you were. But you wouldn't object to a glass of fizz on a sweltering Saturday evening in summer?'

'I don't know what you're talking about.'

He presses on, unperturbed. 'We're simply establishing the possibility of the scenario I gave you. It could have happened to anyone.'

'Not to me.'

'Let's put it to the test. You *have* drunk champagne at some time in your life? You don't deny that?'

You give a shrug that doesn't commit you to anything.

'Presumably you prefer it cooled?'

'Most people do.'

'So if you *did* have a bottle of champagne – a good champagne, a Perrier Jouet 'seventy-nine, shall we say – you'd have sufficient respect to put it on ice?' He spreads his hands to show how reasonable the proposition is.

You refuse to be lured into some admission that will incriminate you. 'Listen, it's becoming more and more obvious that you are talking to the wrong person. I'm not in the habit of drinking champagne on Saturday evenings.'

'Pity. It would make you more co-operative. However, the point is immaterial. As it turned out, nobody drank the champagne.'

A pause.

'As *what* turned out?' you ask.

He gives a long, level look. 'We're coming to that. Let's stay with the champagne a moment. You wouldn't drink it alone, would you? It isn't the sort of drink you have alone. Champagne is for lovers.'

You stare at him and say, 'This is getting more and more ridiculous.'

'Is there someone in your life?'

'If there is, it's no concern of yours.'

'Correction,' he says before you have got out the words. 'It *is* my concern. It assuredly is.'

You press your lips together and shake your head.

He continues to probe. 'Don't tell me you haven't a lover. Look, I may seem old-fashioned to you, but I know what goes on.'

'Not in my life, you don't,' you tell him firmly. 'That's becoming clearer by the minute.'

'All right, if it's the term "lover" you object to, let's settle for friend, then. Intimate friend. Someone who makes your heart beat faster. This is a crime of passion – I'll stake my reputation on that.'

'A *crime*?' Now is the moment to make a stand. 'You're talking about a crime?'

'That's what I said.'

'Involving someone I know?'

'Involving you.'

You are silent for a moment. Then, with an effort to stay in control, you say, 'If you are serious, I think I'd better ask for a solicitor.'

His face creases into a pained expression. 'Don't spoil it,' he tells you. 'We were getting on so well. Let's leave the love angle for the present. We'll go back to Saturday evening. No more beating about the bush. It was about nine. You were at home, alone. But your, em, visitor was expected any minute, so you had the champagne ready in a bucket of ice.'

'All of this is rubbish.'

He lifts a warning finger. 'Have the goodness to hear me out, will you? You're getting the kid-glove treatment, but there are limits. You had the house to yourself because your spouse, is it? – or partner, is that more accurate? – was away for the weekend.'

You sigh loudly and say nothing. Might as well let him continue. He's making a total idiot of himself.

'A romantic evening was in prospect. Soft music in the background. The Richard Clayderman album.'

'I can't stand Richard Clayderman.'

'Your lover can. The candles were lit. After your bath you'd put on something cool and sexy, a white silk caftan.'

You roll your eyes upwards. 'Me in a caftan?'

'Some kind of robe, then. We won't argue over that. Suddenly the doorbell chimed. You went to the front door and flung it open and said, "Darling . . ." Then the smile froze on your lips, because it wasn't your lover on the doorstep. It was You Know Who, back unexpectedly from that weekend away.'

'You're way off beam,' you say. 'This didn't happen to me. This is someone else you're talking about.'

'You don't remember?'

'I haven't the faintest recollection of anything you've said. What's supposed to have happened next?'

'A blazing row. There was hell to pay with all that evidence of infidelity around you. Champagne and soft music wasn't the norm in your house. You just admitted that.'

'Did I?' You feel your mouth go dry. You thought you'd admitted nothing, yet there's a disturbing logic in some of what he is saying.

'You protested your innocence vigorously. You're pretty good at that. And all the time that this row was going on, you dreaded hearing the doorbell again, because you knew this time it would be your lover. Zap! You'd be finished, the pair of you. So what did you do?'

'Don't ask me,' you say acidly. 'I wasn't there.'

'You panicked. You snatched up the full bottle of champagne and swung it with all your strength. Crashed it into You Know Who's skull. Murder.'

'Untrue.'

His eyes open wider. 'How can you say it's untrue if you don't remember anything?' He leaned towards you again. 'You dragged the body across the room and shoved it into the cupboard under the stairs.'

You're sweating now. It's apparent that he's speaking of something that really happened. A murder was committed and you're in grave danger of being framed, or stitched up, or whatever the expression is. But why? What has he got against you? Is there some piece of evidence he hasn't brought up yet? So far it's all been circumstantial. They need more than that to secure a conviction, don't they?

You decide to change tack. 'Listen, it's clear to me that I need some help. How can I convince you that all this absolutely did not happen? Not to me.'

He leans forward and fixes you with his dark eyes. 'You really know nothing about it? You'd swear to that?'

You nod and look earnest.

At last he seems willing to reconsider. 'In that case,' he speculates, 'perhaps I got it wrong. *You* were struck with the bottle. You were concussed, so you remember nothing.'

'Would that explain it?' you blurt out thankfully.

'So it appears.'

'I'm innocent, then?'

He hesitates. 'How's your head? Does it feel sore?'

You rub it, pressing hard with your fingers. 'That part is tender, certainly.'

'At the back?'

'Yes.'

He starts writing in his book, speaking the words aloud. 'A blow on the back of the head, causing concussion and

178

loss of memory.'

You start turning mental cartwheels. 'May I go, then?'

He looks up, grinning faintly. 'No, I can't allow that.'

'Why not?'

'Because there *was* a corpse found in that cupboard and it wasn't yours.'

'A corpse in my house? That isn't possible. Whose corpse, for heaven's sake?'

His tone alters. 'Watch it. You're in no position to talk like that. You asked whose corpse it was. I told you. It was the corpse of the person I referred to as You Know Who.'

'And you hold me responsible? I thought we just agreed that if I was there at all I was out cold.'

He shakes his head. 'You regained consciousness after a minute or two and picked up the bottle and struck the fatal blow – a much harder one. Your victim's skull was heavily impacted. There's no doubt that the bottle was the murder weapon.'

'I deny it.'

'I wouldn't, if I were you.' He closes his book. 'It's my duty to caution you now.' He presses his hands together and stares at you solemnly. 'Speak that which thou knowest and no more, for by thy words shalt thou be judged.'

You gape at him. 'That isn't the proper caution. Those aren't the words.'

'They are in this place.'

You stare around you at the walls, blank except for the stuffed fish above his head. 'Where am I then?'

He gives you a look with genuine pity in it. 'This will come as a shock. You were found unconscious in your house. There was a box of pills beside you. That is to say, a box that had contained pills. Sleeping pills. You swallowed the lot after committing the murder. You've been in intensive care for months, in a coma.'

'A coma.'

'I'm afraid you never recovered consciousness. You died in hospital twenty minutes ago.'

With heavy irony you say, 'Oh, yes, and I suppose you're St Peter.'

But your words are lost in a vaporous mist that swirls over you. The floor sinks away, and you find that you are almost weightless. As you drift lower you glimpse the sandalled feet of your inquisitor. You recall his strange claim to have met Chesterton and the others, all dead writers. Then a man in a red uniform takes a grip on your arm and starts to draw you firmly downwards.

Yes, youdunnit.

The Lady in the Trunk

'I PACKED MY TRUNK . . .'

Inspector Duggan chanted the words as if to a child and pricked up his eyebrows in expectation. He was grinning.

There was no response.

'I said I packed my trunk . . .'

Sergeant George Slim stared at his superior without a glimmer of comprehension.

'. . . and in it I put . . .?'

The sergeant pressed his lips together in a sheepish smile, and shrugged.

'Come on, man. Don't be so dense. I packed my trunk and in it I put . . .' There was a gritting of the teeth now. What had begun as a somewhat tasteless attempt to make light of their unappealing task was fast becoming an aggravation. 'The old parlour game. Don't you ever play it, for heaven's sake?' Inspector Duggan demanded. 'I packed my trunk and in it I put . . .'

'We don't play no parlour games in my house,' the sergeant finally succeeded in saying.

'. . . and in it I put a body, a blood-stained poker and a piece of sacking to cover them up.' Making clear his opinion that he was saddled with a nincompoop, Inspector Duggan folded his arms and gave his attention to the real corpse in a real cabin trunk in the luggage room at Itchingham Station.

The find had been notified by Hegarty, the station-

181

master, a man of exemplary efficiency, whose station held the silver rosebowl as the best-kept on the Brighton line. Today, on this warm July morning in 1927, Hegarty was a troubled man. The presence of a dead body in his luggage room – a body he had personally discovered after his keen nostrils had detected an emanation foreign to the Southern Railway – a *murdered* body, would be no help at all towards his ambition of retaining the rosebowl for an unprecedented third year. Having shown the two police officers what he had found, Hegarty had backed away, and was now outside, inhaling the fresher air on the platform.

'Feeling strong?' Duggan asked the sergeant.

Actually not a vast amount of strength was required to lift the body from the trunk and deposit it on a stretcher. The young woman had been slimly built.

They arranged the limbs decorously. 'You know who she is, of course,' Duggan said in a voice suggesting quite the reverse.

It happened that Sergeant Slim *did* know who she was. As a local man, he recognized the neat features in the still-neat frame of black bobbed hair. The face had not been damaged. The fatal blow must have been to the back of the skull, where blood had dried and caked the hair in a patch that was obvious to the touch. The clothes, fashionable and no doubt expensive, consisted of a lightweight summer coat, red-brown in colour, with accordion-pleated black frills, over a pink georgette dress, white lace gloves, white silk stockings and black patent leather shoes.

'If I didn't know who she is, I ought to be doing another job,' George Slim responded, trying manfully to match the inspector's nonchalance. 'I've seen her hundreds of times in the Wheatsheaf on Saturday nights when they have the dances. She's that singer.'

'Yes – but do you know who she is?'

Duggan was a detective of the old school, not an easy man to work with. His captious style of conversation had seen off numerous detective sergeants in his twenty-five years with the Brighton CID. The black, stoatlike eyes, angular nose and toothbrush moustache reinforced the cantankerous personality.

The sergeant answered limply, 'I believe she called herself the Singing Flapper.'

'That's a lot of help!'

Sergeant Slim stared down at the dead face as if it might whisper a clue, and then admitted, 'I don't know her real name.'

Duggan clicked his tongue and informed the sergeant that the dead woman was Lady Pettifer.

'A titled lady!' said the sergeant on such a piping note of disbelief that it spared him from sarcasm for several minutes.

Duggan explained. 'She was married to Sir Hartley Pettifer, that old boy who used to drive around Brighton in an open carriage. Remember him?'

'The one who always wore a top hat?'

'Yes. Know anything else about him? Evidently not. He made his fortune out of buying and selling hotels. Lived in a suite on the top floor of the Old Ship. Lived is the operative word. Regularly when he spotted a beautiful woman on the prom, he'd stop the carriage and invite her to sit beside him. Not many refused. And not many could resist the invitation to tea and cucumber sandwiches after the drive.'

'In his rooms?'

'Where else? He didn't have time to waste.' Duggan turned his gaze to the body on the stretcher. 'This one was a fast worker too. She insisted on marrying him. The story I heard is that she was just a minor actress – a soubrette – who happened to be appearing in some musical comedy on the West Pier. She became the fourth or fifth Lady P –

and the one who outlived him. The old fellow hopped the twig last year, and left her everything.'

Slim had heard all this in amazement. Although he was a man of thirty, with twelve years' service behind him, he was still capable of being shocked by the eccentricities of the rich. 'If she was so well off, why did she bother to sing in the Wheatsheaf?'

'It was no *bother*. It was her choice. She was convinced she was another Gertrude Lawrence.'

'She wasn't. I heard her.'

'Never mind. She could sing like a drain and no one would argue.'

'She wasn't as bad as all that, sir.'

'The point is that Lady Pettifer *owned* the Wheatsheaf, not to mention six or seven other good hotels, so she could serenade the guests night after night if she wanted. What else did I see at the bottom of that trunk?'

Sergeant Slim leaned over the side and came up with a bloodstained yellow cloche hat.

'Is that all?' Duggan asked.

Slim had another look before confirming that the trunk was now empty.

'Excellent,' said Duggan, obviously savouring his assistant's puzzled reaction before adding in a tone that could only be a provocation, 'Mighty good to have a motive so soon!'

'A *motive*, sir?'

'It's downright obvious, isn't it?'

'Not to me.'

Duggan sighed, shrugged and explained that what was missing was a handbag. No young woman in hat and coat would go out without a bag. From which he deduced that Lady Pettifer had been robbed – probably by someone who knew she was rich. Moreover, the chance was high that her murderer had also robbed her of some jewellery, for none remained on the body, except for her wedding

184

ring, which had been out of sight under a glove – no brooch, earrings, or necklace.

After that impressive flexing of his mental muscle, the inspector ordered his awed assistant to lead a search of the station and its environs. A vanload of uniformed policemen from Brighton awaited orders in the station yard.

'What exactly should we look for?' Slim asked.

Duggan rolled his eyes heavenwards. 'The handbag.'

'If it was stolen, it's gone, sir.'

'No, sergeant. Your intelligent thief gets rid of it. Takes any money out, and then disposes of the bag.'

Left alone, Duggan covered the body with the sacking and unfastened the attaché-case containing his fingerprint kit. Unhelpfully neither the poker nor the trunk responded to the mixture of chalk and metallic mercury that he applied with his camel-hair brush. An hour's work yielded only a few anonymous smudges.

He had more success when he questioned Hegarty. In ten minutes with the stationmaster he established that the cabin trunk, which was brand new, had arrived empty at the station the previous week and was still awaiting collection. Remarkably, its owner happened to be the famous writer, Mr Rudyard Kipling, who lived twenty miles away. Mr Kipling had ordered it from the Army and Navy Stores in London for an overseas trip he was planning, and it had been delivered by mistake to Itchingham instead of Etchingham, Kipling's local station. There was no suggestion that the great man was in any way implicated in the crime.

Kipling's trunk had been left in the luggage office, a room that in reality served as a station glory hole, because little in the way of luggage was ever left on Itchingham station. Instead, the room contained such impedimenta as a broken weighing-machine, a porter's trolley, a set of obsolete destination-boards, a bicycle, Mr Hegarty's golf-clubs, several brooms, a box of light-bulbs and the set of fire-irons that was removed from the waiting room in the summer months. The luggage office was kept unlocked during the hours the station was open.

The fire-irons were incomplete. The poker was missing from its hook. Mr Hegarty, sunk in gloom, confirmed that the blood-stained poker found in the trunk matched the set.

'Splendid!' said the inspector. 'The nature of the crime is unfolding. Lady Pettifer was murdered here on the station – probably in this room – some time last Saturday evening after she sang in the Wheatsheaf and was on her way home to Brighton. She was struck from behind with the poker, robbed of her bag and any jewellery she was wearing and her lifeless body was dumped in the trunk. Tell me, Mr Hegarty, where you were on Saturday evening?'

Hegarty's ashen depression flared into sudden alarm. 'You don't suspect me . . .? Absolutely not. I was off duty by six. I spent the entire evening playing chess with the vicar. You're welcome to ask him.'

Duggan was grinning to himself. 'I was merely seeking to enqire, sir, whether you saw the unfortunate lady.'

Hegarty made it clear that the station had been manned on Saturday night by a booking clerk called Crocker, a conscientious young fellow who had no objection to working late, unlike most Southern Railway employees.

Crocker came on duty at two, and Inspector Duggan interviewed him in the stationmaster's officer. Dapper in Oxford bags and Fair Isle pullover, clean-shaven, and with a confident manner, Crocker impressed Duggan as bright and efficient, the sort of young man who ought to be training as a detective instead of mindlessly sitting at a window issuing tickets for a living. Helpfully it emerged that Crocker's attitude to his work was anything but mindless. He recalled precisely when Lady Pettifer had bought her ticket on Saturday evening.

186

'She was going for the eleven-fifteen to Brighton, which was unusual for her. Most Saturdays she caught the next one, the eleven forty-five. However, she arrived in very good time, at one minute past the hour. I remember because the church clock was still chiming and it's fifty seconds late by Southern Railway time. I wished her a good evening and issued her with a ticket.'

'She didn't already have a return, then?'

'Not to this station.'

Mr Hegarty intervened to explain that Brighton didn't issue return tickets to the smaller stations along the line. The passengers had to purchase a ticket for each journey.

'I understand.' Duggan turned back to Crocker. 'Did the lady seem at all distressed?'

'Not that I noticed. She had a friendly smile for me, as always.'

'You knew the lady?'

'She bought a ticket from me every Saturday. She sang with the band at the Wheatsheaf dances.'

'That much we know,' said Duggan. 'Do you happen to remember what she was wearing?'

'Her yellow hat and brown coat.'

'A necklace?'

Crocker thought for a moment and then said decisively, 'Pearls.'

Duggan arched his eyebrows. The motive of theft looked even more likely now. 'Presumably when she paid for the ticket she took the money from a purse.'

'Quite correct. In a black patent leather handbag.'

'You're certain you saw a handbag?'

'Positive. I just described it.'

'You're being very helpful, Mr Crocker, and I hope you can help me even more. When Lady Pettifer went on to the platform, was anyone else already waiting there?'

'Almost certainly not. Nobody else had passed through the booking hall since the previous train had left.'

Duggan was thinking what an unshakable prosecution witness this young man was going to make. First, there was the burdensome matter of finding an accused. 'And after she had bought her ticket, did any others arrive?'

'Only two.'

'To catch the eleven-fifteen?'

'Yes.'

'Did you happen to recognize either of them?'

'Both,' answered Crocker. 'They're regulars on Saturdays, just as she was. They both come from Brighton to attend the dances. One is the band-leader, Maxie Sands, and the other is a lad known as Leftie. I can't tell you his surname, but he's well known in Brighton as an amateur boxer, hence the name.'

'I dare say we'll find him, then. These two – Sands and Leftie – were the only ones to follow Lady Pettifer on to the platform?'

'Apart from myself.'

'*You* went on to the platform?'

'To meet the train.'

Again, Hegarty found it necessary to explain station procedure. 'Crocker here was the only member of my station staff left on duty. Doubling up is quite normal late at night, when not many people are using the station. As well as issuing tickets, he whistles the trains out and collects the tickets from passengers arriving.'

Duggan commented, 'I wouldn't call that doubling up. I'd say he was a general factotum.' He put another question to Crocker. 'So you must also have seen who boarded the train?'

'Yes, it's a bit of a rush, as you can imagine,' Crocker explained. 'I can't leave the booking office until the last possible moment in case someone arrives late wanting a ticket. I got to the platform in time to see Mr Sands and Leftie stepping aboard. There was no sign of Lady Pettifer. Now, of course I understand why not, but at the

188

time I presumed she'd boarded the train quickly, before the others.'

'The train entered the station before you went on to the platform?'

'That is correct. When I hear it arrive, I pull down the hatch in the booking office, pick up the whistle and the lantern and go through the staffroom to the platform.'

Duggan summed up in the workmanlike style that had taken him so far in the CID. 'So it comes down to this. To your knowledge, one of those two must have attacked Lady Pettifer and robbed her before they boarded the train. You say Sands was the first to buy a ticket?'

'The first after Lady Pettifer.'

'Are those tickets numbered in sequence?'

Crocker confirmed that they were. Because they were the last three tickets issued on Saturday night, and a fresh batch was started the following day, he was able to supply the numbers. Lady Pettifer had been issued with ticket 512, Sands the danceband leader, 513 and the boxer called Leftie, 514.

'In case you needed to see them,' said Mr Hegarty, 'I telephoned Brighton to see if the tickets were collected that night. They were – and here they are.' He held out tickets 513 and 514. 'Sands and Leftie certanly completed their journeys.'

Late the same afternoon – like some explorer who had discovered the lost city of the Incas – Sergeant Slim made his way triumphantly along the railway track at the head of his line of helpers. He was carrying a black patent leather handbag.

'You don't have to hold it by the handle,' Duggan told him without gratitude. 'It makes you look effeminate. Where did you find it?'

'Three hundred yards along the track, sir. It was lying on the embankment. The reason I was holding it by the handle, sir, was that I spotted some fingerprints on the shiny surface.' Even before he had finished speaking, Slim found himself wishing he'd found some better pretext for mentioning the fingerprints. Duggan preferred to make his own discoveries.

'Show me,' said Duggan acidly, producing a magnifying glass. He examined the bag. 'I wouldn't call these fingerprints. Smears is what I'd call them. You couldn't prove anything with these. See for yourself.'

'Yes, they are rather smudged, sir.'

'Wouldn't surprise me if you made them yourself,' Duggan commented loudly enough for Slim's team of helpers to hear. 'Let's look at the size of your hand. Your right, man – not your left. Can't you see it's a right-handed set? Press your fingers against the bag. It's all right. I know what I'm doing. Give me a set of prints above these others and we'll compare them.'

Slim obeyed. It was manifestly clear that the first set of prints had been made by a smaller hand than his own.

'Probably the victim's, then,' Duggan said.

'She was wearing gloves,' Slim pointed out. 'They wouldn't leave this sort of mark, sir.'

Another lapse of tact.

Duggan glared and said, 'No blinking use to this investigation, anyway. No use at all. Smears, that's all they are. You want to see the papillary ridges to make a positive identification. This could be bird-droppings, for all I can tell.' Having earned some laughter for that, he went on to say, 'The bag is empty, I suppose?'

'Empty of money, sir.'

'What else is here, then? Just hold out those petal-like hands, Sergeant.'

The inspector tipped the bag upside down, letting the contents drop into Sergeant Slim's hands. 'Powder compact, lip-salve, rouge, comb, mirror, keys, handkerchief. Nothing remarkable.' He rummaged inside the bag and discovered a railway ticket. 'Ha! This, gentlemen, *is* worth finding – a little item that I don't mind betting Sergeant Slim would have overlooked. Ticket number 512. In court this is going to be Exhibit Number One – the proof that Lady Pettifer was on the platform before' – he paused for dramatic impact – 'before my two suspects bought their tickets.'

'*Suspects?*'

Loftily, Duggan summarized what he had learned from Crocker, the booking clerk, making it sound as if he had prised out the information by interrogative skill. Sergeant Slim's success in finding the handbag was utterly eclipsed.

That evening, while Inspector Duggan was at home rewarding himself with a hot bath, Sergeant Slim traced one of the suspects to a dance hall in Brighton. However, as Duggan pointed out when he eventually arrived there, the finding of Maxie Sands was no great feat when his name was printed in letters six inches high outside the hall.

The two detectives identified themselves at the door and went in. For a few minutes they listened to the Sandpipers, as the band was known. The quality of the music impressed them. It even inspired Duggan to make a witticism: Sands and his band were better on the beat, he said, than most of the police he knew.

The interview with Mr Sands had to be conducted in a series of three-minute intervals between dances; he said he wouldn't answer for the behaviour of the dancers if the music had to be delayed any longer. In the dressing-room, Sands seemed shorter than he had on stage. Dapper in his dark green bandmaster's blazer and white flannels, he made a good impression, confident in his responses, his wide blue eyes regarding the detectives with a steady gaze that gave a strong assurance of integrity.

'I read about this in the paper,' he told them. 'Fearfully sad. I would have come to you if I had anything helpful to say. I'm afraid I haven't. I didn't see a thing.'

Duggan was his usual nit-picking self. 'That's a

191

statement I frequently hear, Mr Sands. It's manifestly untrue, of course. You're not blind and the station wasn't totally in darkness. On the contrary, it was well lit. You must have seen something, even if it was only the platform opposite.'

The bandleader moved his right hand in a downwards direction, as if conducting a *diminuendo* passage, and Sergeant Slim noticed for the first time that it was an artificial hand. 'I don't mean it literally. I mean that I saw nothing of significance.'

Duggan said primly that only he, the investigator, was in a position to judge what was significant and what was not, and Sands obliged by telling them what he had seen that Saturday night. The dance had ended at eleven and he had set off immediately after the last bar of the National Anthem, intent on catching the eleven-fifteen. He estimated that he must have reached the station by eleven-ten.

'You had to step out?'

'Yes.'

'Had Lady Pettifer left before you?'

'She took her bow before we began the last waltz. That's a good ten minutes before the end.'

'She didn't sing the last waltz?'

Sands winched. 'Perish the thought!'

'Why do you say that?'

'The last waltz is meant to be romantic. Dimmed lights and cheek-to-cheek. She was always so far off key that she ruined every number. Most of the time the lads would be doing their best to drown the sound, but you can't battle it out like that in the last waltz.'

'You sound unimpressed by her singing.'

'I have every right to be. Three nights a week she inflicted herself on me and my lads. We're a good band. You wouldn't have known it when she started her caterwauling.'

'Why did you put up with it?'

'We're trying to scrape a living at this. We need every

192

engagement we can get. Lady Pettifer owns – I should say owned – most of the decent hotels along the south coast, but you wouldn't think it from the money she paid. And now if you'll excuse me, I have a one-step to perform.' He picked up his baton and left the room.

The detectives followed him out. Through the strains of 'Horsey, Keep Your Tail Up', Sergeant Slim remarked to Duggan that Sands seemed a decent type, and was rebuked for making a classic error. Some of the meanest murderers ever to have come before the courts, Duggan informed him, had been amiable fellows to meet. When Slim rashly remarked that a man with a love of music couldn't be wholly evil, Duggan reminded him that George Joseph Smith had given a rendering of 'Nearer My God to Thee' on the harmonium shortly after drowning one of his brides in the bath, and the infamous Charlie Peace had been a virtuoso of the violin. Maxie Sands was the obvious suspect, the first person to have followed Lady Pettifer on to the platform on the night she was murdered. 'The blighter hasn't told us anything yet, but I'll have him over a barrel in the next interval,' added the inspector. 'Just watch me.'

The dance ended, the floor cleared and the law swooped.

'Where precisely was Lady Pettifer standing when you arrived on the platform?' Duggan demanded, metaphorically rolling out the barrel.

'I've no idea. I didn't notice her.'

'What do you mean – "*didn't notice her*"? She was the only other person there.'

'She must have stepped into the ladies' waiting room,' Sands said defensively.

'I don't want your opinion,' Duggan told him. 'I can form my own, and I think I have. Did you see anyone else before the train arrived?'

'Only one other. He came a few minutes after me. A big

fellow. The one they call Leftie. He often comes to the dances. Does a very smooth tango. He's heavily in demand as a rule.'

'A gigolo?'

'I'll put it this way: he usually ends the evening with a rich woman.'

'But not last night,' said Duggan.

Sands looked impressed. 'How did you know?'

'You just told me he was alone on the platform. How long was he in your view before the train arrived?'

'Not much over a minute. Maybe two. No more.'

'Did he go into a waiting room, or the luggage office?'

'Not while I was there.'

'You're certain?'

'Absolutely. May I go now? It's time for my foxtrot medley.'

The interrogation over a barrel had ended flatly, if not feebly, and Duggan was quick to explain why, as soon as he and Sergeant Slim had left the dance hall. 'I knew he couldn't possibly be the murderer the moment I clapped eyes on him. Do you know why? I don't suppose you do,' he went on uncharitably, without giving Slim an opportunity to answer. 'Did you notice his right hand?'

Slim, on the lookout for one of Duggan's catch-questions, answered warily, 'He didn't have a right hand.'

'He had a wood and metal one. Remember the fingerprints on the handbag? An artificial hand doesn't leave fingerprints.'

Slim nodded humbly. Privately, he noted that the 'smears' on the handbag were described as fingerprints when they suited the inspector's deductions. But the point was fair. The marks on the bag had clearly been left by a living right hand. He refrained from asking why – if Duggan had known of the bandleader's innocence the moment he had seen him – he had dubbed him as the obvious suspect, and subjected him to such hostile questioning.

194

As if he read the thought, Duggan declared, 'We'll give this amateur boxer a ruthless interrogation.'

'Is he our man, sir?'

'Must be.'

Slim was befuddled. 'But if Sands was telling the truth, the boxer couldn't have done it,' he pointed out. 'He was never out of Sands's sight.'

Duggan gave him a withering look and said, 'I don't think you'll ever have the intellect for this job.'

Sergeant Slim may have lacked brain power, but he was learning some craft. The next day he succeeded in tracing Leftie the boxer, courtesy of a friendly sports reporter on the *Brighton Argus*. He left Duggan with the impression that he had personally tracked the quarry to his lair.

Leftie's real name turned out to be Hooker, which was doubly appropriate for a boxer and fisherman, not to say gigolo. They cornered him that evening in his training quarters, a lock-up under the arches below the King's Parade. He was circling around a punchbag suspended from a beam, ducking, weaving and feinting as if the bag were Bombardier Billy Wells himself.

The two policemen waited, unacknowledged, until it became obvious that Leftie Hooker was in serious want of the most basic civilities.

Duggan cleared his throat and announced, 'I am Detective Inspector Duggan of the Brighton Police Force.'

'I'm busy,' the boxer muttered as he continued sedulously to circumambulate the bag. From his build, he was a heavyweight and the weight was mostly muscle. A tanned, tattooed, good-looking man in his twenties, he must have stood six foot three in his socks.

'Not too busy to talk to the police,' Duggan warned him, making clear that he was not intimidated in the least. 'Stop prancing around like a fairy and come over here.'

This had no apparent effect. The exercising continued.

Sergeant Slim was intrigued to discover how Duggan

would deal with such defiance. When it came, the attack was astonishing considering that the boxer had so far admitted nothing except that he was busy.

'You may suppose you have an alibi, Hooker, but don't depend on it. True, Maxie Sands saw you on Itchingham Station on the night Lady Pettifer was murdered. He saw you come from the booking office and he saw you catch the train, but that doesn't satisfy me.'

Leftie Hooker suspended his training.

Duggan ploughed on relentlessly, 'You see, I believe the lady was already dead when you appeared. I think she was killed *before* Sands arrived at the station. She met her murderer when she first came on to the platform. He'd crept through the booking office while she was buying her ticket. He had no money because for once in his experience he'd been unable to sponge off a starry-eyed female.'

Hooker glared at him, saying nothing.

'You didn't get a girl, did you?' Duggan persisted. 'You didn't get a girl for the last waltz. What a blow to your pride! Leftie Hooker spurned by all the girls. A wallflower.'

'Don't say that,' Hooker said huskily.

Duggan moved towards him. 'You didn't even have the price of a train ticket until you robbed Lady Pettifer. I'm willing to believe you didn't mean to kill her. I suppose she turned her back on you when you asked for money. I'm willing to consider manslaughter rather than murder, but you'd better be straight with me, and truthful, or I'll see you deadheaded, Wallflower.' He placed a hand on Hooker's shoulder.

It was an improvident gesture. The boxer swung his left fist upwards. It struck Duggan's protruding jaw, thrust forward to reinforce the threat. Duggan straightened, curled and crumpled, striking his head on the concrete floor. He lay still.

Sergeant Slim bent over him and looked for signs of consciousness.

Leftie Hooker remarked, 'I shouldn't have done that.'

'But you did,' said Slim, and there was a hint of admiration in his voice.

'Are you going to arrest me?'

'Not yet,' said Slim. 'I'm going to fetch a doctor.' He left.

In the two days that Inspector Duggan was required to pass in hospital, Sergeant Slim put the finishing touches to the Case of Kipling's Trunk, as it was known to the press. Then he visited the hospital.

Duggan was sitting up in bed, arms folded, chin as far out as ever, apparently to demonstrate that nothing had changed. 'You arrested Hooker, I trust,' he said at once.

'Yes, sir.'

'And charged him?'

'Yes, sir.'

'What with?'

'Assaulting a police officer.'

'And . . .?'

'That's all, sir. I did consider charging him with resisting arrest, but I thought you wouldn't want to make too much of the arrest.'

'What do you mean? I got my man. We've nothing to be ashamed of.'

Slim coughed. 'Actually you didn't get him, sir. Leftie Hooker is innocent of murder.'

'*Innocent?* The blighter attacked me.'

'But he didn't attack Lady Pettifer, sir. Somebody else attacked her.'

Duggan sagged appreciably, reclined against the pillow and looked more like the convalescent he was. 'Not Maxie Sands? Surely not Maxie Sands?'

'No, sir. Mr Sands was telling the truth. He and Leftie both told us the truth when they said they didn't see Lady

Pettifer on the station platform that night. She didn't go for the eleven-fifteen train. After her last song, she must have spent some time in her dressing-room. She went for the late train, the eleven-forty-five.'

'But there's a serious flaw in this,' said Duggan, showing more colour. 'She had ticket 512. We found it – I found it – in the handbag. The others had tickets 513 and 514 and caught the eleven-fifteen.'

'Right, sir – but have you considered who issued the tickets?'

'Crocker? You suspect Crocker, the booking clerk, of misleading us?'

'Of murder, sir.' Slim made a rapid summation of the facts. 'He put one ticket aside, knowing Lady Pettifer generally caught the last train and was the only passenger. Then he issued the next two tickets to Maxie Sands and Leftie Hooker, who caught their train. When Lady Pettifer arrived, Crocker issued her with the ticket, followed her on to the platform, struck her with the poker and robbed her. He hid the body in the trunk, to await an opportunity of disposing of it. Just to make it look as if a passenger killed her, he walked along the line and threw the handbag on to the embankment.'

Duggan said faintly, 'What made you think of Crocker?'

'The prints on the handbag. Leftie's hand was larger than mine – much too big to match the dabs we had.'

'Those prints won't satisfy a jury.'

'A confession will, sir. I reasoned that Crocker wouldn't want to keep the jewellery for long, so I put a tail on him and he tried selling a diamond necklace – he lied about the pearls, incidentally – to a dealer in the Lanes this morning. The man is no professional. He didn't know where to look for a fence. He coughed the lot when we collared him.'

After a pause, Duggan said, 'Clever. Deucedly clever.'

Sergeant Slim permitted himself the gratification of a smile. 'Thank you, sir.'

'I meant that trick with the tickets,' said Duggan. 'It takes a rare intelligence to outwit me.'

Pass the Parcel

THE ROADS WERE TREACHEROUS ON Christmas Day and Andy and Gemma took longer than they expected to drive the twenty-five miles to Stowmarket. While Gemma concentrated on keeping the car from skidding, Andy complained about the party in prospect. 'You and I must be crazy doing this. I mean what are we putting our lives at risk for? Infantile games that your sister insists on playing simply because in her tiny mind that's the only permissible way of celebrating. The food isn't anything special. If Pauline produces those enormous cheese straws with red streaks like varicose veins, I'll throw up, I promise you. All over the chocolate log.'

Gemma said, 'We're not going for the food.'

'The games?'

'The family.'

'Your brother Reg, you mean? The insufferable Reg? I can't wait to applaud his latest stunt. What's he planning for this year, would you say? A stripogram? Or a police raid? He's a real bunch of laughs, is Reg.'

Gemma negotiated a sharp bend and said, 'Will you shut up about Reg? There are others in my family.'

'Of course. There's Geoff. He'll be sitting in the most comfortable chair and speaking to nobody.'

'Give it a rest, will you?' Gemma said through her teeth.

'I'd like to. They're showing *Apocalypse Now* on BBC2.

I'd like to be giving it a rest in front of the telly with a large brandy in my fist.'

Andy's grumbling may have been badly timed, but it was not unreasonable. Any fair-minded person would have viewed Christmas with this particular set of in-laws as an infliction. There were four in the current generation of Weavers, all in their thirties now, the sisters Gemma and Pauline and the brothers Reg and Geoff. Pauline, the hostess, eight years Gemma's junior, was divorced. She would have been devastated if the family had spent Christmas anywhere else but in Chestnut Lodge, the mansion she had occupied with her former husband and kept as her share of the settlement. No one risked devastating Pauline. As the youngest, she demanded and received everybody's co-operation.

'I could endure the food if it wasn't for the games,' Andy started up again. 'Why do we put up with them? Why not something intelligent instead of charades and – God help us – pass the parcel? I know, you're going to tell me it's a tradition in the family, but we don't have to be lumbered with traditions for ever more just because sweet little Pauline likes playing the games she did when she was a kid. She's thirty-two now, for Christ's sake. Does she sleep with a teddy-bear?'

When they reached Stowmarket and swung left, Andy decently dipped into his reserve of bonhomie. 'They probably dread it as much as we do, poor sods. Let's do our best to be convivial. You did bring the brandy?'

'On the back seat with the presents,' said Gemma.

Chestnut Lodge had been built about 1840 for a surgeon. Not much had been done to the exterior since. The stonework wanted cleaning and there were weeds growing through the gravel drive.

Someone had left a parcel the size of a shoebox on the doorstep. Andy picked it up and carried it in with their presents.

'So sorry, darling,' Gemma told Pauline. 'The roads were like a rink in places. Are we the last?'

'No, Reg isn't here yet.'

'Wanting to make the usual grand entrance?'

'Probably.'

'You're wearing your pearls. And what a gorgeous dress.'

Pauline always wore something in pink or yellow with layers of net. She was in competition with the fairy on the tree, according to Andy.

She smiled her thanks for the compliment. 'Not very practical for the time of year, but I couldn't resist it. Let's take your coats. And happy Christmas.'

'First I'll park these under the tree,' said Andy. 'The brown paper one isn't from us, by the way. We found it on your doorstep. Doesn't feel heavy enough for booze, more's the pity.'

'I do like surprises,' said Pauline.

'A secret admirer?' said Gemma.

'At my age?'

'Oh, come on, what does that say for me, pushing forty?'

'You've got your admirer.'

Gemma rolled her eyes upwards and said nothing.

'Come and say hello to Geoff.' Pauline cupped her hand to her mouth as she added, 'Hasn't had any work for three months, he told me.'

'Oh, no.'

Their accountant brother, short and fat, with half-glasses, greeted Gemma. 'Merry Christmas,' was likely to be the extent of his conversation for the day unless someone asked him about his garden.

Pauline brought in a tray of tea-things.

Andy said, 'Not for me. I'll help myself to a brandy, if you don't mind. Want one, Geoff?'

Geoff shook his head.

'Any trouble getting here?'

Geoff gave a shrug.

'Roads okay your way, then?'

Geoff thought about it and gave another shrug.

Pauline said, 'It's nearly four. Reg ought to be here. It's not as if he has far to come. Geoff has a longer trip and he was here by three-thirty.'

'Knowing Reg of old, he could be planning one of his stunts,' said Andy. 'Remember the year of the ghost in the bathroom, Pauline?'

'Don't!' she said. 'Will I ever forget? It was so real, and he *knew* I was scared of living alone here.'

Between them, they recalled Reg's party tricks in recent years: the time he arrived with his friend masquerading as an African bishop; the year the Queen's voice came out of the cocktail cabinet; and the live turkey in Geoff's car.

'You've got to give him full marks for trying,' said Andy. 'It would be a dull old Christmas without him.'

'I'd rather have it dull,' said Pauline.

'Me, too,' said Gemma. 'I may be his flesh and blood, but I don't share his sense of humour.'

'Only because it could be your turn this time,' said Andy. 'Poor old Geoff got it last year. The sight of that turkey pecking your hand when you opened the door, Geoff. I'll never forget.'

Geoff stared back without smiling.

Ten minutes later, Pauline said, 'I've had the cocktail sausages warming for over an hour. They'll be burnt to a cinder. And we haven't even opened a single present.'

'Want me to phone him, see if he's left?' Andy offered.

'Of course he's left,' said Gemma. 'He must have.'

Pauline started to say, 'I hope nothing's—'

Gemma said quickly. 'He's all right. He wants to keep us in suspense. We're playing into his hands. I think we should get on with the party without him. Why don't we open some presents?'

'I think we ought to wait for Reg.'

'You could open the one we found on the doorstep,' Andy suggested to Pauline.

'Unless it *is* something personal,' said Gemma.

That induced a change of mind from Pauline. 'I've got nothing to hide from any of you.'

Andy retrieved the parcel from under the tree, turned it over and examined the brown paper wrapping. 'There's nothing written on it. Maybe it isn't meant for Pauline after all.'

'If it was left on her doorstep, it's hers,' said Gemma.

Pauline sat in a chair with the parcel deep in the froth of her skirt and picked at the Sellotape. She was too fastidious to tear the paper.

'You want scissors,' said Andy.

'I can manage.' She eased open the brown paper. 'It's gift-wrapped inside.'

'Where's the tag?' said Gemma. 'Who's it from?'

'There isn't one.' Pauline examined the tinsel-tied parcel in its shiny red wrapper.

'Open it, then.'

She worked at one edge of the paper with one of her long, lacquered fingernails. 'Look, there's more wrapping inside.'

'Just like pass the parcel,' said Gemma.

Andy gave his wife a murderous look.

The paper yielded to Pauline's gentle probing. Underneath was yet another wrapping, with a design of holly and Christmas roses. She said, 'I think you're right. This is meant for a game.'

Andy swore under his breath.

'Let's all play, then,' said Gemma with an amused glance at her husband's reaction.

'After tea.'

'No, now. While we're waiting for Reg. Pull up a chair everyone and sit in a circle. I'll look after the music.'

'Just three of us?' said Andy.

Gemma mocked him with a look. 'You know how Pauline adores this game.'

Andy and Pauline positioned themselves close to where Geoff was already seated, while Gemma selected a CD and placed it on the deck of the music centre.

'What is it – *The Teddy Bears' Picnic*?' said Andy.

Pauline was impervious to sarcasm. '*Destiny*,' she said as the sound of strings filled the room.

'That's an old one.'

'Start passing it, then,' said Gemma. 'I'm not playing this for my amusement.'

Pauline handed the parcel to Andy, who held it to his chest. 'No cheating,' said Pauline.

He passed it to Geoff and the music stopped. Geoff unwrapped a piece of pink paper and revealed a silver layer beneath.

'Tough,' said Andy. 'Play on, maestro.'

As the game resumed, Pauline told her sister, 'You're supposed to have your back to us. It isn't fair if you can see who the parcel has reached.'

'She likes playing God,' said Andy. 'Whoops.' The music had stopped and the parcel was on his lap. He ripped it open; no finer feelings. 'Too bad. Give it another whirl, Gem.'

Geoff was the next to remove a layer. He did it in silence as usual.

'More music?' said Gemma.

'You got it,' said Andy.

Three more wrappings came off before Pauline got a turn. The parcel was appreciably smaller.

'This could be it,' said Andy. 'You can see the shape.'

'But of what?' said Pauline. 'It looks like a box to me.' She was pink in the face as she peeled back the paper, but it was clear that another burst of music would be necessary.

When Andy received the parcel he held it to his ear and gave it a shake. Nothing rattled.

'Come on, pass it,' said Pauline, drumming her shoes on the carpet.

Geoff fumbled and dropped the parcel as the music stopped. Pauline snatched it up.

'Not so fast,' said Andy. 'Geoff hadn't passed it to you.'

But she had already unfolded the tissue paper from around a matchbox, one of the jumbo size capable of holding two hundred and fifty matches.

'One more round, apparently,' said Gemma, and she turned up the music again. To sustain the suspense, a longer stretch of *Destiny* was wanted.

'What could it be?' said Pauline.

'Matches,' said Andy.

'A silk scarf would be nice,' said Pauline.

'Game on,' said Gemma.

The matchbox was sent on its way around the three players.

'No looking,' Andy reminded his wife. 'We're down to the wire now. This has to be impartial.'

'Faster,' said Pauline.

'She's a goer, your sister,' said Andy.

The matchbox fairly raced from lap to lap.

'Do you mind? I didn't know you cared,' said Andy when Pauline's impetuous hand clasped his thigh.

Even Geoff was leaning forward, absorbed in the climax of the game. The music stopped just as he was passing the box to Pauline. They both had their hands on it.

'Mine,' she said.

Geoff apparently knew better than to thwart his younger sister.

'I suppose it's only justice that you get the prize, as it was left on your doorstep,' said Andy. 'Let's see what you've got.'

Unable to contain her curiosity, Gemma came over to see.

Pauline slid the box half-open, dropped it into her lap

and said in horror, 'Oh, I don't believe it!'

'It's a joke,' said Gemma. 'It must be a joke.'

'It isn't,' said Pauline in a thin, strained voice. 'That's somebody's thumb. Ugh!' She hooked the box off her skirt as if it was alive and dropped it on the coffee table.

Large and pale, the offending digit lay on a bed of cotton-wool.

'No it isn't,' said Andy. 'It's too big for a thumb. It's a big toe.'

'A toe?'

'Yes, it's too fleshy for a thumb.'

'It must be out of a joke shop,' said Gemma. 'If Reg is responsible for this, I'll strangle him.'

'Typical of his humour,' said Andy.

Then Geoff spoke. 'I think it's real.'

'It *can't* be,' said Gemma.

'Open it right out,' said Andy.

'I'm not touching it,' said Pauline.

Andy lifted the box and opened it, separating the drawer from its casing.

'I can't bear to look,' said Pauline. 'Keep it away from me.'

'It's the real thing,' said Andy. 'You can see where it was –'

'God in Heaven – we don't wish to see,' said Gemma. 'Put it somewhere out of sight and give Pauline some of that brandy we brought.'

'What a vile trick,' said Pauline.

Andy reunited the two sections of the matchbox and placed it on a bookshelf before going to the brandy bottle. 'Anyone else want some Dutch courage?'

Geoff gave a nod.

Andy's hand shook as he poured. Everyone was in a state of shock.

'He's gone too far this time,' said Gemma. 'He's ruined Christmas for all of us. I shall tell him. Are you all right, love?'

Pauline took a gulp of brandy and gave a nod.

'It's ghoulish,' said Gemma.

'Sick,' said Andy. 'You all right, Geoff? You've gone very pale.'

'I'm okay,' Geoff managed to say.

'Drink some brandy, mate.'

Gemma said, 'Andy, would you take it right out of the room and get rid of it? It's upsetting us all.'

Andy picked the matchbox off the bookshelf and left the room. Gemma collected the discarded sheets of wrapping paper and joined him in the kitchen. 'Where would Reg have got such a ghoulish thing?' she whispered.

Andy shrugged. 'Who knows? I don't imagine a branch manager at the Midland Bank comes across many severed toes.'

'What are we going to do? Pauline's nerves are shattered and Geoff looks ready to faint.'

'A fresh cup of tea is supposed to be good for shock. What am I going to do with this?'

'I don't know. Bury it in the garden.'

'Pauline is sure to ask where it went.'

'Then we'd better take it with us when we go. We can dump it somewhere on the way home.'

'Why should we have to deal with it?' said Andy. 'I'll give it back to bloody Reg. He can get rid of it.'

'If he has the gall to show his face here. Just keep it out of everyone's sight in the meantime.'

To satisfy himself that the toe really was of human origin, Andy slid open the matchbox again. This time he noticed a folded piece of paper tucked into one end. 'Hey, there's something inside. I think it's a note.' After reading the typed message, he handed it to Gemma. 'What do you make of that?'

She stared at the paper. 'It can't be true. It's got to be a hoax.'

They joined Pauline and Geoff in the living-room. 'We

thought you might appreciate some tea,' said Gemma.

'You're marvellous,' said Pauline. 'I should have thought of that.'

'Getting over the shock?'

'I think so.'

'You too, Geoff?'

Geoff gave a nod.

Andy cleared his throat. 'I found this note in the matchbox.'

'A note?' said Pauline. 'From Reg?'

'Apparently not. It says, "*If you want the rest of your brother—*" '

'Oh, no!' said Pauline.

' "*If you want the rest of your brother, bring £10,000, or equivalent, to the telephone box at Chilton Leys at 5.30. Just one of you. If you don't, or if you call the police, you can find the bits all over Suffolk.*" '

'Andy, I think she's going to faint.'

'I'm all right,' said Pauline. 'If this is true, that toe . . .'

'But it isn't true,' said Andy, spacing the words. 'It's Reg having us on, as he does every year.'

'Are you sure?'

'He'll turn up presently grinning all over his fat face. The best thing we can do is get on with the party.'

There was little enthusiasm for unwrapping presents or eating overcooked sausages, so they turned on the television and watched for a while.

'How could we possibly put our hands on ten thousand pounds on Christmas Day?' said Pauline during the commercial break.

'That's the giveaway,' said Andy. 'A professional kidnapper would know better.'

'You've got three hundred in notes in your back pocket,' said Gemma. 'You know you have. You said we needed it over the holiday in case of emergencies.'

'Three hundred is peanuts compared to ten grand.'

'I've got about a hundred and twenty in my bag,' said Gemma.

Geoff took out his wallet and counted the edges of his bank-notes.

'Doesn't look as if Geoff can chip in much,' said Andy.

Gemma said on a note of reproach, 'Andy.'

Andy said, 'No offence, mate.'

Geoff put his wallet away.

'Well, that's it. We couldn't afford to pay the kidnappers if they existed,' Andy summed up. 'How much do you have in the house, Pauline?'

'In cash? About two hundred.'

'Less than eight hundred between us.'

'But I've got a thousand in travellers' cheques for my holiday in Florida.'

'Still a long way short,' said Andy.

'Good thing it's only a hoax,' said Gemma.

'There are my pearls,' said Pauline, fingering them. 'They cost over a thousand. And I have some valuable rings upstairs.'

'If we're talking jewellery, Gemma's ruby necklace is the real thing,' said Andy.

'So is your Rolex watch,' Gemma countered. 'And the gold ingot you wear under your shirt.'

'I notice you haven't offered your ear-rings. They cost a bomb, if I remember right.'

'Oh, shut up.'

'Where the hell is Chilton Leys anyway?'

'Not far,' said Pauline.

'I passed it on my way here,' said Geoff.

The television took over for an interval.

Andy said, 'Well, has anyone spoken to Reg on the phone in the past twenty-four hours?'

'It must be a week since we spoke,' said Pauline.

'What time is it?' asked Gemma.

'Five past five.'

'He would have been here by now,' said Pauline. 'Or if he had trouble with the car he would have phoned.'

'Anyone care for another drink?' asked Andy.

'How many is that you've had already?' said Gemma.

'I want to say something,' said Pauline.

'Feel free,' said Andy, with the bottle in his hand.

She smoothed her skirt. 'I'm not saying you're wrong, but if it wasn't a hoax and Reg really had been kidnapped, we could never forgive ourselves if these people murdered him because we did nothing about it.'

'Come off it,' said Andy.

'I mean, why are we refusing to respond to the note? Is it because we're afraid of making fools of ourselves? Is that all it is?'

'We don't believe it, that's why,' said Gemma.

'You mean you don't want to run the risk of Reg having the last laugh? It's all about self-esteem, isn't it? How typical of our family – all inflated egos. We'd rather run the risk of Reg being murdered than lay ourselves open to ridicule.'

'That isn't the point,' said Andy. 'We're calling his bluff.'

'So you say. And if by some freak of circumstance you're mistaken, how will any of us live with it for the rest of our lives? I'm telling you, Andy, I'm frightened. I know what you're thinking. I can see it in your eyes. I'm gullible, a stupid, immature female. Well I don't mind admitting I'm bloody frightened. If none of you wants to take this seriously that's up to you. I do. I'm going to put all the money I have into a bag and take it to that phone box. If nobody comes, what I have I lost? Some dignity, that's all. You can laugh at me every Christmas from now on. But I mean it.' She stood up.

'Hold on,' said Andy. 'We've heard what you think. What about the rest of us?'

'It isn't quite the same for you, is it?' said Pauline. 'He's my brother.'

'He's Gemma's brother, too. And Geoff's.'

211

Andy switched to his wife. 'What do *you* want to do about it?'

Gemma hesitated.

'Or Geoff,' said Andy. 'Do you have an opinion, Geoff?'

Geoff's hand went to his collar as if it had tightened suddenly.

Gemma said, 'Pauline is right. Ten to one it's Reg having us on, but we can't take the risk. We've got to do something.'

Geoff nodded. He backed his sisters.

Pauline said, 'I'm going upstairs to collect my jewellery, such as it is. We pool everything we have, right?'

'Right,' said Gemma, unfixing her gold ear-rings and turning to Andy. 'Do you want to be part of this, or not?'

Andy slapped his wad of bank-notes on the table. 'I don't believe in these kidnappers anyway.'

'Let's have your watch, then,' said Gemma. 'And the ingot.'

Geoff took out his wallet and emptied it.

The heap of money and valuables markedly increased when Pauline returned. She'd found some family heirlooms including their grandmother's diamond-studded choker, worth several thousand alone. With her own pieces and the travellers' cheques, the collection must have come close to the value demanded in the note. She scooped everything into a denim bag with bamboo handles and said, 'I'll get my coat.'

Gemma told her, 'Not you, sweetie. That's a job for one of the men.'

Andy said, 'Give the bag to me.'

'You're not going anywhere,' said Gemma. 'You're way over the limit with all the brandy you've had. Besides, you don't know the way.'

They turned to look at Geoff. He knew the way. He had said so.

'I'll go,' he said, rising quite positively from the

212

armchair. He looked a trifle unsteady in the upright position, but he'd been seated a long time. Maybe the brandy hadn't gone to his head. He had certainly drunk less than Andy.

Gemma still felt it necessary to ask, 'Will you be all right?'

Geoff nodded. He had spoken. There was no need for more words.

Pauline asked, 'Would you like me to come?'

Andy said, 'The instruction was clear. If you believe it, Geoff's got to go alone.'

In the hall, Pauline helped Geoff on with his padded jacket. 'If you see anyone, don't take them on, will you? We just want you and Reg safely back.'

Geoff looked incapable of taking anyone on as he shuffled across the gravel to his old Cortina, watched from the door by the others. He placed the bag on the passenger seat and got in.

'Is he sober?' Gemma asked.

'He only had a couple,' said Andy.

'He looked just the same when he arrived,' said Pauline. 'He's had a hard time lately. So many businesses going bust. They don't need accountants.'

Gemma said, 'If anything happened to him just because Reg is acting the fool, I'd commit murder, I don't mind saying.'

They heard the car start up and watched it trundle up the drive.

When the front door was closed again, Gemma asked, 'What time is it?'

'Twenty past,' said Pauline. 'He should just about make it.'

Andy said, 'I don't know why you two are taking this seriously. If I believed for a moment it was a genuine ransom demand I wouldn't have parted with three hundred pounds and a Rolex, I assure you.'

213

'So what would you have done, cleverclogs?' said Gemma.

This wrongfooted Andy. He spread his hands wide as if the answer were too obvious to go into.

'Let's hear it,' said Gemma. 'Would you have called the police and put my brother's life at risk?'

'Certainly I'd have called them,' said Andy, recovering his poise. 'They have procedures for this sort of emergency. They'd know how to handle it without putting anyone's life at risk.'

'For example?'

'Well, they'd observe the pick-up from a distance. Probably they'd attach some tiny bugging device to the goods being handed over. They might coat some of the banknotes with a dye that responds to ultra-violet light.'

Gemma turned to Pauline. 'I'm wondering if we should call them.'

Andy said, 'It's too late. The police would have no option but to come down like a ton of bricks. Someone would get hurt.'

Pauline said, 'Oh God, no. Let's wait and see what happens.'

'We won't have long to wait. That's one thing,' said Andy. 'You don't mind if I switch on the telly, Pauline?'

They sat in silence watching a cartoon film about a snowman.

Before it finished, Pauline went to the window and pulled back the curtain to look along the drive.

'See anything?' asked Gemma.

'No.'

'How long has he been gone?'

'Twenty-five minutes. Chilton Leys is only ten minutes from here, if that. He ought to be back by now.'

'Stop fussing, you two,' said Andy. 'You give me the creeps.'

Just after six, Pauline announced, 'A car's coming. I can see the headlights.'

'Okay,' said Andy from his armchair. 'What are we going to do about Reg when he pisses himself laughing and says it was a hoax?'

Pauline ran to the front door and opened it. Gemma was at her side.

'That isn't Geoff's Cortina,' said Gemma. 'It's a bigger car.'

Without appearing to hurry, Andy joined them at the door. 'That's Reg's Volvo. Didn't I tell you he was all right?'

The car drew up beside Andy's and Reg got out, smiling. He was alone. 'Where's the red carpet, then?' he called out. 'Merry Christmas, everyone. Wait a mo. I've got some prezzies in the back.' He dipped into his car again.

'You'd think nothing had happened,' muttered Gemma.

Laden with presents, Reg strutted towards them. 'Who gets to kiss me first, then?' He appeared unfazed, his well known ebullient self.

Andy remarked, 'He's walking normally. We've been suckered.'

Gemma said, 'You bastard, Reg. Don't come near me, you sadist.'

Pauline shouted, 'Dickhead.'

Reg's face was a study in bewilderment.

Andy said, 'Where's Geoff?'

'How would I know?' answered Reg. 'Hey, what is this? What am I supposed to have done?'

'Pull the other one, matey,' said Andy.

'You've ruined Christmas for all of us,' said Pauline, succumbing to tears.

'I wish I knew what you were on about,' said Reg. 'Shall we go inside and find out?'

'You're not welcome,' Pauline whimpered.

'Okay, okay,' said Reg. 'It's a fair cop and I deserve it after all the stunts I pulled. Who thought of unloading all this on me? Andy, I bet.'

Suddenly Gemma said in a hollow voice, 'Andy, I don't think he knows what this is about.'

'What?'

'I know my own brother. He isn't bluffing. He didn't expect this. Listen, Reg, did anyone kidnap you?'

'*Kidnap* me?'

'We'd better go inside, all of us,' said Gemma.

'Kidnap me?' repeated Reg, when they were in Pauline's living room. 'I'm gobsmacked.'

Pauline said, 'Andy found this parcel on my doorstep and—'

'Shut up a minute,' said Andy. 'You're playing into his hands. Let's hear his story before we tell him what happened here. You've got some answering to do, Reg. For a start, you're a couple of hours late.'

Reg frowned. 'You haven't been here all afternoon?'

'Of course we have. We were here by four o'clock.'

'You didn't get the message, then?'

'What message?'

'I've been had, then. Geoff phoned at lunchtime to say that Pauline's heating was off. A problem with the boiler. He said the party had been relocated to his place at five.'

Pauline said, 'There's nothing wrong with my boiler.'

'Shut up and listen,' said Gemma.

Reg continued. 'I turned up at Geoff's house and there was a note for me attached to the door. Hold on – I should have it here.' He felt in his pocket. 'Yes, here it is.' He handed Gemma an envelope with his name written on it.

She took out the note and read to the others, ' "*Caught YOU this year. Now go to Pauline's and see what reception you get.*" It's Geoff's handwriting.'

'He's a slyboots,' said Reg, 'but I deserve it. He was pretty annoyed by the turkey episode last year.'

'You're not the only victim,' said Gemma.

'Were you sent on a wild goose chase?'

'No. But I think he may have tricked us. He *must* have.

He led us to believe you were kidnapped. That's why he went to this trouble to keep you away.'

'Crafty old devil.'

'He took ten grand off us,' said Andy.

'What?'

'He persuaded us to put up a ransom for you.'

'Now who are you kidding?'

'It's true,' said Gemma. 'We put together everything we had, cash, jewellery, family heirlooms, and Geoff went off to deliver it to the kidnappers.'

'Strike me pink!'

'And he isn't back yet,' said Andy.

Pauline said, 'Geoff wouldn't rob his own family.'

'Don't count on it,' said Reg. 'He doesn't give a toss for any of us.'

'Geoff?'

'Did you know he's emigrating?'

'No.'

'It's true,' said Reg. 'He's off to Australia any day now. I picked this up on the grapevine through a colleague in the bank. I think the accident made him reconsider his life plan, so to speak.'

'What accident?'

'There you are, you see. I only heard about that from the same source. Old Geoff was in hospital for over a week at the end of September and the last thing he wanted was a visit from any of us.'

'A road accident?'

'No, he did it himself. You know how keen he is on the garden. He's got this turfed area sloping down to the pond. He ran the mower over his foot and severed his big toe.'

You May See a Strangler

HELEN'S MIND WAS MADE UP. Three times today she had got to the point of picking up the phone to call the police. She had pressed the first two numbers of the emergency code, then stopped, her finger poised over the third. Some loss of nerve had impelled her to hang up.

This time she would not falter. She stretched out her hand.

The phone bleeped before she touched it. Reacting as if she had disturbed a snake, she backed against the wall.

Outside in Carpenter Avenue, the kids from next door were skateboarding. Bees were plundering the lavender bush. Her neighbour Sally walked by on her way to the art class. Sally modelled nude for five pounds an hour and thought nothing of it. She was Helen's closest friend, a free spirit, unencumbered by her four kids. Before the firstborn arrived, Sally had organized a baby-sitting circle. Helen could discuss anything with her. Or almost anything. Cool, liberated Sally wouldn't fathom how any woman could be afraid to pick up a phone.

She braced herself. 'Yes?'

'Helen?'

'Speaking.'

'So you don't know who this is.' The voice was difficult to place. Female, youngish, with a trace of the north. There was background noise of voices laughing and talking animatedly, and music.

'I . . . I'm sorry. Your voice is familiar, but . . .'

'Come on, you can do better than that, love. Picture a blousy dame with pink-rimmed specs and a blonde pony-tail.'

She dredged the name from her troubled mind. 'Immy.' Imogen had been her mainstay through that dreary history course at university. 'It's over ten years. It must be.'

'Eleven this June since we chucked our course-notes into the Avon and got totally Brahms and Liszt. Remember? How are things with you, Helen? You don't sound too chipper from here.'

'It's nothing.'

'An off-moment? What's your news? I know there's a man in your life now. Nelson, am I right?'

'How do you know that?'

'From the Christmas card you sent one year. You caught me out. I didn't think we were the sort who sent cards.'

'That was the only year I sent.'

'Properly hitched, are you?'

'Yes.'

'Kids?'

'No.' Helen made an effort to switch the questioning. 'How about you, Immy? Did you marry?'

'Me? Can you imagine it? I lived with a footballer for a bit. He was the striker for Manchester City Reserves, whatever that means. All the training kept him really warm, specially on those freezing nights in January. Talk about cosy. I didn't use the electric blanket all winter. But he got sweaty when the weather improved so I blew the whistle. That's meant to be a joke, sweetie. You're supposed to fall about laughing.'

'Sorry.'

'You would have laughed in the old days. You *are* down. It isn't your health, is it?'

'I'm fine.' Helen was trying to decide whether this call from Imogen was just for the chat or whether a visit was imminent. In her present crisis she couldn't face doing the hostess bit, not even for Immy. 'Where are you speaking from?'

'Got you worried, have I?' Imogen said, laughing.

'Of course not.'

'Go on – you've got a mental picture of me standing on your doorstep with two enormous suitcases and a dog.'

'Normally I'd love to see you, but . . .'

'It's all right, kiddo, you can relax. Put your feet up, wash your hair, have nookie with Nelson on the bearskin rug. I'm not about to descend on you.'

'You're just as daft as ever,' Helen said, trying to sound matey and not succeeding. 'Where *are* you speaking from? It sounds like a party there.'

'The mental picture gets worse – two suitcases and a dog, and a carload of drunks with funny hats. I said relax. There's no way I'm going to make a nuisance of myself.'

'The last I heard you were back in the north.'

'And so I am. Granadaland. Back to my roots. I'm a television researcher. The history degree got me in, but I make sod all use of it. I don't know why they keep me on.'

Manchester. At least two hundred miles away. While Imogen was outlining the pleasures and perils of TV research, Helen's thoughts became less guarded. The voice from the past, chattering freely, confiding failure as readily as success, revived that time in their second year when they had opened their minds to each other. Talking to Immy had been a balm at that vulnerable stage of her life. She had kept nothing back.

Then wasn't this a God-sent opportunity? All the reasons she had for not confiding in Sally next door didn't apply to Imogen. Immy was remote now, eleven years and two hundred miles away. Remote, yet close in spirit. A sympathetic ear. No, that wasn't the point – it wasn't sympathy she wanted. An understanding ear. Immy understood her. She might even know what to do.

'Now what about you, poppet?' Imogen ended by saying. 'What's your news?'

'Mine?' In her anguish Helen covered her mouth with her hand and pressed her fingers into the flesh under her cheekbones.

'Helen, it's bloody obvious I must have got you at a difficult time,' Imogen said. 'Typical of me, wittering on like that. Look, I'll call back another day.'

'No. No, I want to talk,' Helen managed to say. 'God knows, I want to talk. It must be fate that you called.'

Concern flooded into Immy's voice. 'Darling, what is it?'

Helen started by saying, 'What would you do if . . .?' and then switched to a blunt statement. 'Immy, I believe Nelson is a murderer.'

She heard the intake of breath from Imogen. The background voices shrilled and giggled inanely.

'I know it must sound crazy spoken cold like this. You must have seen all that stuff in the papers about the Surrey Strangler, the man who killed those women. I think it's Nelson.'

When – after another pause – the voice at the end of the phone responded, it was compassionate, but sceptical, with the tone of a mother attempting to coax the truth from her child. 'Helen, how do you know?'

Helen made an effort to sound rational. Now that she'd confided her appalling secret she had to convince Immy that she was still sane. For a start she needed to convey something of Nelson's personality. She described how she had met him four years ago in the cinema queue for the latest James Bond, how he had offered to keep her place when the rain started tipping down, just when she was about to give up for the sake of her hair. He'd got drenched, along with the others who'd kept their positions, but she'd been able to shelter in the cinema entrance. And when they'd finally got their tickets he hadn't done the expected thing and used his gallantry as a

221

ploy to sit beside her. (She was doing her best to be just to Nelson.) He hadn't forced the pace of their relationship at all. He'd found a seat a couple of rows behind her and they'd only spoken in the foyer as they came out. She'd caught his eye and smiled and only then had he asked her to join him for a coffee in the pub across the street. That was how tentative his first approach had been.

'He isn't dishy, or anything. I mean, he isn't ugly, but you wouldn't look twice at him. He's about average height, dark, with a dent in his nose from falling off his bike when he was a boy. What appealed to me was his personality. Immy, he gave me this wide-eyed look – his eyes are brown, by the way – like he'd just arrived from another planet and never seen a woman before. It made me go quite dopey. From the beginning he treated me like someone special, as if I was the first girl he'd ever known. He still does. That's what makes this so creepy. He's never hurt me, or anything, never been violent in any way. If we have a row, as everyone does from time to time, he just goes out of the room until we both see how ridiculous it is to fight.'

'What makes you think he . . .?' Immy declined to supply the rest.

'The dates, the places. Each of those women was killed within thirty miles of here. It's happened each time on a night when Nelson got in really late – I mean well after midnight. He spend ages in the bathroom showering – I hear the tank filling in the loft – and then he sleeps downstairs on the sofa. When I ask him about it in the morning he says he didn't want to disturb me after getting in so late.'

'Do you ask him why he got in late?'

'Clients, he says. He's a sales rep for a firm that makes computer games. Sometimes he has to see people in the evenings.'

'Does he tell you which client he's been with? Maybe you could check in some way.'

'It's not so simple as that. He doesn't go in for talking about his work.'

'And you say all the dates fit?'

'Yes.'

'Listen, I never read things like that in the papers. How many women has this guy killed?'

'Three.'

'It could be coincidence. Has Nelson been out other evenings when a woman wasn't killed?'

'Never so late. Generally he's back by eleven at the latest. And he hardly ever takes a shower before going to bed.'

'But is that all you've got to go on? Just the dates? I mean, these poor women must have fought the guy who attacked them. They were raped as well as strangled, weren't they? Have you noticed scratches, marks, any signs?'

'There was a scratch down the side of his face a few months ago, but I can't say exactly when it got there. I didn't have these suspicions then. Nelson said he got clawed by a cat.'

'A cat?'

'In a pub. He picked it up and it scratched him.'

'Have you looked at his clothes? What about spots of blood, hairs and so on? Scent?'

'I tried to find his shirt last Wednesday, after that nurse was killed in Dorking. He got in terribly late, like the other times. Next morning when I heard on the radio what had happened, I looked in the laundry basket, feeling really sick at what I was doing, and found that the shirt he'd been wearing wasn't there. It wasn't in his room either. Nor were his underpants. I think he must have got rid of them somehow. They weren't in the rubbish sack. Immy, did you see the detective on the television news speaking about it? He said someone must be withholding information, someone who suspects that the man they live with could be this murderer. He said by remaining silent they could have the deaths of more women on their conscience. I've got to speak to them, haven't I?'

Imogen sidestepped the question. 'You won't mind if I ask a personal question?'

'What is it? Go ahead.'

'What's the sex like with Nelson?'

Helen had always found it difficult to talk about such things. If anyone but Imogen had asked her that question she would have slammed down the phone. 'He's never tried to force me, if that's what you're getting at.'

'But you do allow him to make love to you?'

She saw the drift. 'I'm not frigid, for God's sake. I mean it was never *that* passionate, and when it happens it's sometimes more like a duty than a pleasure, or it is for me, but we do sleep together, yes.'

'So the satisfaction isn't there?'

'Did I say that? I suppose it's true.' Not for the first time, Helen found herself wondering whether she was partly to blame. She wasn't experienced or comfortable as a lover. She hadn't the confidence to be anything but passive. Since the latest episode she couldn't imagine herself wanting Nelson ever again.

Through the net curtains she could see the accountant who lived at the end house. He always got back from the City about this time. Several paces in the rear came his Vietnamese wife. Each day she walked to the station to meet him and trail respectfully home behind him, carrying his briefcase. Most couples' relationships aren't paraded so obviously.

'If you go to the police, that's the end of your marriage,' Imogen said. 'Even if he's totally innocent, the point is that you believed this ghastly thing was possible. That's a betrayal in itself.'

Helen was silent.

'Do you really want my advice, love?'

'Immy, I do.'

'You're sure he wouldn't hurt you?'

'He never has.'

'Then I think you owe it to Nelson to talk to him.'

'Tell him what I believe?'

'If I were faced with this, I hope I'd have the guts to do the same.'

'They issued one of those photofit pictures,' Helen said, shrinking from the advice. 'I don't think it looks much like him apart from his eyes and hair.'

'So you want to be certain, and the only way is to find out the truth from Nelson.'

She wavered. 'How can I say such a terrible thing to him?'

'You mean you'd rather say it to the police?'

Inwardly, Helen admitted the truth of this. Until Immy had suggested confronting Nelson, such a course of action had been too hideous even to contemplate. The most she had been prepared to do was to turn Nelson in. Faced with the biggest crisis in her life she had looked for the easy solution, the coward's way.

'Where is he right now?' Imogen asked.

'Out on the road somewhere. He should be back in the next hour or so.'

'Then why don't you talk to him when he gets in? If he's innocent – and he could be – it's the only way to save your marriage, if that's what you want.'

'I don't know if I can face it.'

'You must, poppet, you must. You asked for my advice and that's it.' Having delivered it, Immy steered the call to an end with a promise that she would phone back next day to find out what happened. Helen thanked her and managed to say that they must meet some time. She put down the phone.

It was seven-fifteen. Generally Nelson got in by eight. Immy had convinced her. Helen started rehearsing what she would say. She could broach it indirectly, claiming that she'd looked for his pink shirt with the red stripes – the one he'd been wearing Tuesday – to put in the washing machine. She could remind him that Tuesday was the night he'd got in really late. His responses might give him away. He might even be willing to talk about what had happened. If only it could be so simple . . .

The hour of eight passed. It was getting dark, but she didn't draw the curtains. She stood waiting, staring out of the window. A red Toyota like Nelson's slowed as if to stop, then turned into the drive of one of the neighbours.

She went to make herself some tea and realized when she handled the warm pot that she'd already had two mugs since Immy's call. She'd be awash with the stuff. Instead she did something quite out of character by going to the cupboard where they kept the drinks and pouring herself a gin and tonic. With growing intimations of dread she took up her vigil at the window again.

Another hour went by.

For distraction she dusted the surfaces in the front room, still in darkness, looking out intermittently for the gleam of headlights in the street. She dusted everything twice, moving the ornaments by touch, like a blind person.

It must have been getting on for ten when she heard the heavy tread of a man in the street. She couldn't see enough to tell if it was Nelson, but her pulse raced faster when she saw the shape of someone coming up the garden path. An explanation leapt into her brain: the car had broken down and he'd had to come home by train.

She waited for the sound of his key in the latch. What she heard instead was the doorbell. He was never without his key.

The light in the hall dazzled her when she switched it on. She blinked as she opened the door.

'Sorry to disturb you, Helen,' the man on the doorstep said.

He was the neighbour, Gerald. She stared at him blankly.

'I'm slightly puzzled,' he told her. 'Sally isn't back. She's always in by now. I wondered if she said anything to you about what she was doing tonight.'

Her thoughts had been so focused on Nelson that it was an effort to register Sally's existence, let alone her movements that day. Finally she succeeded in saying, 'I thought she was modelling at the tech. I saw her go past at the usual time.'

'Have you spoken to her at all today?'

'Er – no.'

'Maybe she's gone for a drink with somebody in the class,' said Gerald. 'I wouldn't think twice about it normally, but you can't be too careful these days, you know?'

She gave a nod. She knew what was on his mind. There was no need to say more.

Gerald repeated his apology and left. After she'd closed the door, Helen wondered whether she should have offered to babysit, giving Gerald a chance to walk down to the tech and enquire about Sally. Maybe that had been his real reason for calling. She could have gone after him, but she didn't want to be out when Nelson got back. Besides, she told herself in justification, if Sally *was* having a drink with someone from the class, she might not be overjoyed at her husband turning up. Not that Sally was wayward; simply that she'd balk at being treated as if she were in moral danger.

If the unspeakable had happened, and Sally had met the strangler, what could Gerald do? What could anyone do?

More than three hours had passed since Helen had been on the point of calling the police about Nelson. The appalling thought occured to her that if Sally had met Nelson as she was leaving the tech, she might easily have accepted a lift. Sally knew Nelson. She'd assume she was safe with him. The words of that detective on the television taunted Helen. *'Someone out there knows this man. By remaining silent, they put more women in danger. If they have any conscience at all they should come forward and prevent another murder.'*

Instead of listening to Immy, she should have spoken to the police. Immy had been wrong, catastrophically wrong. She hadn't considered the possibility that if Nelson was the strangler he might kill again tonight.

But it was wrong to blame Immy. The responsibility was her own. She, Helen, should have sensed the dangerous flaw in the advice.

Nelson finally got in at ten to one. He hadn't abandoned the car, apparently. He closed the garage doors quietly – furtively, Helen thought – and let himself in. He was clearly startled when she turned on the light.

'I thought you'd be in bed.'

'I thought I'd wait,' she said in a flat voice.

'Is something the matter?'

'You tell me, Nelson. Look at you. Your hand is bleeding.'

Two long scratches were scored across the back of his right hand. He covered them with his left. His tie was twisted askew and there were buttons missing from his shirt-front. 'I need a drink,' he said.

She followed him into the front room and watched him help himself from the whisky bottle.

'You haven't even pulled the curtains,' he remarked. It seemed to matter to him that they should not be seen from the street. His right hand went up to the cord and tugged at it, displaying the scratches.

Helen said, 'I was looking out for you. I didn't expect you to be so late.'

'I can't predict what's going to happen.'

She found herself saying, 'Maybe a psychiatrist could.'

The hunted look that was already in Nelson's eyes gave way first to horror, then, unexpectedly, to tears. He bowed his face and covered it with his hands. He was sobbing.

228

Helen had no need of her strategies, the questions about the times he'd been late before, and the missing clothes. She had tapped the truth.

And now she had to find out all of it. She still felt safe with him; some instinct told her that he wouldn't attack her, whatever he'd done to those other women. 'Where is she, Nelson? Where did you leave her?'

He said in a broken voice, 'The river, in the park.'

'Ashdown Park?'

He nodded, still sobbing. The local park was just a ten-minute walk away. Sally's children played there often.

'Is she dead?'

'Yes.' After a pause he added. 'You're right – I'm mentally ill. I was locked up for six years before I met you. I should have told you.'

Stunned, she still knew that he was telling the truth. She understood why he'd so often stared at her as if she belonged to another species. She'd allowed herself to be flattered instead of sensing what that wide-eyed regard really meant.

Nelson said, 'I'm going to call the police. I've been wanting to call them. Believe me, I planned to call them. That's why I did it so close to home tonight. I was making sure they'd get me, if you can understand.'

She took the phone to him and waited while he dialled the number and spoke. He told them who he was and where he lived and what he had done. Then he replaced the phone and told Helen, 'They're sending a car.'

She said, 'I knew it was you. I should have turned you in. I'm always going to blame myself. How could you, Nelson, knowing she had four young children?'

He looked at her without a spark of communication. 'Who?'

'Sally.'

'Sally?'

'Sally next door.'

229

'What are you talking about? It wasn't Sally,' he said. 'It was some north country woman staying in the King's Arms. That's where I picked her up.'

Helen registered first that Sally was spared; she must after all have gone out with some people from the art class. Then she played Nelson's words over in her mind. 'This woman – what did she look like?'

'About your age. Blonde hair and glasses. She didn't know the town. She was something in television. Said she was at a loose end tonight. She'd planned to drop in on an old college friend, only it wasn't convenient.'

The Curious Computer

IT WAS ALREADY FOUR A.M.

George Harmer, better known as 'Grievous', was having a sleepless night in his penthouse suite in Belgravia. His brain had been working like a teleprinter for the last two hours. He was in despair.

So he tossed and turned: tossed caution to the winds and turned to the naked blonde who lay beside him. She was Silicon Lil, a stripper of manifest charms who performed nightly in his chain of night-clubs and afterwards by special arrangement.

'Lil.'

She barely stirred.

'Lil.'

She stirred barely.

'Lil, are you awake?'

'Tie a knot in it, Grievous.'

'I want to talk to you. I've got something . . .'

'What?' She snatched at the light switch and sat up. 'What did you say?'

'. . . something on my mind. I can't think of anything else.'

'Don't you ever give up?' Lil flicked off the light and resumed the attitude of slumber. 'What you want is a cold shower.'

If anyone had spoken to Grievous like that in daylight they wouldn't have lasted long enough to complete the

231

sentence. He was the undisputed boss of organized crime in Britain. Undisputed and unforgiving. But at four in the morning he was pathetic. He said in a voice like a choked-up waste disposal unit, 'Lil, I just want to bend your ear.'

She sighed, rolled over and said, 'You must be desperate. What's bugging you, then?'

'Holmes.'

There was a pause.

'What sort of homes? Stately or mental?'

'Holmes with an "l", Lil.'

'As in Sherlock?'

'Right.'

Lil smiled to herself in the dark. 'Him with the deerstalker, Grievous?'

'Not him exactly.' Grievous flicked on the light again, hopped out of bed, switched on the TV and slammed a cassette into the video.

'Give me a break, Grievous,' Lil protested. 'I'm not watching some old detective movie at four in the morning.'

'Shut your mouth, bint!' said Grievous savagely. He was becoming his normal, psychotic self. 'This ain't Peter Cushing. This is a top secret video that was smuggled out of Scotland Yard for me. It's being shown to every chief constable in the country.'

The TV screen flickered. A countdown of numbers appeared, then a famous head in profile, with pipe and deerstalker.

'That's no secret. That's in the tube at Baker Street,' Lil commented.

Grievous silenced her with a growl.

The title of the video was superimposed.

Introducing Holmes . . .

A voice-over spoke in the ponderous tones peculiar to documentary films: 'Everyone has heard of Mr Sherlock Holmes, the world's greatest consulting detective. In his day, if Sir Arthur Conan Doyle is to be believed, this celebrated sleuth consistently outwitted everyone, including the police. He was streets ahead of the best brains at Scotland Yard.'

Stills of wooden-faced Victorian policemen were superimposed over Old Scotland Yard. A hansom cab stood waiting.

'In the modern police, it's another story.'

A clip of New Scotland Yard, with buses and cars cruising past.

'Holmes is working for the police. Holmes is a computer system for use in large-scale enquiries. Home Office Large Major Enquiry System.'

The words appeared on the screen with the initials blown up to triple size.

'They've got to be joking,' said Lil.

The commentary continued, 'Holmes is the most valuable aid to the detection of crime since fingerprints were classified. Holmes will range beyond the boundaries of the police forces, providing instant information on suspicious persons and vehicles. Through free text retrieval, it will provide data on, say, all bald-headed men on record over forty owning D registration Rolls-Royces.'

'My God, that's you,' said Lil.

Grievous fumbled for a cigar.

The screen was filled by a close-up of the computer's interior.

'Holmes is more powerful and more flexible than the Police National Computer,' the commentary continued as the camera panned over crowded logic boards. 'It is a means of linking different forces engaged on similar investigations. Holmes can issue descriptions of persons interviewed or noticed, listing their previous convictions, addresses, telephone numbers and vehicles. It can collect information received from any source, whether it amounts to a verifiable fact or a mere opinion. No member of the criminal fraternity can sleep easily now that Holmes is working for the Yard. The game's afoot!'

The screen went blank. Grievous had pressed the 'stop' button.

He said in a voice laden with doom, 'This is the end of crime as we know it.'

'Come off it!' piped up Lil. 'It's only a computer, for crying out loud. You wouldn't let a piece of hardware get you down, would you?'

'It isn't just me,' moaned Grievous. 'It's the movement I represent. It's employment for thousands of skilled professionals. It's generations of experience and hard graft. It's major industries like prostitution and drugs and pornography. Nothing's sacred no more, Lil. We're all under threat.'

'Strippers?' enquired Lil, betraying some concern.

'With Holmes on the trail? I wouldn't care to be caught in a G-string.'

Lil gave a shudder, and the motion had the effect of distracting Grievous. He enfolded her in a sudden clinch.

'Grievous, my love, you've got to think big,' Lil panted.

'You're big enough for me,' came his muffled reply.

'This is just a cop-out. You must convene a secret meeting of the crime bosses from all over Britain and tell them about Holmes.'

He drew away from her. 'I can't do that. They'll go berserk.'

'And if you *don't* tell them . . .?'

'They'll roast me,' Grievous admitted. 'You're right, Lil. I've got to face it.'

'I'll help.'

'I wouldn't let you within a mile of that lot.'

'No,' Lil explained. 'I'll get to work on Holmes.'

'You?' he sneered. 'What do you know about computers?'

She puffed out her chest provocatively. 'Why do you

234

suppose I'm known as Silicon Lil?'

Grievous grinned. 'It stands out, don't it?'

'Are you talking about my figure?'

'I'm talking about a silicone job.'

She slapped his face. 'Bloody cheek. There's nothing false about these. Silicon without an "e", get it? Ever heard of silicon chips?'

'Naturally, Lil.'

'So?'

He stared at her open-mouthed. His face was giving him gyp. 'You're a computer freak?'

'In my spare time,' she admitted casually. 'More to the point, I have some helpful contacts in the electronics world. Give me a week or two and I might be in a position to save your bacon, Grievous Harmer.'

So a meeting was convened at a secret location in the capital. They were the top men in their respective fields: terrorism, drugs, armed robbery, protection and vice. Grievous ran the video and the air was thick with denunciations and obscenities. They denounced and swore for two days and well into a second night before deciding on the proper response of organized crime to this vile threat to its very foundations: they formed a sub-committee.

Within a week, one of the sub-committee was caught red-handed tunnelling into the Bank of England, and the word got round that Holmes was responsible.

'Already they're pointing the finger at *me*,' Grievous told Silicon Lil. 'They want action. What am I going to do?'

She gave him a serene smile. 'Don't panic, sweetheart. If they want action, they can have it. I've found the only guy in the world who is capable of helping you.'

'Thank God for that! Who is he?'

'Hold it a minute. What's in it for me?'

Grievous said cautiously, 'What have you got in mind, Lil?'

235

'A trifling consideration., Six months' paid leave at the Palm Beach Hotel in the Bahamas.'

'You sure this fellow can nobble Holmes?'

'Nothing is certain, darling, but you won't find a better hacker than this one. He's a professor.'

'Fair enough. You've got your holiday. Now introduce me to this genius.'

The safest place in the world for a secret rendezvous is a metropolitan railway terminus, so Grievous and Lil made an assignation the same day with the Professor under the station clock at Victoria.

To be truthful, the Professor on first acquaintance was a disappointment, if not an affront. He shuffles into our story in decrepit shoes, a shabby raincoat with the buttons missing, a battered violin case under his arm and an ancient bowler on his head. He is obviously very old indeed, desperately thin, tall, but round-shouldered, with deeply-sunken, puckered eyes. Around his neck on a piece of string hangs a notice with the words *Accident Victim*.

'He's a common busker!' said Grievous in disgust.

'Possessed of extraordinary mental powers,' murmured Lil.

'He's as old as the hills!'

' "... from whence cometh my help," ' said Lil opportunely. She wasn't religious; some previous inmate had inscribed the psalm on the door of the cell she had occupied last time she was in Holloway.

And helpful the Professor proved. Over a couple of beers in the station bar, he enlightened them both as to how he could outwit Holmes. In a soft, precise fashion of speech that produced a conviction of sincerity, he said that he regarded the prospect as an intellectual treat. 'I was endowed by Nature with an exceptional, not to say phenomenal, faculty for mathematics,' he informed them. 'At twenty-one, I wrote a treatise upon the Binomial Theorem which earned me a European reputation. I was offered, and accepted, the Chair of Mathematics at one of the better provincial universities. Later, I was obliged to be attached to the military, but I retained my grasp of numerical analysis.'

'What about computers?' put in Grievous anxiously. The old man was rabbiting on too much for his liking.

The Professor gave him a withering stare, and continued to rabbit on. 'In middle age, I had the singular misfortune to suffer a climbing accident in Switzerland. I might easily have perished, for the drop was sheer and I struck a rock in the descent, but I fell into water, which saved me. I was carried downstream by the force of the torrent and deposited in the shallows, where I was ultimately found by a Swiss youth. I spent some weeks in a coma. The Swiss doctors were beginning to despair of me when I opened my eyes one morning and asked where I was. Happily, none of my faculties were impaired. I recovered all my powers.'

'Luckily for us,' said Lil.

'If we ever get to the point,' said Grievous.

The old man appeared to sense that some acceleration was necessary. He made a leap of many years. 'With the advent of computers, I rediscovered all my old zest for numerical analysis. Are you familiar with the terminology? Have you heard of hacking?'

'Breaking into computers?' said Grievous with enthusiasm.

'Crudely expressed, yes. It is an activity peculiarly suited to my present capacities. Physically, I am not so active now. Mentally, I am as alert as ever. Hacking is my chief joy in life. No computer has yet been invented that is proof against my ingenuity. The Bank of England, the Stock Exchange—'

'But have you heard of Holmes?' asked Grievous.

'The name is not unknown to me,' answered the Professor with a strange curl of the lip.

'The police computer – can you nobble it?'

'Give me a month,' said the Professor, adding, with a fine grasp of modern vernacular, 'So long as the bread is up front.'

In the next weeks there was astonishing activity. With Lil acting as the Professor's buyer, vast sums were invested in computer hardware. Such was the drain on resources that Grievous had to order a million-pound bank job to finance the operation.

'He must be knee-deep in chips by now,' Grievous commented.

'It's a mammoth assignment, sweetheart,' Lil told him, 'but progress is spectacular.'

They installed the machinery in a Surrey mansion owned by a forger who was unavoidably detained elsewhere. In this secret location, the Professor worked undisturbed apart from occasional visits from Lil. After three weeks, word came through that he had succeeded in getting a line into Holmes.

Grievous lost no time in summoning the underworld bosses for a demonstration. One month to the day that the Professor had agreed to help, a stream of limousines with dark-tinted windows arrived at the Surrey mansion. The mobsters and villains hurried inside and stood uneasily in the ornate pillared entrance hall muttering obscenities and dropping cigar-ash on the Persian carpet.

Grievous let them wait a full twenty minutes before making his entrance down the marble staircase. So that there should be no confusion who took the credit for outwitting Holmes, he was alone. Silicon Lil was already on her flight to the Bahamas and the Professor had been given his fee and shown the door. This was the moment of triumph for Grievous, his confirmation as the Godfather of British crime.

'Today, gentlemen,' he announced, 'I will show you why Holmes is no longer a threat. Come this way.'

He led them into a vast room as cluttered with computer

hardware as the last reel of a James Bond movie. 'Take your seats,' he said in a voice resonant with authority. 'There should be a VDU for each of you.'

Porno Sullivan, the vice king, gave him a filthy look. 'I didn't come here to be insulted.'

'A visual display unit,' Grievous explained. 'A box with a glass front just like the telly, right? Now, comrades in crime, don't touch the keyboards yet. What you have at your fingertips is the underworld's answer to Holmes. Let's face it, a month ago we were in dead lumber. Holmes could have put us all away for the rest of our naturals. Holmes: don't let the name worry you – that was just a public relations exercise. Sherlock Holmes was said to be infallible, but we know he was just a work of fiction. Some nutters believe he really existed, and that he's still living in retirement somewhere on the Sussex Downs keeping bees. He'd be over 130 by now. I've heard of honey being good for your health, but that's ridiculous.' He paused to let the audience appreciate his wit, but nobody laughed.

'Get on with it,' Porno urged.

'All right. When I heard about Holmes, I didn't panic. I happen to know a little about computers, gentlemen. I've been working on the problem, and I'm glad to say I've cracked it. What you see in front of you is our own computer, plugged into the private circuit out of Scotland Yard. I call it Moriarty.'

'Morrie who?'

'Moriarty, Sherlock Holmes's greatest enemy.'

'Professor Moriarty, the Napoleon of crime,' said Porno, who had done some reading in his youth. 'Not the happiest of choices, Grievous. He came to a nasty end, didn't he? Got pushed off a ledge by Holmes.'

This came as a shock to Grievous. He was less familiar with the works of Sir Arthur Conan Doyle than he made out. He hadn't known, until Porno spoke up, that Moriarty had been a professor. Was it possible . . . For one distracting moment, he remembered the *Accident Victim* notice around his saviour the Professor's neck. He pulled himself together. 'Never mind about him. This computer is known as Moriarty, and you want to know why? Listen: Microcomputer Output Rendered Impotent And Rot The Yard.'

A burst of spontaneous applause greeted this popular sentiment.

Grievous basked in their approval a moment and then went on, 'To keep it simple, Moriarty gives us total access to Holmes. By using the password, we can call up our own police records and examine them. Better still, we can alter them, erase them—'

'Or give them to some other bleeder?' suggested Porno.

Grievous gave him a withering look. 'That wouldn't be comradely, would it? Now I shall key in the password and you can type out your names on the keyboards and examine your form.'

It worked like a dream. The coos and whistles that presently ensued were music to Grievous's ears. The delegates were like kids on Christmas morning. For a happy hour or more Grievous went from one to another giving instruction and encouragement as they learned how to make their criminal records unintelligible.

It was 'Hash' Brown, the drugs supremo, who had the gentlemanly idea of calling up Silicon Lil's record and erasing it for her. After all, she wasn't there to do it for herself.

He entered her name.

Instead of a criminal record, there flashed onto the screen a quaintly worded instruction:

PRAY BE PRECISE AS TO DETAILS.

With a frown, Hash cleared the screen. He called out to Grievous, 'What's Lil's full name?'

'Lilian Norton.' Grievous spelt it for him.

This time, Hash got the following:

NORTON, LILIAN

A.K.A. SILICON LIL. BORN 1/4/54, KNIGHTS-BRIDGE. PARENTS: JAMES & MARY NORTON. NIGHT CLUB PERFORMER & ASSOCIATE OF GEORGE 'GRIEVOUS' HARMER (SEE FILE). PRISON RECORD: MAY, 1985, 1 MONTH, DRUNK AND DISORDERLY; DEC, 1986, 3 MONTHS, HARBOUR-ING A KNOWN CRIMINAL. NOTE: GREAT-GRANDFATHER RUMOURED TO HAVE BEEN CHILD OF GODFREY NORTON & IRENE ADLER. SEE: A SCANDAL IN BOHEMIA.

'What's this about a Scandal in Bohemia?' said Hash.

'One of the Sherlock Holmes stories,' said Porno. ' "To Sherlock Holmes she is always *the* woman." '

'Who?'

'Irene Adler.'

'Let me look at that,' said Grievous. 'Move aside a minute.'

He keyed in the name Irene Adler and got the following response:

NOW, WATSON, THE FAIR SEX IS YOUR DEPARTMENT.

'Who the hell is Watson?' asked Hash.

Grievous was already tapping out another message:

AM I IN COMMUNICATION WITH MR SHER-LOCK HOLMES?

Instantly came the response:

IT IS AN OLD MAXIM OF MINE THAT WHEN YOU HAVE EXCLUDED THE IMPOSSIBLE, WHAT-EVER REMAINS, HOWEVER IMPROBABLE, MUST BE THE TRUTH.

'Well, that beats everything,' said Grievous.

All the others had left their VDUs to see what was happening. They watched in fascination as Grievous typed in:

ARE YOU REALLY WORKING FOR SCOTLAND YARD?

Holmes responded:

I SHALL BE MY OWN POLICE. WHEN I HAVE SPUN THE WEB, THEY MAY TAKE THE FLIES, BUT NOT BEFORE.

'I don't like this,' said Porno. 'I don't like it at all.'

Precisely at that instant the screen went blank as if the power supply had been cut. Every other machine in the room behaved likewise.

Then a voice announced over an amplifier, 'This is the police. We are armed, and we have the building surrounded. Listen carefully to these instructions.'

Grievous rushed to the window. The drive was cluttered with police vans. He could see the marksmen and the dogs. Resistance would be pointless.

That, in short, was how the entire leadership of the underworld was taken into custody. While they were sitting in the van on their way to be questioned, Grievous blurted out the whole extraordinary story to Porno, and then asked, 'Where did I go wrong?'

'You trusted Lil. She was working for Holmes.'

'The computer?'

'No, the guy who fancied her great-grandmother.'

'Come off it, Porno. He isn't still around.'

Porno gave him an old-fashioned look. 'I've been thinking about this Professor of yours. Holmes was a master of disguise and he played the violin. He retired to Sussex, which happens to connect with Victoria Station.'

Grievous was wide-eyed. 'Still alive? And into computers? Unbelievable!'

'Elementary,' said Porno dismally.

The Man Who Ate People

NO ONE KNEW THE GIRL. She turned up at the rec one Friday morning in the summer holiday when the hard lads from Class 5 were doing nothing except keeping the younger kids from using the swings. Gary and Clive were taking turns at smoking a cigarette. Podge Mahoney was trying to mend a faulty wheel on his skateboard. Daley Hughes and his brother Morgan were on the swings – not using them in the conventional way, which would have been soft, but twisting them so that the chains entwined. The rest of the bunch, including Mitch – by common consent the most mature – lounged on the grass talking about the bikes they wanted to possess.

None of the girls from Class 5 ventured anywhere near. This incautious miss strolled up to the unoccupied swing, backed against it to push off and started swinging, her eyes focused far ahead, excluding the lads from her vision. Thin, pale-skinned, with a straw-coloured pony-tail, she was in black jeans and a white tee-shirt.

Several heads turned towards Mitch for a lead. Mitch possessed the coveted first floss of a moustache and he generally spoke for all of them if required. He leaned back on his elbows and said, 'Someone wants a swing. Give 'em some help.'

Paul, the boy Mitch had addressed, said, 'Come on,' to Clive. The pair got behind the girl on the swing, waited for it to come to them, tucked their fingers over the seat and heaved it forward. When it had soared high and swung back, they gave it another push, straining high to catch it at the peak. The rest of the lads chorused support with a rising 'Wooooo!'

Against expectation, the girl didn't scream. Indeed, as the swing soared to the high point of its arc, almost level with the crossbar, she brought her knees up to her chest to secure a footing. Then she braced and stood upright – an acrobatic feat that few, if any, of the watchers would have essayed.

The ironwork groaned. Paul and Clive stepped out of range, for the girl was imparting her own momentum to the swing, hoisting it still higher by getting leverage bending her knees and virtually kicking the seat upwards. She looked capable of going right over the top. She was fearless. The mocking chorus had already died in the throats of the watchers. The girl kept the display going for long enough to demonstrate that she was doing it from choice. When at length she signalled the end of the ride by straightening on the swing, making herself a dead weight, there was an awed silence. After the swing was still again, she remained standing on the seat, arms folded, only her left shoulder lodged against the chain to keep her balanced.

'What's your name?' Podge Mahoney asked. He'd given up fiddling with his skateboard.

'Danny.'

'That's a boy's name.'

'Danielle.' She made it sound like Daniel.

'What school?'

'Grantley.'

'Never heard of it.'

'It's a private boarding school.'

Roger, who was a good mimic, repeated the statement in the accent of the private boarding school.

The girl was undeterred. 'What are your plans for

today? What are you going to do?'

'Nothing much,' said Podge.

'That's our business,' Mitch said, sensing that the girl was trying to gatecrash.

'Mind if I join in?' Danny asked.

'Course we mind,' said Mitch. 'Piss off.'

'I can get cigarettes.'

'Fags?' said Clive. 'You can get fags?'

'We wouldn't take bribes,' said Mitch, and several faces fell.

'What are you, a gang, or something?'

'No,' said Mitch, who was known, and respected, for the honesty of his statements.

'I want to join.'

'Don't be so dumb.'

Clive added, 'Find some girls to play with.'

She shifted her position on the swing just a fraction and braced her legs, imparting a shudder to the structure. 'Who's going to make me?'

No one answered. Podge walked across to his skateboard and started taking an interest in the wheels again.

She was a scrap of a girl really, but her manner unsettled everyone. She said in her elegant voice, 'Anyway, you look like a gang to me. If you were a gang, what would one have to do to join?'

All eyes turned in Mitch's direction. No one else was capable of answering such a hypothetical question. Until now nobody had thought of the group as a gang. They were just the kids from Class 5 obliged to hang about the rec until they thought of something better to do. At the end of the summer they would go to secondary schools and be dispersed among a number of classes that would be called 'forms'. For these few remaining weeks they clung to the familiar.

Mitch pondered the possible entrance requirements of

the hypothetical gang. He was sure it wouldn't be enough to say that girls were excluded. This one was unlikely to accept the logic that she was different.

He had to think of something she wouldn't contest. At length he said, 'If we were a gang, which we aren't, I'd make a rule that anyone who joined had to show their thing.'

The rest didn't share his seriousness. There were cackles of amusement. Morgan said, 'Girls haven't got things.'

'Shut up, toerag.'

The laughter stopped, quelled by the force of Mitch's putdown. Nobody wanted to catch his eye.

The girl Danny said, 'If I do, am I in?'

Mitch was finding it difficult to cope with her erratic reasoning. Clinging doggedly to reality, he said, 'It isn't a question of being in or out. We don't have a gang, okay?'

'Anyway,' added Clive to the girl, 'you wouldn't dare.'

Nobody anticipated that she would take them up on the dare at once, in broad daylight, in the rec, in full view of any grown-ups who happened to be passing. She unfastened the top button of her jeans and called across to Mitch, 'You won't see from over there.'

She proposed to display herself standing on the swing. For a moment everyone held back in awe. Then Podge Mahoney took a step closer. It was the signal for a general advance. Daley and Morgan disentangled themselves from the other swings. A half-circle formed in front of the girl. Mitch, on his dignity, had to decide how to react. The others had left no doubt of their commitment. If he missed this, he'd be like the kid sent early to bed the night they showed *Jaws* on TV. He was the last to his feet, but nobody noticed, or cared. The girl Danny had turned an intended humiliation into a show of power.

She gripped the front of her jeans and said, 'Ready?'

A couple of heads nodded, but no one spoke.

In a slick movement she slid jeans and knickers down a

short way. Most of Class 5 had been initiated into *la différence* at some time in their lives; none so publicly, nor with such nonchalance.

'All right,' she said as she drew the jeans up again, 'someone else's turn.' She pointed to Mitch. 'Yours.'

The tension broke to howls of laughter, gleeful at Mitch's discomfiture and relieved that Danny hadn't pointed to anyone else.

'On the swing, Mitch!'

Mitch glared at Clive, who had made the remark. Of all the lads, Clive was the one he would have counted on to support him. How could loyalty be so brittle? 'Shut up! Shut up, the lot of you!'

They didn't shut up, so he had to continue to shout to be heard. 'This ain't a bloody game. It was to see if she could join some gang, but there ain't a gang, is there?'

Someone said, 'Chicken.'

Someone else said, 'Get 'em off.'

It only wanted someone to shout, 'Debag him!' and they would be on him like wolves.

Then Danny the girl, still aloft on the swing, spoke up. 'Mitch is right. There isn't a gang, but if there was, I'd be in. Who's going to give me another swing?'

Shouts of, 'Me!' sprang up all round her.

Mitch's dignity was preserved. His authority was in tatters, and he couldn't think where he had made his mistake.

In the week that followed, Danny dispelled the summer boredom with marvellous suggestions. She knew a way into the dump where the scrapped cars were heaped high. It was her idea to cross the railway lines and build a camp on the embankment out of old sleepers and slabs of turf someone had left there. She turned the multi-storey car park into a Cresta Run, using supermarket trolleys as sledges. When they were told by the attendant to stop, she negotiated a fee of twelve pounds with the fête secretary for pushing leaflets under the wipers of cars. The experiences unified the group as never before. They actually were becoming a gang.

Yet Danny's influence was discreetly managed. She made no overt bid for the leadership; rather, she made a show of deferring to Mitch, seeking his approval. She would let him distribute the cigarettes she brought with her most mornings. Sometimes she let Mitch carry the day with his own suggestions. Unfortunately when the daily cry of 'What shall we do?' went up, Mitch could never think of anything they hadn't done before, so there were days when they played football or went fishing complaining that it was a drag.

He knew he ought to do better. His lack of originality depressed him. He lost sleep trying to think of new challenges. In the bleakness of the night all he could see in his mind's eye were the faces of Class 5, mouths downturned, eyes glazed in boredom. It wasn't as if they lived by the sea, or in the country, where adventures were to be had. No circuses ever came through their suburban town. No pop concerts, No marathons. Not even Billy Graham.

The idea, when it came, almost escaped Mitch. Like a butterfly it fluttered within range and eluded his grasp. He captured it clumsily at the third attempt.

Over breakfast one Monday, submerged in gloom at the prospect of another meeting in the rec, he failed to hear his father the first time.

'Wake up, lad.'

'Wha'?'

'I was saying that somebody slipped a leaflet about the fête under my windscreen wiper – in my own garage.'

Mitch did his best to produce a sunny smile. 'That was me, Dad. I had a few left over. Me and some of the kids—'

'Some of my friends and I.'

'We were going round the car park Saturday.'

Mr Mitchell's eyebrows bobbed up. 'Helping the church fête committee? Making yourselves useful for a change? Whose idea was that – yours?'

'Em, one of the others', I think.'

'Never mind. I like it. I won't be going to the fête myself, but I approve the spirit of the venture.' Mr Mitchell had long nursed an ambition to see his son as a boy scout, but Mitch, with a distaste for uniforms, had refused to join.

'Why aren't you going, Dad?'

'On principle, son. I don't approve of a certain gentleman they've invited to open it.'

'Sam Coldharbour?' Mitch was stunned. He had long been convinced that his father revered people who achieved things. Sam Coldharbour had climbed Everest and walked across America. He had boxed for Britain in the Olympics. He was the most famous person for miles around. Moreover, the Mitchells hadn't missed a fête in Mitch's lifetime. Mitch's father had twice been chairman of the committee. 'Don't you like him, Dad?'

'It isn't a question of like or dislike. I don't know the man personally. It's just that I'm unwilling to shake the hand of a man who behaves as he does.'

'Now, Frank,' said Mitch's mother in the voice she used to stop conversations that threatened to offend.

'What does he do?' asked Mitch.

'Not over breakfast,' said Mitch's mother.

'The man may be a hero to some, but he isn't to me,' Mitch's father insisted on saying, more to Mrs Mitchell than the boy. 'He isn't even discreet with his philandering.'

'What's philandering, Dad?'

'It's misconduct.'

'Frank, please!'

'But it's true. The man preys on women – ladies, I mean.'

'Prays – like in church?'

'No, you stupid boy. I used the word "prey" in the sense

249

of hunting.'

'Hunting – like a tiger?'

'A wolf, if you ask me.'

'Frank!'

At the rec an hour or so later, Mitch related to an enthralled audience what he had learned about Sam Coldharbour, the man chosen to open the church fête. 'My Dad calls him a wolf.'

'A werewolf?' said Roger, eyes popping.

'I said a wolf. He goes philandering. Any of you lot heard of philandering before? No? I thought not. Well, I'll have to tell you, won't I? It's hunting ladies. Mr Coldharbour goes around hunting ladies.'

There was a thoughtful silence.

'What does he do if he catches one?' Podge asked.

There was some coarse laughter. Class 5 knew what men and women were supposed to do together.

'You're wrong,' said Mitch with his regard for the literal truth. 'What do wolves do if they catch people?'

'Kill them?' said Clive, after a pause. Class 5 also knew a lot about horror and fantasy.

'Eat them?' said Daley.

Mitch opened his hands in a gesture that seemed to say there was no accounting for the things grown-ups got up to.

Morgan pulled a face and said, 'Ugh.'

'I don't believe it,' said Danny. 'People don't eat each other in Worcester Park.'

Mitch rose to the challenge he had anticipated ever since Danny had gategrashed. 'Why not?' he demanded. 'He didn't always live here.'

'He'd have to be a cannibal, and you can see he isn't,' said Danny. 'How many of you lot have seen Mr Coldharbour?'

Half a dozen hands were hoisted.

'Well, then,' she said, as if the matter were settled. She walked to the swing and gave it a push.

Mitch was about to defend his assertion by claiming that

anything his Dad said was the truth when he thought of a better riposte. 'He's travelled all over the world, Sam Coldharbour has. He's been up in the mountains and through jungles and on desert islands. He must have met some cannibals on one of his expeditions. If a cannibal asks you to come to a feast, you don't say no. That's how it started, I reckon.'

'You reckon?' said Podge.

'Yes,' said Mitch with decision. 'I reckon. He joined in a cannibal feast.'

Clive came to his aid. 'And then he got a taste for it. Once you've tasted human flesh, everything else tastes like old socks.'

'Podge's socks,' said Roger, and everyone laughed, including Podge. They needed to laugh.

Boys of that age are not fastidious about much, and they'll talk about anything. They argued lustily whether cannibalism could be justified for survival, but it was clear that whatever they claimed to the contrary, few, if any, cared to think of it close to home.

Danny the girl listened, contributing nothing else. She waited for the arguments to run their course and then said, 'Isn't it time we decided what to do?'

Mitch proposed cops and robbers and everyone groaned.

That evening Mitch heard his father on the phone talking about the fête. Someone from the committee was evidently trying to get him to reconsider his decision to stay away, but he was adamant. 'I don't need telling Coldharbour's fame will increase the attendance no end, but I have my principles, Reggie. I don't approve of the fellow. I don't care for the way he conducts his life . . . The women are what I'm talking about, and what he gets up to at that disagreeable house of his in Almond Avenue . . . All right, I may be behind the times, but I try to lead a decent life. I've seen Coldharbour in action. I was at the tennis

251

club dance last autumn when he was supposed to be partnering Hettie Herzog. He got a sight of that pretty little girl who works in the cakeshop – Linda? Belinda? – something like that. She's married to the chap who runs the bar. He cut Hettie stone dead and started nuzzling Linda in front of her husband. I didn't enquire what happened later, but I've a pretty good idea. What could the husband do? Coldharbour boxed for England. He's had four different women since then, to my certain knowledge. Married or single, they're all meat and drink to Sam Coldharbour. No, I don't wish to meet him. I don't wish to go within a mile of the man.'

Mitch listened with fascination that turned to awe. If there had been any doubt before of the news he had conveyed to Class 5 – and he *had* rather overstated his confidence – such doubt had just been removed. Four women . . . all meat and drink to Sam Coldharbour.

The next morning found Mitch in Almond Avenue staring through the railings at Coldharbour's house, a modern construction with flat roofs and arched windows distinctly out of keeping with the mock-Tudor 1930s houses on either side. The grounds were spacious enough for a tennis court and a good-sized swimming pool, with a diving-board. While Mitch was staring in, thinking about the owner, he had his idea.

He came straight to the point when the gang assembled at the usual place. 'You know what Clive said about eating people?' Since nobody appeared to remember, he said, 'Once you get a taste for it, you can't stop. It's like drugs. Sam Coldharbour's had five women this year.'

'*Eaten* them?' piped Roger in horror.

'My Dad says they're meat and drink to him, married or not.'

'Who said?' asked Danny the girl. It took a lot to alarm her, but there was a gratifying glint of concern in her eyes.

'I told you. My old man.'

Danny said nothing else and no one questioned the statement. After all, Mitch was always so scrupulous about the truth.

'I've thought of a brill dare,' Mitch went on. 'On Saturday, when old Coldharbour opened the fête, he isn't going to be at home for an hour or so, is he? Well, who's coming for a swim in the cannibal's pool?'

He might, perhaps, have phrased it more invitingly.

'Can't swim,' said Podge.

'Just a dip in the shallow end, then.'

'I'm going to the fête with my Mum,' said Paul.

'Chicken.'

'It's a great dare,' said Clive with more craft. 'If all of us do it, I'm in.'

'I got athlete's foot,' said Morgan. 'I'm supposed to keep it dry.'

It was Danny who swung the decision by simply saying, 'I'll be there, Mitch.'

Seven others were shamed into enlisting.

The fête organizers were rewarded with brilliant sunshine on Saturday. From behind a builder's skip in Almond Avenue at one fifty-five p.m., eight of the would-be bathers watched Sam Coldharbour drive out between the stone pillars of number eleven in his BMW.

'All right, who's coming?' Mitch challenged the others.

Podge said, 'Danny ain't here yet.'

'She must have chickened out,' Clive said. He gave Mitch a supportive smile. 'What do you expect from a girl? We can't wait for her.'

Mitch led them in, sprinting full pelt up the drive and across a stretch of lawn to the green-tiled surround of the pool. Lattice patterns of sunlight made the water look specially inviting. Mitch stripped completely, ran to the diving board and took a header in. Clive followed. Some of the boys had prudently put on swimming-trunks under their clothes, but no one wanted to risk derision, so everything came off. Immersion made them feel secure. Soon they were shouting and splashing each other as if it were the town pool.

At some point Mitch came up from a dive and saw Danny standing by the edge. She was dressed as if for church, in blouse, skirt, socks and shoes. Her hair was in bunches tied with white ribbon. He grabbed Clive's arm and pointed. Clive wasn't going to miss an opening like this. He called out derisively to the others, 'Look who's finally turned up.'

'My mother made me go to the fête,' Danny explained. 'I only just got away.'

'Coming in?' Mitch called out.

'There isn't time.'

'Course there's time.'

'There isn't. He'll be back soon. When I left, he was walking round the stalls, but it won't take him long to get round. You'd better get out.'

They hesitated, each boy swivelling his head to see if one of the others was willing to climb out first. Truth to tell, the hard lads of Class 5 had turned coy. Their naked state in front of the girl – the girl with no inhibitions about her own body – was a more immediate concern than being caught and eaten by Sam Coldharbour.

She said, 'I think I can hear the car.' She turned to look along the drive.

There was turmoil in the water. Modesty abandoned, everyone struck out for the side. Lily-white bottoms were everywhere exposed, bent over the tiled edges of the pool in the scramble to get out.

'It's him!' Danny shouted.

To shrieks of alarm, the bathing party broke up. No one had time to put on clothes. They grabbed their things and scampered across the grass, dropping garments as they fled.

A squeal of brakes from Sam Coldharbour's BMW

added to the panic. The car skidded and stopped, raising dust. Coldharbour leapt out and sprinted after someone. Mitch saw enough to convince himself that it would be suicidal to try and get through the gate, so he made for the railings some way down. He flung his clothes over, grabbed the top and hauled himself up. He perched up there a moment before leaping to the pavement. The sense of relief at getting out was so overwhelming that it took him a second or two to realise that he was standing naked in a suburban street. He went behind a tree and struggled into his clothes. He was a sock short, but he didn't care.

Further along Almond Avenue, Podge had made a similar escape. He'd left both shoes in the garden.

Daley and Morgan came running from the other direction. 'Anyone get caught?' Morgan asked.

'Don't know,' Mitch admitted. 'Let's go back to the rec. That's where we'll meet.'

'If he *did* catch anyone—' Podge started to say.

'Your shirt's inside out,' Mitch interposed.

Members of the bathing party arrived at the swings at intervals and told of narrow escapes and grazed flesh and missing garments. Clive insisted that he'd been thrown to the ground by old Coldharbour and only got away because he was still wet and too slippery to hold. Nobody placed much reliance on things Clive said.

Roger had gone straight home feeling sick, but all eight of the bathers were accounted for.

'What about Danny?' Mitch said. 'Did anyone see Danny get out?'

'He was chasing her,' said Podge. 'I saw the cannibal chasing her.'

'She's an ace runner,' said Clive. 'She'll turn up soon.'

His optimism wasn't justified. The shadow of the swing lengthened and faded in the dusk and Danny didn't come.

'She must have gone straight home,' Clive said eventually.

'We ought to make sure,' said Podge.

'How can we, you fat git?' Mitch rounded on him. 'We don't know where she lives.'

'We ought to tell the police or something.'

'If she doesn't come home, her mum will report it.'

Mitch's faith in grown-ups prevailed. It was conceded that nothing could be done and they dispersed, after vowing to assemble again at the same place next day. 'And I bet she turns up as usual,' said Clive.

In reality Mitch had a horrid conviction that Clive was mistaken. Danny would not turn up, and he was responsible for the adventure that had gone so tragically wrong. In bed that night, he struggled to reassure himself that somehow his father must have been misinformed and cannibalism had not broken out in suburban Worcester Park. No one could get away with it, even if they were so ghoulish as to try. But the fears returned at intervals through the night.

In the morning everyone except Danny turned up at the rec. The optimists among them said they should wait. Clive wanted to go to the police right away.

'No,' said Podge. 'They don't believe kids like us. We'll get done for trespassing, and it'll all get in the papers, and our new schools will know about it.'

'What are we going to do, then?' said Clive. 'We can't just forget about Danny. She's in the gang.'

'It was never a gang,' said Mitch.

'Was.'

'Wasn't.'

'Was.'

'While you're arguing,' said Clive, 'Danny might still be alive. She could be killed any minute.'

Mitch may have been short of original ideas, but he was sharp enough to tell when his leadership was under threat. This was a moment for action. 'We're going back to the house.'

'What?'

'We're going to get Danny out. If we stick together, there's enough of us to take on anyone, even old Coldharbour. Strength in numbers, right?' He held a fist aloft.

'Right,' said Clive raising a fist.

'Right,' said the others with less animation.

For mutual encouragement, they marched like a platoon to Almond Avenue, swinging their arms high and trying to stay in step. At the railings of Sam Coldharbour's house they halted.

'Look,' said Morgan.

Anyone cherishing the hope that the man who ate people might have slipped out for an hour, to church, or the paper shop, or to walk the dog, must have felt a draining of enthusiasm at the sight of the prominently muscled figure reclining beside his swimming pool on a sun-lounger.

Mitch, however, was equal to the challenge. He believed that they were capable of rescuing Danny if she was still alive. And he did accept responsibility for what had happened to her. This was the right way, the man's way, to put things right. He felt like a leader now.

He explained how they would take care of Sam Coldharbour.

They climbed over the railings at the place where the foliage was thickest and crept like Indians around the perimeter, using the shrubs as cover, and staying close to the railings. The reclining figure continued to recline. No one else was in the vicinity of the pool.

A toolshed stood close to the railings near a kitchen garden, and this was where they headed first. Their luck was in. It was unlocked, and there was room for everyone inside. Better still, the shed was well-equipped. The boys started arming themselves with garden tools. Roger had a large wooden mallet. Morgan and Daley started to wrestle for possession of a scythe.

'What do you think you're doing?' Mitch said in a voice that shamed them all. 'Put those things down. We don't want to get in a fight.'

'We might,' said Podge. 'We need to arm ourselves.'

'Bollocks,' said Mitch. 'We need both hands free. Our weapon is surprise.'

So it was that in a moment the Class 5 assault team emerged from the toolshed armed with nothing more lethal than several lengths of rope and a narrow-mesh net, of the sort used for keeping birds off redcurrant bushes. This was the most dangerous stage of the operation, for they had to cross an open stretch of lawn.

Mitch led the advance, his eyes fixed on the recumbent figure of Sam Coldharbour. The eight small boys moved stealthily but rapidly towards the ex-Olympian, who still didn't stir. His eyes opened only when Mitch was so close that he blotted out the sun.

This was Mitch's first close sight of the cannibal's face, and it was not so frightening as it had been in his mind's eye. The teeth were not the vampire-fangs he had pictured and the eyes weren't, after all, narrow slits edged with red. Close up, Sam Coldharbour was unremarkable, the more so when an oily rag was spread over his face and the net thrown across the entire length of his body and held down by six boys, while two others passed ropes around, to secure him to the frame of the sunlounger. Morgan, who was strong in the arm and good at knots, drew the ends of the ropes tightly together and fastened them. Sam Coldharbour was efficiently trussed, his protests muffled by the rag. It had all been done so rapidly that Mitch doubted if any of them had been recognized.

'Leave him,' he ordered. 'We're going into the house.'

With a perceptible swagger, he led his commandos across the patio and up to the house. The patio window was slightly open. It squeaked as he pushed it aside. He had never been inside a house so modern-looking, or so large. There was steel and leather and stripped pine and huge plants in white containers. 'You three take the downstairs,' he told Clive, Daley and Roger. 'We'll try the bedrooms. And remember,' he said in an afterthought to Clive, 'to look in the freezer.'

The house was silent except for their footsteps on the spiral staircase, which was made of wrought iron, painted white. With a silent prayer that they would find Danny still alive, Mitch progressed to the landing and opened the first door. The room was some sort of office, with maps on the walls. He tried the next. A bathroom. Then discovered a bedroom with a single bed, a featureless room devoid of anything notable except what Podge noticed – a pair of blue and white trainers half hidden under the bed.

'Those are Danny's.'

'She's here, then,' said Mitch.

'She was,' said Podge in a low voice.

Mitch shuddered. 'We'll try the other rooms.'

Two more unoccupied bedrooms.

The last door on their left was ajar. Mitch pushed it open, and stood staring. The room contained a huge circular bed, out of keeping with the other furnishings, which in Mitch's opinion were silly for a bedroom – a glass-fronted cocktail cabinet, a fridge, a music centre and pink-tinted mirrors the length of two of the walls. When his gaze travelled upwards, he saw that another vast, pink mirror was attached to the ceiling.

It was in the reflection on the ceiling that Mitch noticed something stir in the untidy heap of bedclothes. 'Someone's there!' he told Podge. 'Come on.'

He approached the bed, with Podge observing a judicious step behind him. For a worrying second or two Mitch wondered if he was in error. The bedclothes were quite still.

Then they were flung aside and a red-haired woman sat up and shouted, 'What in the name of Satan . . .?'

The words didn't trouble Mitch so much as the sight of her rearing up from the bed, not unlike a ship's figurehead he had once seen in a maritime museum. She was bare-breasted and gave every appearance of being carved out of oak and painted bright pink with dabs of crimson on the points of her chest. No doubt the effect was partly due to the light from the mirrors and partly to Mitch's immaturity. Female torsos in general had yet to persuade him that they were anything but grotesque.

Without even covering herself, the woman demanded, 'Just what do you think you're doing here?'

'Looking for someone,' answered Podge, over Mitch's shoulder.

Mitch found his voice. 'Our friend Danny.'

She said, 'Danny? You're friends of Danny? Bloody liberty – I'll have her guts for garters. Get out, the lot of you. Out!'

He heard the others act on the order. Before going after them, he stood his ground long enough to say, 'You want to watch out. It could be you next.' Far from being grateful for the advice, the woman gave signs of rolling out of bed in pursuit. That was too much for Mitch. He fled.

Downstairs, Clive was waiting with the others. 'She ain't here,' they said in chorus, and Clive added, 'We're too late.'

'Did you look in the freezer?'

'It's stacked to the top with peas and things from Sainsbury's. We couldn't move all the stuff.'

From the bedroom upstairs the woman shouted, 'I'll call the police.'

'We've got to get out,' said Podge. 'There's nothing we can do, Mitch.'

'Danny must be dead by now,' said Clive. 'If the police come, they'll find out.'

'That lady upstairs won't call them,' Mitch said, trying to calm his troops. 'She's in it. She knew about Danny. Is

260

there anywhere we haven't looked – a cellar, or a garage?'
He knew as he spoke that any gang-leader worthy of the
name would have said something more positive.

Morgan said, 'I don't bloody care. I'm off.'

'Me, too,' said his brother Daley. 'Who's coming?'

Not everyone was so frank. One or two muttered
inaudible things before they followed Morgan out.

'Wimps!' Mitch called after them.

If the slur was heard, it was not heeded. The 'gang', all
of it, including Clive, deserted. Mitch stepped out to the
patio and watched his friends in flight, the seven he would
have claimed as his closest mates, haring along the drive
towards Almond Avenue. He knew for certain that his
authority, his credibility as leader, was gone for ever. They
were the quitters, yet he would be blamed.

He still felt driven to find out what had happened to
Danny. He was about to go around the side of the house in
search of a cellar when he became conscious of something
that shouldn't be. Some part of his brain was functioning
independently, trying to convey information, an observa-
tion. He stared about him uncertainly.

Then he realised what was amiss: the swimming pool
was deserted. Sam Coldharbour was no longer beside it,
tied to the sun-lounger. The sun-lounger itself was gone.

If Coldharbour was free, danger was imminent.

He heard a sound close by, and swung around. It wasn't
Sam Coldharbour standing behind him, and it wasn't the
woman from upstairs. It was Danny.

She was in shorts and a tee-shirt, and was barefoot. She
said solemnly, 'Thanks, Mitch.'

'We thought you were dead,' he said in a whisper. His
real voice wouldn't function. 'Come on, let's run for it!'

She said in her flat, unexcited way, 'There's no need to
run.'

'He'll get us.'

'He won't.'

'There's a woman as well.'

'She's my mother,' said Danny, then added, 'I know what you're thinking and you're right. Your Dad was right, too. She's another stupid woman who got tricked by Sam Coldharbour. He told her she was adorable, and stuff like that. She moved in here four weeks ago. School had broken up and I had nowhere else to go.'

'You mean you lived here all this time?'

'Stayed here.'

'Why didn't you tell us?'

'I was ashamed.'

'When you didn't come out last night, we thought you were caught. Podge saw him chasing you.'

'He did. He was in a foul temper. He grabbed my hair and pulled me inside and spanked my bum. *Him!* My mother thought it was a real joke. She locked me in my room for swearing at him. She sided with him.' Danny's lips drained of blood as she pressed her mouth shut.

Mitch said, 'We thought he was going to kill you and eat you.'

'That was dumb.' She gave a faint smile. 'But I'm glad about what you did.'

Mitch shook his head. 'We did bugger all except tie him up.'

Then Danny surprised him by catching hold of his wrist. 'I want to show you something.'

Still keeping hold of him, she led him across the patio and over a stretch of lawn to the tiled surround of the pool. She pointed into it.

A breeze was sending ripples across the surface and for a moment Mitch thought the body underneath was struggling. It was not. Sam Coldharbour, roped to the lounger, his face still covered by the oily rag, was motionless at the bottom.

Mitch turned to look at Danny, his eyes huge with the horror of what was down there. 'We only tied him up. We

262

didn't do that.'

'I know,' said Danny.

Mitch glanced down at the smooth surface of the tiled surround and saw how simple it must have been to push the lounger over the edge. He knew what Danny had done, and he knew why. But he stopped himself from speaking prematurely. He turned away from the pool, biting his lip. Finally he said in his usual considered way, 'It must have moved because he was wriggling. He wriggled to try and get free and it sort of moved. He couldn't see where it was going. It was an accident.'

His eyes glistened. He despised himself, even when Danny squeezed his arm.

Supper with Miss Shivers

THE DOOR WAS STUCK. SOMETHING inside was stopping it from opening, and Fran was numb with cold. School had broken up for Christmas that afternoon – 'Lord dismiss us with Thy blessing' – and the jubilant kids had given her a blinding headache. She'd wobbled on her bike through the London traffic, two carriers filled with books suspended from the handlebars. She'd endured exhaust fumes and maniac motorists, and now she couldn't get into her own flat. She cursed, let the bike rest against her hip and attacked the door with both hands.

'It was quite scary actually,' she told Jim when he got in later. 'I mean the door opened perfectly well when we left this morning. We could have been burgled. Or it could have been a body lying in the hall.'

Jim, who worked as a systems analyst, didn't have the kind of imagination that expected bodies behind doors. 'So what was it – the doormat?'

'Get knotted. It was a great bundle of Christmas cards wedged under the door. Look at them. I blame you for this, James Palmer.'

'Me?'

Now that she was over the headache and warm again, she enjoyed poking gentle fun at Jim. 'Putting our address book on your computer and running the envelopes through the printer. This is the result. We're going to be up to our eyeballs in cards. I don't know how many you

264

sent, but we've heard from the plumber, the dentist, the television repairman and the people who moved us in, apart from family and friends. You must have gone straight through the address book. I won't even ask how many stamps you used.'

'What an idiot,' Jim admitted. 'I forgot to use the sorting function.'

'I left some for you to open.'

'I bet you've opened all the ones with cheques inside,' said Jim. 'I'd rather eat first.'

'I'm slightly mystified by one,' said Fran. 'Do you remember sending to someone called Miss Shivers?'

'No. I'll check if you like. Curious name.'

'It means nothing to me, but she's invited us to a meal.'

Fran handed him the card – one of those desolate, old-fashioned snow-scenes of someone dragging home a log. Inside, under the printed greetings, was the signature *E. Shivers (Miss)*, followed by *Please make my Christmas – come for supper 7pm next Sunday, 23rd.* In the corner was an address label.

'Never heard of her,' said Jim. 'Must be a mistake.'

'Maybe she sends her cards by computer,' said Fran, and added, before he waded in, 'I don't think it's a mistake, Jim. She named us on the envelope. I'd like to go.'

'For crying out loud – Didmarsh is miles away, Berkshire or somewhere. We're far too busy.'

'Thanks to your computer, we've got time in hand,' Fran told him with a smile.

The moment she'd seen the invitation, she'd known she would accept. Three or four times in her life she'd felt a similar impulse and each time she had been right. She didn't think of herself as psychic or telepathic, but sometimes she felt guided by some force that couldn't be explained scientifically. A good force, she was certain. It had convinced her that she should marry no one else but Jim, and after three years together she had no doubts.

265

Their love was unshakable. And because he loved her, he would take her to supper with Miss Shivers. He wouldn't understand *why* she was so keen to go, but he would see that she was in earnest, and that would be enough.

'By the way, I checked the computer,' he told her in front of the destinations board on Paddington Station next Sunday. 'We definitely didn't send a card to anyone called Shivers.'

'Makes it all the more exciting, doesn't it?' Fran said, squeezing his arm.

Jim was the first man she had trusted. Trust was her top requirement of the opposite sex. It didn't matter that he wasn't particularly tall and that his nose came to a point. He was loyal. And didn't Clint Eastwood have a pointed nose?

She'd learned from her mother's three disastrous marriages to be ultra-wary of men. The first – Fran's father, Harry – had started the rot. He'd died in a train crash just a few days before Fran was born. You'd think he couldn't be be blamed for that, but he could. Fran's mother had been admitted to hospital with complications in the eighth month, and Harry, the rat, had found someone else within a week. On the night of the crash he'd been in London with his mistress, buying her expensive clothes. He'd even lied to his pregnant wife, stuck in hospital, about working overtime.

For years Fran's mother had fended off the questions any child asks about a father she had never seen, telling Fran to forget him and love her stepfather instead. Stepfather the First had turned into a violent alcoholic. The divorce had taken nine years to achieve. Stepfather the Second – a Finn called Bengt (Fran called him Bent) – had treated their Wimbledon terraced house as if it were a sauna, insisting on communal baths and parading naked around the place. When Fran was reaching puberty there were terrible rows because she wanted privacy. Her

266

mother had sided with Bengt until one terrible night when he'd crept into Fran's bedroom and groped her. Bengt walked out of their lives the next day, but, incredibly to Fran, a lot of the blame seemed to be heaped on her, and her relationship with her mother had been damaged for ever. At forty-three, her mother, deeply depressed, had taken a fatal overdose.

The hurts and horrors of those years had not disappeared, but marriage to Jim had provided a fresh start. Fran nestled against him in the carriage and he fingered a strand of her dark hair. It was supposed to be an Intercity train, but BR were using old rolling-stock for some of the Christmas period and Fran and Jim had this compartment to themselves.

'Did you let this Shivers woman know we're coming?'

She nodded. 'I phoned. She's over the moon that I answered. She's going to meet us at the station.'

'What's it all about, then?'

'She didn't say, and I didn't ask.'

'You didn't? why not, for God's sake?'

'It's a mystery trip – a Christmas mystery. I'd rather keep it that way.'

'Sometimes, Fran, you leave me speechless.'

'Kiss me instead, then.'

A whistle blew somewhere and the line of taxis beside the platform appeared to be moving forward. Fran saw no more of the illusion because Jim had put his lips to hers.

Somewhere beyond Westbourne Park Station they noticed how foggy the late afternoon had become. After days of mild, damp weather, a proper December chill had set in. The heating in the carriage was working only in fits and starts and Fran was beginning to wish she'd worn trousers instead of opting decorously for her corduroy skirt and boots.

'Do you think it's warmer further up the train?'

'Want me to look?'

267

Jim slid aside the door. Before starting along the corridor, he joked, 'If I'm not back in half an hour, send for Miss Marple.'

'No need,' said Fran. 'I'll find you in the bar and mine's a hot cuppa.'

She pressed herself into the warm space Jim had left in the corner and rubbed a spy-hole in the condensation. There wasn't anything to spy. She shivered and wondered if she'd been right to trust her hunch and come on this trip. It was more than a hunch, she told herself. It was intuition.

It wasn't long before she heard the door pulled back. She expected to see Jim, or perhaps the man who checked the tickets. Instead there was a fellow about her own age, twenty-five, with a pink carrier bag containing something about the size of a box file. 'Do you mind?' he asked. 'The heating's given up altogether next door.'

Fran gave a shrug. 'I've got my doubts about the whole carriage.'

He took the corner seat by the door and placed the bag beside him. Fran took stock of him rapidly, hoping Jim would soon return. She didn't feel threatened, but she wasn't used to those old-fashioned compartments. She rarely used the trains these days except occasionally the Tube.

She decided the young man must have kitted himself in an Oxfam shop. He had a dark blue car coat, black trousers with flares and crêpe-soled ankle boots. Around his neck was one of those striped scarves that college students wore in the sixties, one end slung over his left shoulder. And his thick dark hair matched the image. Fran guessed he was unemployed. She wondered if he was going to ask her for money.

But he said, 'Been up to town for the day?'

'I live there.' She added quickly, 'With my husband. He'll be back presently.'

'I'm married, too,' he said, and there was a chink of

amusement in his eyes that Fran found reassuring. 'I'm up from the country, smelling of wellies and cow-dung. Don't care much for London. It's crazy in Bond Street this time of year.'

'*Bond Street?*' repeated Fran. She hadn't got him down as a big spender.

'This once,' he explained. 'It's special, this Christmas. We're expecting our first, my wife and I.'

'Congratulations.'

He smiled. A self-conscious smile. 'My wife Pearlie – that's my name for her – Pearlie made all her own maternity clothes, but she's really looking forward to being slim again. She calls herself the frump with a lump. After the baby arrives, I want her to have something glamorous, really special. She deserves it. I've been putting money aside for months. Do you want to see what I got? I found it in Elaine Ducharme.'

'I don't know it.'

'It's a very posh shop. I found the advert in some fashion magazine.' He had already taken the box from the carrier and was unwrapping the pink ribbon.

'You'd better not. It's gift-wrapped.'

'Tell me what you think,' he insisted, as he raised the lid, parted the tissue and lifted out the gift for his wife. It was a nightdress, the sort of nightdress, Fran privately reflected, that men misguidedly buy for the women they adore. Pale blue, in fine silk, styled in the empire line, gathered at the bodice, with masses of lace interwoven with yellow ribbons. Gorgeous to look at and hopelessly impractical to wash and use again. Not even comfortable to sleep in. His wife, she guessed, would wear it once and pack it away with her wedding veil and her love letters.

'It's exquisite.'

'I'm glad I showed it to you.' He started to replace it clumsily in the box.

'Let me,' said Fran, leaning across to take it from him.

269

The silk was irresistible. 'I know she'll love it.'

'It's not so much the gift,' he said as if he sensed her thoughts. 'It's what lies behind it. Pearlie would tell you I'm useless at romantic speeches. Hey, you should have seen me blushing in that shop. Frilly knickers on every side. The girls there had a right game with me, holding these nighties against themselves and asking what I thought.'

Fran felt privileged. She doubted if Pearlie would ever be told of the gauntlet her young husband had run to acquire the nightdress. She warmed to him. He was fun in a way that Jim couldn't be. Not that she felt disloyal to Jim, but this guy was devoted to his Pearlie, and that made him easy to relax with. She talked to him some more, telling him about the teaching and some of the sweet things the kids had said at the end of term.

'They value you,' he said. 'They should.'

She reddened and said, 'It's about time my husband came back.' Switching the conversation away from herself, she told the story of the mysterious invitation from Miss Shivers.

'You're doing the right thing,' he said. 'Believe me, you are.'

Suddenly uneasy for no reason she could name, Fran said, 'I'd better look for my husband. He said I'd find him in the bar.'

'Take care, then.'

As she progressed along the corridor, rocked by the speeding train, she debated with herself whether to tell Jim about the young man. It would be difficult without risking upsetting him. Still, there was no cause really.

The next carriage was of the standard Intercity type. Teetering towards her along the centre aisle was Jim, bearing two beakers of tea, fortunately capped with lids. He'd queued for ten minutes, he said. And he'd found two empty seats.

270

They claimed the places and sipped the tea. Fran decided to tell Jim what had happened. 'While you were getting these,' she began – and then stopped, for the carriage was plunged into darkness.

Often on a long train journey there are unexplained breaks in the power supply. Normally, Fran wouldn't have been troubled. This time, she had a horrible sense of disaster, a vision of the carriage rearing up, thrusting her sideways. The sides seemed to buckle, shattered glass rained on her and people were shrieking. Choking fumes. Searing pain in her legs. Dimly, she discerned a pair of legs to her right, dressed in dark trousers. Boots with crêpe soles. And blood. A pool of blood.

'You've spilt tea all over your skirt!' Jim said.

The lights had come on again, and the carriage was just as it had been. People were reading the evening paper as if nothing at all had occurred. But Fran had crushed the beaker in her hand. No wonder her legs had smarted. The thickness of the corduroy skirt had prevented her from being badly scalded. She mopped it with a tissue. 'I don't know what's wrong with me – I had a nightmare, except that I wasn't asleep,' she said. 'Where are we?'

'We went through Reading twenty minutes ago. I'd say we're almost there. Are you going to be okay?'

Over the public address system came the announcement that the next station stop would be Didmarsh Halt.

So far as they could tell in the thick mist, they were the only people to leave the train at Didmarsh.

Miss Shivers was in the booking hall, a gaunt-faced, tense woman of about fifty, with cropped silver hair and red-framed glasses. Her hand was cold, but she shook Fran's firmly and lingered before letting it go.

She drove them in an old Maxi Estate to a cottage set back from the road not more than five minutes from the station. Christmas-tree lights were visible through the leaded window. The smell of roast turkey wafted from the door when she opened it. Jim handed across the bottle of wine he had thoughtfully brought.

'We're wondering how you heard of us.'

'Yes, I'm sure you are,' she answered, addressing herself more to Fran than Jim. 'My name is Edith. I was your mother's best friend for ten years, but we fell out over a misunderstanding. You see, Fran, I loved your father.'

Fran stiffened and told Jim, 'I don't think we should stay.'

'Please,' said the woman, and she sounded close to desperation. 'We did nothing wrong. I have something on my conscience, but it isn't adultery, whatever you were led to believe.'

They consented to stay and eat the meal. Conversation was strained, but the food was superb. And when at last they sat in front of the fire sipping coffee, Edith Shivers explained why she had invited them. 'As I said, I loved your father Harry. A crush, we called it in those days when it wasn't mutual. He was kind to me, took me out, kissed me sometimes, but that was all. He really loved your mother. Adored her.'

'You've got to be kidding,' said Fran grimly.

'No, your mother was mistaken. Tragically mistaken. I know what she believed, and nothing I could say or do would shake her. I tried writing, phoning, calling personally. She shut me out of her life completely.'

'That much I can accept,' said Fran. 'She never mentioned you to me.'

'Did she never talk about the train crash – the night your father was killed, just down the line from here?'

'Just once. After that it was a closed book. He betrayed her dreadfully. She was pregnant, expecting me. It was traumatic. She hardly ever mentioned my father after that. She didn't even keep a photograph.'

Miss Shivers put out her hand and pressed it over Fran's. 'My dear, for both their sakes I want you to know the truth. Thirty-seven people died in that crash, twenty-five years ago this very evening. Your mother was shocked to learn that he was on the train because he'd said nothing whatsoever to her about it. He'd told her he was working late. She read about the crash without supposing for a moment that Harry was one of the dead. When she was given the news, just a day or two before you were born, the grief was worse because he'd lied to her. Then she learned that I'd been a passenger on the same train, as indeed I had, and escaped unhurt. Fran, that was chance, pure chance. I happened to work in the City. My name was published in the press, and your mother saw it, and came to a totally wrong conclusion.'

'That my father and you . . .'

'Yes – and that wasn't all. Some days after the accident, Harry's personal effects were returned to her, and in the pocket of his jacket they found a receipt from a Bond Street shop, for a nightdress.'

'Elaine Ducharme,' said Fran in a flat voice.

'You *know*?'

'Yes.'

'The shop was very famous. They went out of business in 1969. You see—'

'He'd bought it for her,' said Fran, 'as a surprise.'

Edith Shivers withdrew her hand from Fran's and put it to her mouth. 'Then you know about me?'

'No.'

She drew herself up in her chair. 'I must tell you. Quite by chance on that night twenty-five years ago, I saw him getting on to the train. I still loved him, and he was alone, so I walked along the corridor and joined him. He was carrying a bag containing the nightdress. In the course of the journey he showed it to me, without realizing that it wounded me to see how much he loved her still. He told me how he'd gone into the shop—'

'Yes,' said Fran, expressionlessly. 'And after Reading the

273

train crashed.'

'He was killed instantly. The side of the carriage crushed him. But I was flung clear, bruised, cut in the forehead, but really unhurt. I could see that Harry was dead. Amazingly, the box with the nightdress wasn't damaged.' Miss Shivers stared into the fire. 'I coveted it. I told myself if I left it, someone would pick it up and steal it. Instead, I did. *I* stole it. And it's been on my conscience ever since.'

Fran had listened in a trancelike way, thinking all the time about her meeting in the train.

Miss Shivers was saying. 'If you hate me for what I did, I understand. You see, your mother assumed that Harry bought the nightdress for me. Whatever I said to the contrary, she wouldn't have believed me.'

'Probably not,' said Fran. 'What happened to it?'

Miss Shivers got up and crossed the room to a sideboard, opened a drawer and withdrew a box, the box Fran had handled only an hour or two previously. 'I never wore it. It was never meant for me. I want you to have it, Fran. He would have wished that.'

Fran's hands trembled as she opened the box and laid aside the tissue. She stroked the silk. She thought of what had happened, how she hadn't for a moment suspected that she had seen a ghost. She refused to think of him as that. She rejoiced in the miracle that she had met her own father, who had died before she was born. Met him in the prime of his young life, when he was her own age.

Still holding the box, she got up and kissed Edith Shivers on the forehead. 'My parents are at peace now, I'm sure of it. This is a wonderful Christmas present.'

274

THE LAST DETECTIVE

Peter Lovesey

Detective Superintendent Peter Diamond is the last
detective: 'not some lad out of police school with a
degree in computer studies' but a genuine gumshoe,
given to doorstopping and deduction. So when the naked
body of a woman is found floating in the weeds in a
lake near Bath with no-one willing to identify her,
no marks and no murder weapon, his sleuthing abilities
are tested to the limit.

Struggling with a jigsaw of truant choirboys, teddy bears, a
black Mercedes and Jane Austen memorabilia, he alienates
his superiors, forensic scientists – and many of his suspects.
He even persists when 'the men in white coats' decide they
have enough evidence to make a conviction. It's just as
well: for despite disastrous personal consequences, and by
following the real clues hidden amongst Bath's historic
buildings and intertwined with its literary past, the last
detective exposes the uncomfortable truth . . .

'Admirably unpredictable (Lovesey keeps you guessing
until the very end) and entertaining all the way'
Philip Oakes, *Literary Review*

'Lively . . . Articulate'
Sunday Times

DIAMOND SOLITAIRE

Peter Lovesey

Peter Diamond, the short-fused detective who stormed out of the CID in *The Last Detective*, takes a job as a Harrods security guard and loses it one night when a little Japanese girl sets off the alarms in his section.

The child Naomi is a challenge, for she is autistic and a mystery. Diamond, strongly committed to helping her, arranges a TV appeal to discover her true identity, but she is kidnapped. By interpreting pictorial clues left by Naomi, Diamond tracks her to New York, where a murder is discovered, and to Tokyo, where Japan's most famous sumo wrestler helps bring the quest to a sensational climax.

'Lovesey sustains his reputation as a deft mystifier in one of the choicest crime-shelf entertainments of the year'
Guardian

'Lively . . . entertaining'
Marcel Berlins, *The Times*

'Too few writers seem capable of delivering a crime novel that is not only entertaining but also delicate and witty. An exception is Peter Lovesey'
Sunday Express

☐	The Last Detective	Peter Lovesey	£4.99
☐	Diamond Solitaire	Peter Lovesey	£4.99
☐	Bertie and the Crime of Passion	Peter Lovesey	£4.99
☐	Pieces of Justice	Margaret Yorke	£5.99
☐	Almost the Truth	Margaret Yorke	£4.99
☐	Widow's Peak	Gillian Linscott	£4.99
☐	Stage Fright	Gillian Linscott	£4.99

Warner Futura now offers an exciting range of quality titles by both established and new authors which can be ordered from the following address:

Little, Brown and Company (UK),
P.O. Box 11,
Falmouth,
Cornwall TR10 9EN.

Alternatively you may fax your order to the above address. Fax No. 01326 317444.

Payments can be made as follows: cheque, postal order (payable to Little, Brown and Company) or by credit cards, Visa/Access. Do not send cash or currency. UK customers and B.F.P.O. please allow £1.00 for postage and packing for the first book, plus 50p for the second book, plus 30p for each additional book up to a maximum charge of £3.00 (7 books plus).

Overseas customers including Ireland, please allow £2.00 for the first book plus £1.00 for the second book, plus 50p for each additional book.

NAME (Block Letters) ....

....

ADDRESS ....

....

....

☐ I enclose my remittance for ....

☐ I wish to pay by Access/Visa Card

Number ☐☐☐☐☐☐☐☐☐☐☐☐☐☐☐☐

Card Expiry Date ☐☐☐☐